Miss Spencer and the Con Man

by

Sandra Sookoo

MISS SPENCER AND THE CON MAN © 2016 by Sandra Sookoo
Published by New Independence Books

ISBN-13: 978-0692613894

ISBN-10: 0692613897

Contact Information:
sandrasookoo@yahoo.com
newindependencebooks@gmail.com
Visit me at www.sandrasookoo.com

Edited by: Victoria Miller
V.millerartist@gmail.com

Book Cover Design by Victoria Miller
V.millerartist@gmail.com

Victorian, Kieran and jax | Period Images.com
Old pharmacy by silvanoaudis | Deposit Photos.com
abstract blue background of elegant dark blue vintage by milanares | Fotolia.com

Publishing History:
First Digital Edition, 2016
First Print Edition, 2016

Other Victorian romances by Sandra Sookoo

Cairo Nights
Winner Takes All
Caribbean Heat
Unraveled Souls
A Wolfish Scandal
A Wolfish Tangle

Praise for Sandra Sookoo's historical work

Sandra Sookoo has created a strong and independent heroine who never expected to find herself in the position she is in. However, once in it she does not give up or give in to her circumstances or love very easily. I would recommend this book to readers who love an adventure and to romance lovers who enjoy a strong female heroine to match up against a sultry bad boy hero. -- Kathryn Bennett, Readers Favorite (for *Act of Pardon*)

Ms. Sookoo has written an incredible story for the history geek in me and the werewolf lover too! She never once makes the Civil War look rose-colored, nor does she hold back from some of the real descriptions of prisoners with lice. She doesn't once become so gritty as to turn the reading into something horrible enough to make me want to close the book. I have to say, I loved how, Southern Lady and all, Caroline is very much a match to our hero, Franklin. Not only did she give us two characters worth reading, she continued with a story gripping us to the end -- Teresa T, The Romance Studio (for *A Wolfish Tangle*)

There is something to be said about a romance book that can keep you enthralled page after page where everyone is fully clothed and no one is cursing. This was truly a delight to read, and it reminded me that there used to be a simpler time, a purer time, where people thought about family and obligation and not just lust. The book wasn't full of contrived drama or misunderstanding after misunderstanding. This book was an easy read, but a nice one. – Peyton, The Romance Reviews (for *Marriage Minded Lord*)

I was swept along with this story and the characters' grand affair and passions. It is a lively love story but starts off very carnal... The characters are full-bodied and well-developed. Maggie is passionate, scandalous, stubborn and strong-willed, while Stephen is a rogue in every way and both are sure they will not fall in love. – Linda, The Romance Studio (for *Lady Parker's Grand Affair*)

Dear Readers,

The day is finally here. I can hardly believe it. This book is out in the wild for people to read it. It's been a long road with this intrepid little project. Though I'd finished it four years ago, I had no idea what to do with it. After all, I'd been told time out of hand that Victorian romances wouldn't sell and that nobody wanted to read a historical unless it was a Regency.

So, this book sat on my hard drive, waiting. Then a miracle occurred, or what I thought was a miracle at the time. I thought my hard work and dedication to improving my craft had finally paid off. An agent made an offer! After much deliberation, I accepted the contract.

And then, the dream distorted. I was forced to cut out a subplot and retitle the book. No problem. These are little things. When that wasn't enough, I was told I needed to uproot the whole story and dump it into a different country, which would essentially change the plot and the characters' motivation and how they acted.

I declined respectfully. The publishers it had been queried to rejected it on the grounds that they didn't know how to categorize it, the story wasn't edgy enough, etc. Eventually, I parted ways with my agent over creative differences regarding my writing.

In the fall of last year, I was done with trying to fit into molds I'd never been made for with my stories. If I never landed an agent or hit the "big time" with a "big" publishing house, so be it. There's more to life than that. I tell the stories that need to be told in the way they should be told regardless of whether that's not slick or marketable.

So, I took back my original title, sent this baby to an editor and now here we are. After a long road of heartache and disappointment, I'm doing things on my terms. I might do the extracted subplot as a supplemental short in the future. I'm so pleased this book has been released for your enjoyment, because I know that you — my fans and friends — do enjoy my work in its original intent.

Everything has history; even books. It's the struggle that makes the payoff more worthwhile. Thank you for listening and happy reading!

Sandra

Dedication

For every reader who has ever felt different from others. For every person who has for too long carried around secret shame you think makes you unworthy. This book is for you. Love is for everyone, no matter what has happened in your life. Let the past go and embrace your future.

You won't regret it.

Maybe falling in love is the greatest con of all.

Julia Spencer may be new at her journalist's job, but that doesn't mean she can't spot a rat when she sees one. When she investigates a con-artist's lies, her own terrible past resurfaces. Despite the acute desire she feels for him, she has to decide if he's trustworthy or if he intends to ruin her life.

Tyler Browning needs money — quick. He's a first-rate fraud who has charm and charisma on his side. After making a hasty promise to a dying friend, hawking a bogus tonic seems the easiest way to meet the financial dilemma. All goes well until a chance meeting with a pretty but far too conscientious reporter sends his plans and passion into a tailspin.

As their unlikely relationship deepens and they give into mutual need, Tyler begins to reap what he's sowed, while kidnap and extortion schemes push Julia back into her dark past. Together she and Tyler will have to learn to trust each other in order to overcome the obstacles, before they do something they might regret.

Chapter One

Indianapolis, Indiana, September 10th, 1900

"Damn it, Julia. Stop the babbling!" The bellow resounded through the cramped quarters of the *Indianapolis Sentinel* newsroom. Loud enough to cut through the frantic clacking of typewriter keys, the command demanded to be obeyed.

Julia Spencer blew out an irritated breath. Her current stream of conversation died away as she sat on the other side of her uncle's desk. The clutter of his office covered his desktop. Onionskin, pencils and copies of the past weeks' newspapers teetered on piles, had slid off the furniture and now littered the floor around it. "It is quite unfair of you to expect me to write the fluff pieces you and your sycophant pups won't simply because I am the only woman in this office, and your niece to boot." Tendrils of strawberry-blonde hair escaped from her chignon, and she tucked them back into place.

Uncle George, a barrel-chested man sporting a bristle-brush mustache, shot up from behind his massive desk. Currently the junior editor of the paper, he had his eye on the editor-in-chief position, but since the paper was about to be under new management, he hadn't gained the title though he did most of the work. The quick movement dislodged even more paperwork from the precarious piles scattered across the top, and they fell down in a raspy avalanche, adding to the accumulation on the floor. "At least the pups bring in interestin' stories. You, on the other hand, give me drivel about the latest fashions, the newest thing in home goods, or couples gettin' hitched. Who the

1

hell wants to read about that?" A marked Southern drawl trailed every sentence, and well it should since her father and his brother came from the Atlanta area. They migrated to Indiana after the Reconstruction when she was a tyke of five, but she'd never forget the journey.

A chorus of raucous male laughter erupted outside the cramped office from the bullpen.

"I give you those articles because that's all you let me do." Julia's cheeks burned at the insult. When he put up his hand, palm outward, she sighed and stood.

"Spare me the excuses." He came around the desk, and dropped a heavy arm around her shoulders. "Look, sweetness, I appreciate your efforts, but right now, we have *real* news to contemplate. The hurricane that struck Galveston, Texas a couple days ago killed hundreds of people and—"

"If you would just listen—"

Uncle George's bushy brown brows crashed low and barely controlled anger glittered in his blue eyes. "Damn, Julia, if you want to be taken seriously as a journalist, you must remember to stop interruptin'. Otherwise, you'll never learn enough information to dig into the good parts. You have to let people talk because there's nothin' folks like better than to brag about themselves."

"I apologize." She turned into her uncle's substantial side. He reeked of cigar smoke and stale cooking—typical scents for the man who worked most of the day and into the night. He'd always smelled thusly, ever since she was little. In those days, Uncle George and her father were forever together, running from one political event and interesting issue to another. One thing she could count on was Uncle George's tireless dedication to getting out the news.

"Think nothin' of it." He steered her out of his office, then to the far side of the bullpen, finally maneuvering her behind a grouping of potted plants. "Your work is important in its own way, but the hurricane takes precedence. It's big news. Fascinatin' news. People want to know details. Even now, we're gettin' some of those winds as it moves inland. Both telephones are ringin' so much I can't keep up. I'm sending Gerald and Frank down there. Reporters in the field."

"Send me instead." She tugged on his tweed jacket sleeve, much like she used to do as a child when she wanted a treat from him. Now that she'd barely passed her twenty-eighth birthday, it was exceedingly immature, but she knew it would garner his attention. "I promise to do the paper proud."

"Sorry, darlin'. Not this time." He patted the top of her head. "I'll think about givin' you a better shake at writin' somethin' else soon."

"But—" When he glared, she focused her gaze on a leaf on one of the plants.

"You just keep putterin' around here, and maybe soon I'll give you a real interview." Again, he gave her head a pat as if she were that same small child she remembered. "Don't make me regret handin' you a job. Your daddy will take me to task if I have to respectfully ask you to leave. You're my responsibility while he's out of pocket, you know."

"I know. I don't need the lecture." A renewed blush swept over her cheeks and neck as Uncle George walked over to one of the other reporter's desks in the back corner and immediately became surrounded by a few of the young men. She clenched a fist then relaxed her hand, resisting the urge to stomp over the cluttered floor.

Look at them, all yapping around Uncle George, waiting for his approval like the dogs they are. Without a chance to spread her wings in journalism, there was no point in her being at the paper. How did she make her uncle—or any man of her acquaintance for that matter — see her as more than a woman, more than a potential wife, mother or sexual object to be possessed? She had much to offer the world and damn it, she wanted to leave her own mark.

There was a time ten years ago when she'd attempted exactly that. It hadn't ended the way she'd wanted. Shame burned her cheeks and the old guilt and unease bubbled into her stomach. Thank the Lord her family had never found out about those three mindless years at the finishing school. She'd garnered the attention she'd sought, but not from the right people. Her mother would probably die of heart palpitations if that scandal ever broke. Not to mention her dear father, the man she'd wished would have noticed her but never did. He'd always seemed surprised to find her beneath the same roof whenever he was home, as if he couldn't quite place her in his busy life.

Tears blurred her vision. Ruthlessly, she dashed them away. It wouldn't do her any good for the men to see her acting like the overly emotional woman they thought she was. Regret didn't hold sway in journalism. Her parents were well-respected in their community, and therein laid the problem. They lived in a beautiful house, did proper things, entertained socially acceptable people. While her father was involved in the political scene of the city and loosely connected to the paper, doing political commentary when needed, he was rarely home. Julia kept her mother company, but most of the time, she wasn't sure that stately lady even remembered she was alive, so involved in her charity work was she.

Julia had spent a good portion of her formative years trailing around their two story townhouse in the company of various nannies or housekeepers. Yet she couldn't seem to quit trying to gain her parents' regard or love. She'd settle for a modicum of respect or a moment of their undivided attention, had longed for it all her life, but it was a losing battle. Making a name in the community would always come first to them, then social graces and niceties, followed by securing connections that would cushion their future. Any other energy her parents could scrape together went into their devotion to each other, as evidenced by their imminent return from an exotic vacation to Panama.

It was delightful and very fairytale-ish to think of her parents' romance as so enduring, but at times she wondered if her birth happened by accident or as an afterthought. If not, and they'd truly loved her, wouldn't they wish to spend time with her, their only child?

Deliberately shoving those sobering thoughts to the back of her mind, Julia wrinkled her nose at the thick cloud of acrid cigarette and cigar smoke that obscured the top few feet of the air in the building. Apparently, smoking helped the men think. A couple of the reporters sat at typewriters and frantically pecked their way through the articles. The poor fellows worked so hard, but if her uncle signed off on the article, it still needed to gain the favor of the new owner in order to make the deadline, and no one had seen that gentleman yet.

She glanced at a scarred, wooden editor-in-chief's door. A pulled-down shade obscured its pane of glass. Jackson C. Hayes was a bit of a mystery to her. He worked off hours at the paper and never seemed to be in the office when she was even though he oversaw every aspect of the *Indianapolis Sentinel*. Bored with watching the young pups jockey for Uncle George's attention, Julia wandered over to Frank's desk. He flinched but didn't glance up from his typewriter. Annoyance swept through her chest from the snub. She planted both hands, palms down, on his desk and leaned over his typewriter, obscuring his view. Out of all the reporters the *Sentinel* had, he'd be the most likely to let her under his wing, especially since he thought himself in love with her anyway. "Let me cover the labor rally tomorrow, Frank, uh, I mean Mr. Adams." Her cheeks heated. So used to being around her uncle, she always forgot to call the others by their surnames to maintain proper protocol. "With all of your other assignments, you can't possibly have the time."

Finally, Frank gave her a dark glance with a leer on his classically handsome face. "I can't, Miss Spencer. Incensed females are more likely to go to dinner with me if I pretend to believe in their cause." He lifted a blond eyebrow. "Unless you would do me that honor?"

She sprang back in disgust. "Not even if you paid me." Narrowing her eyes, she frowned. "Must you be such a pig?" For almost every day of her short, three-month career at the newspaper, Frank had pestered her about going to dinner, picnics or any manner of outing he could think of that could be construed as courtship.

"I don't need to be, but I've found it is much more fun." He rifled through the detritus on his desk and thrust the morning's edition at her. "Look, I know how hard it is to have George take you seriously. He did the same to me a year ago when I first started. The longer you keep turning in society pieces, the longer he'll keep making you do them. But then, better you than us." As he laughed, a few other journalists joined in.

"Thanks for that thrilling bit of insight." Julia snatched it from him and stomped away. Being treated as an equal in this bunch would be next to impossible. As much as she would like to beat the wretched man about the shoulders with the paper, she held her temper in check. "Uncle George, I'm going out to find something newsworthy to write about. I'll be back by close of business."

Her uncle waved a hand but didn't glance up. "Stay out of trouble, darlin'."

"Gah." What would it take to have someone really notice her? She sailed through the door and slammed it behind her, then strode through the waiting room, crossing its black-and-white checked floor. Julia slammed the street door as well. If it was the last thing she did, she *would* make a difference, she *would* realize her dream of independence and she *would* become the object of someone's undivided attention.

There was nothing else she desired.

Tyler Browning chuckled softly to himself as he slid a fat wad of bills into the pocket of his waistcoat. Quite a tidy haul he'd taken in today, and all because of the insecurities and fears — real or imagined — of the misinformed public.

His chuckle turned into a full-fledged laugh when he spied a succinct article on the back page of the paper, which lay innocently on the counter of his apothecary shop. Drawing the periodical closer, he scanned the scant few paragraphs, and read bits aloud to his companion. "Listen to this, Victor. 'In a tiny apothecary nestled on bustling Washington Street, Mr. Tyler Browning is operating a little side business, and it has nothing to do with the usual tinctures, poultices or potions in which he usually dabbles.'"

His friend from childhood, and military chum, crossed his arms over his chest and leaned a shoulder against a shelf. "Is that the end of it?" A man of little words, his physical design was as utilitarian as his speech. Tall, lean and fit, Victor Archer had been likened to a ghost in military campaigns. The description was no less pertinent in a city setting with his pale skin and blond hair so light it would be angelic on a different person.

"No." Tyler smoothed out a crease and continued reading. "'We have it on good authority Mr. Browning is conducting illicit physical "adjustments" in his back room, so gentlemen, if your lady folk go missing for a couple of hours during the day without explanation, seek out Mr. Browning.'"

"Ah, I see." Victor pushed off the shelf in order to pace about the small space. "You are apparently running a brothel. I cannot imagine how that escaped my notice." Sarcasm dripped from his words, but then, Victor's philosophy in life could be summed into one phrase: everyone had an angle.

"If only that were the truth." Tyler's grin widened as he crumpled the paper and disposed of it beneath the counter. "It would seem the individual at the *Sentinel* who wrote this drivel believes me to enjoy a much seedier reputation than I actually do. The journalist hasn't been back here since and hasn't asked for an interview."

Which didn't necessarily bother him. A mysterious standing meant he became a greater curiosity to the public; therefore, they would seek him out in bigger numbers, padding his bottom line. That was a very good thing, not only for his livelihood but also because he did indeed have something else to sell them, and it wasn't the secret bouts of sex the paper cited.

Things were different now. Priorities had shifted, turned upside down and smacked him in the face. Still, some old habits died hard, which had led him to this pass.

Feeling Victor's gaze on him, Tyler gave a forced laugh. "Trust me when I say my latest scheme has absolutely nothing to do with the sexual arts. I draw the line at charging for that sort of service."

"Then you have two options. Threaten to sue the paper for slander or become the man they, in fact, want you to be."

Tyler raked a hand through his hair and wished for the thousandth time he didn't have the curls that seem to attract an excess of female attention. "I'll consider both."

"I would caution you to remember a man's reputation is sometimes the one thing most difficult to overcome."

"People will think what they want regardless of what I do or say. It has always been so." He hated the bitterness seething in the pit of his stomach. After all this time, he was his own worst critic. "Perhaps I should entertain the thought of selling illegal goods."

"Do you want to dabble in the morphine trade? I don't condone it. The price is much more expensive than you're willing to go." His friend's eyes were hard. "Are you having financial difficulties? Is that what this is about? I still owe you a huge debt, which you refuse to let me pay."

Along with the elation the remembrance brought, a flood of guilt plowed into him. The same day he'd saved Victor's life in Cuba, a full two years before the official conflict of the Spanish-American War began, he'd also been the cause of a needless death on the battlefield. Never would he forget the expression of pain on Joshua's face or the haunted, sad look in his eye as blood oozed from the gaping wound in the young man's chest.

"You have already repaid it. You hauled my sorry ass back to camp and accompanied me home. We're even." But the debt he owed the widow and child of his fallen compatriot still loomed heavy on his mind and heart.

Shortly after he'd lost his friend, a bullet from an enemy who'd gotten too close tore up his left leg and did permanent damage to his kneecap. Two years later, though he regained most of the use of that limb, he walked with a limp and needed the aid of a cane—an everyday reminder that a momentary distraction could result in hideous repercussions.

Which was exactly the crux of his current flim-flam. How to convince the general populace a miracle tonic existed when he couldn't cure his own injury?

He cleared his throat, hoping to marshal his scattered thoughts. "Forget it."

Victor's gaze never wavered. "I'm determined to save your ass—again—when the time comes. I have a feeling you'll need help in the coming weeks. Now, are you going to tell me what you're dealing, or will I need to read about it in tomorrow's paper?"

"I came across the most amazing thing in the woods behind my house a few days ago." Tyler cast a furtive glance at the window where a pair of older women chatted on the wooden walkway beyond. Their shadows in the evening light stretched over the shop's floor. "Mineral water." When the expected praise and accolades didn't come from his friend, he frowned. "It's quite brilliant."

"How so?" Victor crossed his arms over his chest as an incredulous expression shadowed his face. "Please tell me you don't intend to scam the people of this city."

"Not all of them. Only the ones who aren't as well-adjusted as the rest." He grinned and warmed to his subject. "I bottle the product from a small waterfall where I think it's the freshest. What's more, I successfully sold the first bottles not ten minutes ago." Feeling Victor would respond better by having hard proof, he pulled the bills from his pocket. "Just think, in a month, I could be well on my way to owning one of those classy homes near Brookside Park." Except that was a bald-faced lie. His funds were tied up in other things.

"Is real estate your goal?" Victor unfolded his arms and yanked his bowler hat from the counter. "What are you really after, Tyler? I've known you all our lives. Hell, I live next door to you, and the neighborhood is perfectly acceptable."

"True, but lately I suspect there's more to life than working for the pittance here and—"

Victor held up a hand, interrupting. "What happens to your money?"

Hot guilt and remorse churned in Tyler's gut. "You wouldn't believe me if I attempted explanation." He'd never told Victor about his responsibility toward Joshua's family, never uttered a word regarding the nightmares he suffered. Best to keep it to himself and act cavalier instead of being perceived as weak and spineless. "Remember when we ran a scam and sold the same horse to twelve different Spanish officers in Cuba?"

"Yes. You always had talent to make money out of nothing. Remember when our commanding officer caught wind and made us dig latrines by ourselves for the next six months? Not to mention, we had to do it naked as punishment." Victor's lips twitched.

"Well, it was still the best con we've done."

"True. I'm not up for any more." He glanced at his pocket watch. "I have an appointment at the bank, but let me say this. Don't do something you'll regret later. You have a good life now, and whatever is addling your brain, dump it."

What's another regret to add to the pile? Tyler nodded and shoved the money into his pocket. "I'll bear that in mind." Once Victor closed the door behind him, he slumped onto a tall stool.

Absently rubbing the scar on his left thigh, he retreated once more into melancholy thoughts. He'd been exceedingly lucky to find the post in the apothecary. Discharged from the military, and knowing he'd never be whole again to fight, he'd returned home to the States with Victor tagging along for moral support. By fate, or maybe wanderlust, they both ended up in Chicago. After running a few cons in order to buy lodging and food, they'd decided to go south. Tyler figured Victor kept on with him in the attempt to fulfill his alleged debt. When they'd pulled into Union Station in Indianapolis, Tyler liked the feel of the small, bustling crossroads city. The two men had started their new lives the next day.

Victor pursued a banking career while Tyler, not having a firm grasp on what he wanted from the future, ran a few more cons. He'd won the apothecary shop in a game of poker, which was lucky indeed. Finally, his skills as a remedial medic came into play, yet he was woefully unprepared for pharmacology.

Desperate and in need of cash, he went to the local lending library and devoured all he could regarding herbs, short-term medicines and homeopathic remedies — everything that wouldn't necessitate the need for actually practicing medicine. A few weeks later, and taking his newly acquired knowledge into the venture, he'd opened the shop and realized he enjoyed the daily interactions with the various people who visited.

Two years had gone by since that endeavor began, and always Joshua's family preyed on his mind. Never able to forget, he'd paid them monthly visits, hoping his widow and child would overcome their grief. Locked in a guilt-induced haze, he'd made a promise of financial assistance before the reality of that covenant sank in.

Thus was born the need for funds above and beyond his monthly salary.

The bells attached to a leather strip hung on the doorknob jangled and yanked Tyler out of his introspection. The two women who'd been gabbing in front of his store ambled to his counter.

"Good evening, ladies. May I help you?" As they talked quietly to each other, cataloguing their complaints, Tyler stifled the urge to hurry them along.

The yearning to be content slipped away while demons from his past pressed in. Just once, he wanted to be accepted for who he was, despite the physical deformity, in spite of his less-than-honest past and his propensity for what he could give the other person.

Perhaps then he would finally be happy and free.

Chapter Two

The next morning, Tyler sat on the cool bank of the stream where he'd made his find. Barely a foot wide, the stream meandered through a wooded area and undoubtedly emptied into White River at some point, but he'd never had the wherewithal to follow it to the source. The ribbon of crisp water flowed over an earthen shelf. Limestone and other rocks created a small, fairy-like waterfall that tinkled with the faintest of whispers.

It had been that feature which had drawn him deeper into the woods. Before the idea for the con took hold, he'd spent many hours reading or napping by the waterfall. Now, it was still early yet as sunrise had occurred thirty minutes before.

A glance around confirmed he was alone and, assured of privacy, he began the task of filling twelve glass bottles. He held up one of them and gazed through the clear liquid. How was it possible the public could be so gullible thinking this ordinary water a cure-all? A half-grin lifted the corners of his mouth. It didn't matter as long as they kept offering him money.

One by one he filled the bottles, corked them, then placed them in a wooden box divided into twelve separate compartments by pieces of wood. Today, he intended to hawk the water at his shop. Unlike the few he'd already sold, this new venture would hopefully bring new interest not only to his apothecary but to the "miracle tonic" he peddled outside the City Market on the weekends. If he didn't procure customers soon, he'd need to think up a new con quick.

The cold flow of water on his fingers recalled him to the here and now. When his task was finished, he levered himself off the ground, dusted off the seat of his trousers and stretched. On the surface, life had the potential to be idyllic. The early morning silence in the woods, a gentle breeze and sweet-smelling air all conspired against the erratic swirl of thoughts in his brain.

Hefting his box by its handle in one hand and gripping his cane with the other, Tyler meandered down a path of mashed and mangled brush that had been flattened from his frequent passing. Only two people were acquainted with the existence of the mineral spring, and he knew, above all, Victor as well as his housekeeper, Hilda wouldn't betray his trust.

The snap of a twig nearby was as loud as a gunshot. Tyler's heartbeat accelerated. A quarter of a mile from his townhouse, it was too far off for passersby leisurely morning stroll. Shoving the box beneath a large bush, he moved closer to where he'd heard the sound. Seconds later, a small, brown-and-white animal shot out of the underbrush and hurtled toward him. The dog yapped. His pink tongue hung out of his mouth as he jumped against Tyler's legs.

"Who are you?" Stooping, he scooped the beagle under his free arm. The dog squirmed and yapped again, this time licking Tyler's hand. He'd no sooner taken another few steps forward when the sound of female conversation met his ears, punctuated by someone frantically calling out the name "Fitzwilliam."

He lifted the dog and stared into the soulful brown eyes. "*That's* your name?" When he received a lick on his cheek in answer, Tyler chuckled. "Let's find your owner."

It would do no good if his sanctuary was discovered. Visions of picnics and social events shattering the tranquility raced through his mind, not to mention the destruction of his spring. He quickened his pace as best he could despite the cane and the rambunctious, squirming dog.

"Gretchen, this is the absolute last time I intend to help you track down your oatmeal-for-brains dog. Why you let him jump out of the carriage is beyond me."

Tyler grinned at the blatant annoyance in the female's voice. He looked at the tail-wagging runaway. "You don't appear to have oatmeal for brains." When the dogged yapped and squirmed, Tyler let him loose. The beagle rolled over, then darted through the underbrush toward the sound of what now amounted to full-blown arguing.

"It wasn't my fault Fitzwilliam was bored as we sat in traffic. He's a smart dog and hates to be inactive." This speaker was different than the first woman. "You simply cannot understand the workings of his mind, Julia. You've always hated him."

"That's because Fitzwilliam is only competent in two things. Defecating then turning about and playing with said defecation wherein the result is vomiting. I want no part of that."

Tyler's grin widened at her matter-of-fact tone. Though the timbre was pleasing enough, it conjured images of a woman who knew her own mind and would do whatever it took to make her dreams happen. As incongruous as it was pairing a woman who brought out ferocious feline predators with an apparently gastro-intestinally troubled canine, an acute desire to meet the woman for nothing else than to assuage his own curiosity grew.

He came upon them just as Fitzwilliam barked in a series of high-pitched yaps and longer woofs. A black-haired woman kneeled in the brush while cradling the dog to her chest. The brim of her dainty hat hung haphazardly over one ear while the dog chewed its ribbon. Standing nearby, with an expression of annoyance, was another woman—the owner of the capable voice, he presumed.

Blonde hair lay pinned beneath a wide-brimmed navy hat. A valiant black satin ribbon fluttered off the back. No other accessory graced the brim like so many popular forms of headgear. Shapely arched eyebrows gave way to high cheekbones, an average-sized nose that turned up in a slightly impertinent fashion while full lips pulled down in a frown were the color of a tulip he'd once seen. Would they feel as soft as the flower they resembled? Endless seconds ticked by as he imagined them yielding beneath his in a kiss.

She gathered the navy, wool skirt of her plain dress in both hands, lifting it off the forest floor in an apparent attempt to keep it clean of debris. Such an action showed off the fine, ruffled lace of her petticoats and slim ankles encased in serviceable black boots. Such a sight captivated his mind.

Tyler pasted the grin guaranteed to charm almost anyone to his lips and cleared his throat. "If I had known the wood would hide such beautiful visions, I'd endeavor to spend all my time here."

Both ladies' attention leapt to his face, and the dog owner smiled as she set the animal down. "What a delightful greeting." Her cheeks colored. A tad shorter and a bit stouter than her friend, she didn't seem to mind that her precious Fitzwilliam alternated between digging up dirt and jumping onto her skirt, leaving muddy paw prints on the cream-colored fabric.

"Don't be such a loon, Gretchen." The other woman's vivid blue eyes bore into his soul. "The man merely gave a flowery speech to distract us from asking him what he's doing in this same wood at such an early hour." A faint Southern drawl blended through the musical tones.

Tyler's smile slipped at her boldness. He narrowed his eyes. "I didn't think it a crime to take the air before one consigns himself to the rigors of the workaday world. If a man decides to commune with nature, does that make him a criminal?" Did she suspect he was, in fact, just that?

"Not necessarily, but if that's true, we needn't explain our presence either." She stepped close enough that dark indigo lining her irises became evident. "You look familiar. Have we met before?"

Foreboding spread from his stomach through his bloodstream. He didn't mind her forward attitude or bold manners. The fact she refused to hide behind shyness and flirting piqued his interest. It was her dogged determination to place him that made him wary. "You may have seen me around the city. I run the apothecary on Washington Street." He held out a hand. "Ty—"

"Ah. Mr. Tyler Browning." She frowned and caught her bottom lip with her teeth ever so slightly. The gesture sent a low-grade fever sailing over his skin. "You were recently mentioned in the paper."

Anger warmed his neck. A firm denial sprang to his lips. Then he remembered Victor's words and he smiled. For the time being, he'd become the stories. "Indeed I was." Realizing she had no intention of shaking his hand, he let it drop to his side and decided to concentrate his charms on the woman's friend. Perhaps if he ignored her, she'd be more receptive to his questions. "Good morning. I'm Tyler Browning, and what is your name?"

"Gretchen Schmidt. This," she grabbed her friend's upper arm and thrust her forward, "is Julia Spencer. She writes for the *Indianapolis Sentinel*."

The call of a bird sent the dog running. Gretchen murmured an apology and followed after the animal at a more sedate pace, yelling the unfortunate canine's name.

"Well, well." Tyler's mind raced at the mention of the paper. He stifled the urge to cringe, but instead, transferred his attention to Julia. The woman hid secrets behind her inscrutable eyes. "You're a journalist?" Had it been she who had written the column proclaiming the rumors? He couldn't recall the byline.

A rosy bloom suffused her cheeks and gave personality to her otherwise cold expression. "Yes, I do write… just not features." Her gaze dropped for a few seconds. She pinned him as quickly. "Make no mistake. I *will* be a serious reporter. I only need a big break and time."

"I don't doubt you'll find both." He assessed her, marked the determined gleam in her eyes, and his grin widened. If he could convince her to believe in him and his elixir, it would take the stigma off his back, driving added business to his shop. Not to mention having an ally on the paper could catapult his luck into a new realm. "Tell me, Miss Spencer, what are you and your friend doing out here so early? Spying on me for the paper?"

She raised an eyebrow. "My, you're full of so much arrogance I'm surprised you haven't choked yourself."

"Some would say it isn't arrogance, only confidence." Impressed by the way she didn't back down, he took her hand and pulled it through the crook of his arm. "Let's catch your friend. With that wayward dog of hers, I can only imagine the problems they'll find." At the last second, he stifled the urge to whistle a tune. "A word of warning. There are vagrants who frequent this area. Not the kind of place for two finely bred young ladies to be lost."

"Why do you assume we're lost?"

"I'm attempting to ascertain if you are." He patted her hand. "Were the two of you out here for business or pleasure?"

She wrenched from his grasp. "Why would you phrase your question in that manner?" Her eyes rounded. In the morning sun, emotion darkened the depths, but he couldn't identify it. "It's none of your business why Gretchen and I are out here."

"I apologize." Tyler continued his walk. The sooner he led her away from his spring and the hidden bottles of mineral water, the better. He had a feeling this woman would stop at nothing to ferret out the truth from anyone she met, and there was too much at stake. Until he could figure what her intentions were, he'd consider her a potential enemy. "In light of your reluctance to talk about your plans for the day, I'll leave you and Miss Schmidt to your business. Good day, Miss Spencer."

One thing he could count on about human nature was curiosity for the unknown. The moment he exited the protection of the trees and the tip of his cane hit the walking path, Julia crashed through the leaves behind him.

"Forgive my poor manners, Mr. Browning. You caught me off guard."

Tyler smiled as he waited patiently for her to join him. "Think nothing of it. Now, suppose you enlighten me about your early morning jaunt."

Rule one to live by as a flim-flam artist: always leave your audience hungering for more.

Julia glanced up and down the street as she searched for some sign of her friend. From somewhere nearby, Fitzwilliam's bark sounded, but she couldn't place the direction. Beyond that, she didn't care. Her companion was much more interesting. She walked on his left side, the one he favored slightly, and though her mind spun, creating wild tales of how he came by the limp, for once she bowed to manners and didn't inquire.

Yet the raging curiosity wouldn't go away. "You said you run an apothecary. How did you come to be in that profession?" She peered at him from beneath the brim of her hat and stifled a sigh of appreciation.

A mop of thick, black curls ran riot from under his bowler. Clean shaven cheeks flowed into a strong chin while brown eyes twinkled as if he knew exactly what she thought.

Over the years she'd had just cause to size men up and could determine in a glance what sort of person they were—this she'd also learned from her uncle. Many men lied to build themselves into the people they wished to be. Some fibbed to hide the lives they were unhappy or ashamed of living. Even more stretched the facts to manipulate. With Tyler, did he, indeed, tell falsehoods? He didn't appear to be a vagrant, but some drifters were skilled in passing themselves off as upstanding members of society.

As a half-smile graced his sensual lips, she allowed her mind to wander. Would he be a gentle lover, content to torment her by kissing every shivering inch of her skin and bringing her inches from release before she begged for mercy? Or would he choose to boss her by hard, passionate embraces, showing her with every touch of his hands and stroke of his tongue that he was master as he possessed her, body and soul?

God forgive me. Desire tingled between her thighs only to be swept away by her mental determination not to think of him along those lines. She never wanted to feel that way, never wanted to be used as an object for a man's pleasure again. It led to trouble, and she had too many dreams to realize now. *Give me strength.* The fact she was compelled to pray to a higher power brought home her desperation to be free from those bonds.

No matter how much she wanted to escape the past, it followed her everywhere.

Julia refocused on Tyler. "I beg your pardon." She couldn't help but admit his impressive form and charming manners screamed a warning. In short, he had the potential to be dangerous.

"No need. Silence is appreciated as well as day-dreaming."

She dropped her gaze from his face, only to have it land on the broad sweep of his shoulders and how they filled every inch of his tweed jacket to perfection. Tyler possessed the body of a man used to physical taxation, which was in direct opposition to his profession. Not many pharmacists spent their leisure time out of doors. The mystery of his person increased exponentially. She'd burn into ash from her less than austere thoughts if she wasn't careful.

"Is that what you're doing now — day-dreaming?"

Realizing she had to say something, she blurted, "Do you live in this area?"

"I do, but let me answer your earlier question." When she offered no comment, he continued. "I could bore you by telling stories of the years I'd had to study for this position. Suffice it to say, I came to be an apothecary by way of a fortunate game of poker." He drew to a halt and turned to face her. "I find the work fascinating and satisfying."

Julia nodded. "How nice for you. Have you always been interested in the field?" She noted the way he gripped the curved brass handle of his cane so hard his knuckles turned white. What was his true story? "I ask because it seems odd you would choose to pursue such a career when it's obvious you're a man of much different pursuits." It was risky, this digging for information, but she'd learned at her uncle's knee and from life's tutelage. She could do nothing less.

Emotion flashed in his eyes, so fleeting she didn't have a chance to read it. "Ah, and now you treat me to the reporter you claim not to be." Tyler's grip on the cane relaxed, and he strolled forward once more. "You're correct in your assumptions. At one time, I had chosen to remain in the military until I reached my dotage. Fate had other plans." To emphasize the point, he lifted the cane, spun it through his fingers like a circus performer before replacing the tip on the hard-packed earthen path.

Julia chewed the inside of her lip as she digested his words. He had natural charisma and a cavalier charm, to be sure. A military career explained his fit form, yet it was the almost haunted expression, the ghosts of horrors reflected in his eyes, which compelled her to ask, "What of the rumors? If the articles in the paper are to be believed, what exactly do you offer your female clients in addition to medicinal and homeopathic services?"

Again, he paused in his forward motion. "Is it the negative connotations of the column that have spiked your notice, or is it interest in my alleged actions that prompts you to ask?" His gaze bore into hers as if the fate of the world depended on her answer.

"You'd be surprised at how low I have seen society act. Nothing shocks me." Heat jumped into her cheeks from his scrutiny and, again, tendrils of heat seeped between her thighs. Annoyed that she would feel any sort of reaction to him, she turned and took two steps before his next words brought her to a halt.

"Is that why you dream of becoming a journalist? Because you desire to worm the truth out of everyone you meet?" A trace of sarcasm and bitterness fell from his words. "Do you value honesty over everything else, no matter the circumstances involved? Can you not accept a person at face value and hope he or she is a good person deep down? Would you ever befriend someone regardless of their past?"

A heavy swath of guilt cut through her stomach, obliterating the wave of lust that had threatened moments earlier. What the hell did she know about honesty anymore? There were parts of her life so steeped in untruths it would take days to unravel the falsehoods. But he would never know any of them—no one would if she could help it. Turning to face him, she closed the distance until she stood toe-to-toe with the man. She raised her chin and glared, boldly holding his gaze. "Don't assume to understand me. What I do and why I do it is none of your concern."

Tyler came close enough that his lips were but a hairsbreadth from hers. His soft exhalation warmed her face, scented faintly of peppermint. "I ask you to adopt the same attitude toward me." Stepping away, he touched a forefinger to the brim of his hat and slightly bowed. "I bid you good day. Next time, think twice before you and your friend go traipsing through wooded areas." A hint of a smile touched his mouth, but it held no mirth. "Perhaps in the future you should stick close to the well-to-do neighborhoods or even your precious newspaper office."

"Wait." She laid a hand on his sleeve before he could fully leave. Instant warmth crept through her fingers and she yanked her hand away.

Is that how he saw her? An uptight woman from a good home who took herself too seriously? She went forward a step. Or did she immediately turn him off by her attitude and pushy questioning? She narrowed her eyes. And damn it, he'd nearly gotten away without answering her question regarding the article in the paper.

"Is there something else you wished to say, Miss Spencer?"

"Yes, in fact there is." She refused to give up so easily. Tyler Browning had something to hide, and she intended to find out what it was. "Are you, or are you not, what the paper claims?" Why did she desperately want him to say he wasn't a womanizer and that everything he did was above board?

Had she lost all faith in humanity? Nevertheless, Julia held her breath in anticipation. Her pulse tripped, stampeding through her veins as he grabbed her hand and brought it to his lips. He barely brushed her skin, but she trembled as if he'd caressed the length of her body.

"That is something you'll need to find out for yourself. I trust I'll see you around town. Until then, Miss Spencer." This time, there was no mistaking the dismissal in his tone.

She relaxed when he disappeared around the corner of a building. Of all the people she'd met, Tyler was the most inscrutable. All the mystery did was make her want to delve deeper to find out the real story.

"Julia!" The spell broken, she swung around at the sound of Gretchen's voice. Her friend rushed down the path with Fitzwilliam in tow. "Do you know who that man was?"

By sheer willpower she refrained from verbally berating her friend. "I have a general idea." She frowned when the dog yapped and began circling around them.

Gretchen grabbed Julia's arm and shook it. "He's the man everyone says conducts," she lowered her voice to a mere whisper, "sexual lessons in his shop. They say he charges ten dollars for thirty minutes of pleasure under the guise of body realignment and reinforcing positive mental health."

Julia rolled her eyes. As if intercourse could ever be misconstrued as that sort of thing. "Who are 'they?'" she asked as she gently detached Gretchen from her person.

"The gossips." Her friend waved a hand in a vague attempt to encompass the area around them. "Who did the article for the *Indianapolis Sentinel*? He must have had inside information if his article was published."

"Is that what you think?" She burst into laughter at Gretchen's naiveté. Unfortunately, her opinion was probably also that of the general public. "I'm not sure which of those goons wrote the article. I can tell you they don't have all the facts. Maybe one of them actually paid Mr. Browning a visit, but he didn't do any sort of investigation. That article is mere speculation. A good journalist will keep tabs on their quarry, follow them, find out what they do every minute of their lives before they write their piece." She stopped to draw a breath. "Why do you stare at me like that?"

Gretchen stood, her hands on her ample hips, and pursed her lips. "If you believe he is innocent, why not convince your uncle to let you do a new article?" She bent and picked up Fitzwilliam, then buried her nose in his fur.

"I..." Julia looked back in the direction where she'd last seen Tyler. "I have a feeling he wouldn't give up the information to me either." As her stomach churned, she shook her head. "I have no plans to give Mr. Browning another thought. He deliberately keeps himself an enigma simply to have the people talk about him, thereby drawing crowds of the curious, which in turn helps his bottom line. It's not necessarily a crime."

"So you say now, but I know you, Julia. Discovering this man's story will eat at you until you cannot stand it any longer. Sooner or later, you'll visit his shop for your own piece of mind." Gretchen walked with determined strides, pulling her behind.

Julia remained silent. She had no business becoming involved in a man's life. Nothing good lay down that path. Only heartache, guilt and tragedy, and she doubted if she had enough strength to immerse herself into such drama again.

Chapter Three

That afternoon, Julia sat typing one of her breezy, society pieces, this one on the happenings where Hoosier poet James Whitcomb Riley would attend. Uncle George stood at his office door and rapped the frame with a knuckle.

"Julia darlin', Mr. Hayes wants a meetin' with me, so you mind the bullpen. Afterward, I'll treat you to dinner at the Carlisle." Not waiting for her acknowledgement, he crossed the room and knocked on the owner's door. Seconds later, he entered and closed the portal behind him.

On a different day she would have enjoyed sitting back and watching the young reporters struggle with their typewriter keys and ribbon, but this afternoon, with her fingers busy on her own work and her mind mired in thoughts that alternated between her article and Tyler's enigmatic responses, she had difficulty concentrating, let alone observing. To say the secrets of his eyes captivated her would be an understatement, yet she firmly told herself she was interested in him only as a potential column for the paper.

Bored, and her mind pre-occupied, her fingers flew over the keyboard. When the "h" and "t" arms on the typewriter stuck, she frowned and began the tedious task of gently untangling the hammers and starting again. The models Uncle George purchased for the office weren't the latest available on the market. When a person typed with any sort of speed, the hammers oftentimes became frozen into a mix of metal and inky ribbon. Most days, by the time she went home, her fingers were stained black. Today, she borrowed the one at her uncle's desk.

Uttering a few choice phrases she'd heard her uncle say on occasion, Julia plopped back into her chair to continue her task despite the few snickers from some of the reporters. She ignored them in the quest to poke at the outdated typewriter with her index fingers only. For a moment she considered telling Uncle George she quit in favor of seeking employment in one of the many offices in the area. Surely they had a budget to purchase better equipment. As soon as the thought popped into her mind, her gaze fell on the morning's edition of the paper and the urge to see her name as a byline overwhelmed her.

No, she needed to remain determined and focused. Only as a journalist could she make a difference in the world, state her opinion on society reform and give voice to the people who were silent. Rights for women, children and minorities were exactly the angles she needed for a new column. Or perhaps she should focus her attention on the apothecary. Surely there'd be enough interest there for an article, something beyond the society pages.

She'd no sooner settled her fingers over the keys once more when loud, angry voices erupted from the owner's office. Something crashed against the wall, and two seconds later, the door flew open and Uncle George hurtled out, slamming the door behind him. He stormed across the bullpen, not looking at anyone. When he entered his office, Julia scuttled out of his chair. He acknowledged her with a curt nod, then threw himself into the chair. The springs protested at the savage treatment.

Julia peeked into the newsroom. The five reporters kept their heads down, attending to their work. Occasionally, one would look up furtively before returning to their papers. She peered at her uncle, cringing when he gripped his pencil so hard he broke it in half.

Growling in disgust, he threw the useless writing utensil at a wastebasket. It missed, rolling over the floor and coming to rest in a corner.

She chewed her bottom lip. Not exactly the best of times to inform Uncle George of her new idea, but it couldn't be helped. What was life without taking a risk? Now or never. As she approached her uncle's desk, his bleak expression worried her. Not able to recall a time when he'd seemed so shaken or perhaps even depressed, her first inclination was to comfort him. As she glanced again out the door toward the owner's office, foreboding washed over her skin. What had the two men argued about?

"Uncle George?" Her knees knocked together while flutters filled her stomach. His emotions had become an almost palpable entity, ebbing through the air toward her. Whatever he and Jackson had discussed, it must have been shattering. When he grunted, she continued, the urge to prove herself outweighing common sense. "I have an idea for an article. I believe it will appeal to the general public, and it will be edgy enough to make people feel outrage. You always say pull at their heartstrings. Could I—"

"Damn it, Julia!" He slammed a thick fist onto his desktop. Pencils scattered in all directions. A stack of papers slid to the floor. "Dump the notion out of your head, child. What I told you yesterday still stands. You are not ready to write hard pieces on your own. Until you put in the time learnin' the ropes, I refuse to waste *my* time and space on the paper. You stay with the silly little pieces about the latest party or fashion development."

"I'm not interested in shallow things such as those, so why should I waste *my* time?" Her cheeks burned. The noise in the newsroom slackened as if the men waited to see what would happen next. "My idea far surpasses society pieces. I want to write—"

"No. I don't care." His face turned a few shades of red as he stared at her. "Go back to your desk."

"Uncle George, keeping me tucked away in your office isn't fair! Why are you trying to hide me away?" She stomped her foot. "I have just as much talent as those poor excuses." Julia gestured to the door. "Give me a chance like you did them."

"I wish I could. I really do." He rubbed a hand along the side of his face. "And maybe I would have until a few minutes ago when things turned ugly. You don't understand the situation here." Unfathomable sadness swallowed his gaze.

What had changed? "Tell me why. I refuse to give up. I require a sound explanation."

"Your stubbornness is appreciated. This…matter is between Hayes and me." For one fleeting moment, such uncharacteristic vulnerability lined her uncle's face that her heart ached. In another second it was gone, replaced by the hard set to his lips and impassive glare. "The *Sentinel's* readership has dropped off over the past two years. The paper's in financial hardship. Chances are high it'll be sold to the *Indianapolis Star*. That's why Mr. Hayes is here."

"Oh no! I thought he was the new owner."

"No. He'll fill the editor-in-chief position, but the gossips say he's from the other paper as a spy."

"I'm sorry." What else could she say? "What will happen then?"

Her uncle shrugged. "We'll be let go. We're too small a paper to cover the news with any sort of competency. We need—"

"But this is exactly why…" Belatedly, Julia realized she'd once again interrupted him. "Please continue."

He cleared his throat. "We need to develop big, shockin' articles to garner interest to stimulate sales.

Whatever your idea is won't be enough. I apologize. This is the way of the world. People would rather not have to think of what side of an issue they are on. They want to let others form an opinion so they may follow like sheep." He gave her a hard look. "No articles on rights. No controversial subject, especially not from a female writer."

"The people need to see the world as a whole, not simply the slice of life the paper wants to show them." Why wouldn't he at least listen to her? "You of all people should know that ignoring issues is wrong. Don't do the people of Indianapolis a disservice by ignoring them." She shifted her weight from foot to foot. "There is a whole, untouched demographic out there who would take out a subscription to the paper if you would report on things they want to read about."

"Enough, Julia." Uncle George grabbed a new pencil from the collection on his desktop and pulled a small notebook from the inside pocket of his jacket. "I admire your fervor. It's just not the time for it."

The resignation in his voice made her bottom lip quiver and tears clog her throat. She swallowed them, refusing to give the men in the room cause to laugh. "Please, let me have a chance. If I fail, at least it will be my mistake."

He reached into the wastebasket beside his desk and took out a wrinkled sheet of paper. "Here." He shoved the bulletin across to her. "Someone's been postin' these flyers all over town. It's the same fellow one of the boys went out to report on earlier in the week. They were supposed to get an interview, not a speculation piece."

Scooping up the paper, she glanced at the black and white printing. "For Sale. Marvelous Mystery Tonic. Guaranteed to heal whatever ails you. From depression to measles and even unmentionable 'female' complaints, buy a bottle now! Available at Browning's Apothecary on

Washington Street." She pinned her uncle with a glare. "*This* is who you want me to write about?" Why not? Hadn't she entertained the same idea not ten minutes before?

"It'll keep you out of the office. Julia, I'm tryin' to protect—"

"No!" This time, all noise in the bullpen ceased. She didn't need to turn about to know every eye was directed on her. "You pulled this out of the trash because you know it is not worth looking into. Where's *my* respect, Uncle George? Why won't you treat me with the same courtesy you give to the rest of your staff?" Her breath came in short spurts as tears sprang to her eyes. She crumpled the advertisement in her fist.

"What you don't understand is I am givin' you respect." He rubbed a hand over his jaw and lowered his voice. "I'll tell it to you straight. Stop hidin' behind the words you think are pretty because if you keep on, the past will catch you up, if it hasn't already."

The vague uneasiness that plagued her stomach reared to the forefront. She narrowed her eyes. "What did Mr. Hayes say to you in there?"

"Don't worry your pretty little head about it. For the time bein', I'm only considerin' it as ugly gossip by a bully." He shot out of his chair, came around the desk and threw a familial arm around her shoulders, tugging her out of his office, through the newsroom and into the waiting area. "This salesman is your first assignment. Dog his steps. Follow him. Find out what the man is really about. Don't come back until you have a fully realized article. If I'm not here, you stay in my office with the door closed. Understand?"

She nodded, troubled by the urgency behind the question. At the outer door, he called her name and she turned toward him. "Yes?"

"Remember, a good story is based on eighty percent fact, fifteen percent heartfelt emotion and five percent gut instinct. Once you have all that, you'll have an article people will talk about."

Maybe doing a piece on Tyler Browning wouldn't be that bad. After all, he was an interesting individual.

Tyler grinned while, using his mortar, he ground dried passion flowers. Remains of several flower heads and leaves rested in the bowl of the pestle. A native plant to South America, it was one of the most popular dried flowers he ordered, as it was purported to calm a person's anxieties and reduce the inflammation of a headache. When he had enough to fill the order, he gently laid the marble mortar on his countertop, poured the plant detritus on a slip of waxy paper then folded it into a sort of envelope.

He'd taken the post of pharmacist as a means to an end. Now, he found he actually did enjoy the work. Each time a customer walked into his store and listed their complaints, he'd take the time to research cures in several of his text books until he came across the exact one he thought would do the trick.

Which made his decision to hawk the mineral water distasteful. If he hadn't needed the money so badly, none of this would have occurred. He frowned, turning to one of the shelves behind him. Scanning the many brown, glass bottles, he lifted a small vial of peppermint oil and laid it next to the packet of ground flowers. That wasn't necessarily the full truth. He enjoyed the challenge of running a con, staying one step ahead of the authorities, figuring out ways to turn an ordinary object into something the public practically salivated over owning.

Yet, the thought of being forced out of the city due to fleecing hard-working people didn't have the same ring of excitement it did in years past. Victor refused to take part in the schemes, but mostly because his friend enjoyed Indianapolis and felt he could put down roots here.

"Mrs. Samuels, I have your items ready." He tore a length of brown paper from a bolt on the counter and stretched it out before him. "I'm sorry to hear of the headaches plaguing you. These two items should provide some relief."

"That's very good news, Mr. Browning. Between my husband and the four children, it will take nothing short of a miracle to make my poor head settle." As the middle-aged woman spoke, she rubbed her left temple.

"Mmmhmm." He wrapped the flowers and the vial into the brown paper, tying it off with twine. "Steep one teaspoon of the passion flower in boiling water for ten minutes before drinking. Do this a few times a day until the headaches subside. It's said to calm the drinker. If you find it doesn't help, put five drops of the peppermint oil in a basin of cold water. Dampen a cloth, wring it out, then press the compress to your forehead for a few minutes and breathe in the aroma."

He handed the parcel to his customer and moved to the cash register. "Barring that, you'll probably need to see the doctor, but I thank you for the business. That'll be eighty-five cents." Tyler rested his gaze on her matronly frame. Lines of tiredness crossed her face, and he mentally excused her. He half-suspected if she'd discipline her unruly brood and tell her louse of a husband to stop drinking his salary, most of her headaches would go away on their own.

As the woman counted out exact change, the bells on the front door jangled. A cluster of three women entered the apothecary, chattering like magpies, complaining about real or imagined ailments and what they should do about them. All darted sly glances at him before dropping their voices to a whisper.

Damn the press and their rumors.

"Oh, Mr. Browning, I'm fifty cents short. If it wouldn't be too much trouble, could I open an account?" The woman's nasal tone languished dangerously close to a whine.

Shopkeepers were always shortchanged. Chances were, the customer would never come back to pay on her bill, yet if he was amiable enough, she might tell her friends to drop by for the attentive service, which could lead to future sales. Pasting on a smile, he slid the coins she did give him into the cash drawer and closed it before she could weasel the money back. "Never you worry, Mrs. Samuels. I will indeed open an account and you just come on by to pay when you're able." His smile widened. Now was the perfect time to try out his new speech for the tonic.

Being mid-afternoon, the women still had plenty of time to cool their heels before haring off to care for their families. And the best part of the plan? No frowning males, who would try to be the voice of reason, accompanied them. No rambunctious children were in tow to distract their attention.

His luck had suddenly turned.

Ladies, may I have your attention for one moment?" Tyler thumped his cane on the floor. When all four of them looked at him, expectation in their expressions, he gave them the grin that had gotten him out of trouble more times than he could count. The charm came natural and he used it to his advantage. "As you may or may not have heard, I can offer you the unique opportunity to buy something completely different from my shop."

A few murmurs went through the small crowd and heads nodded.

Tyler stifled a laugh. It was almost too easy. Thanks to the ridiculously inaccurate article in the newspaper, everyone was naturally curious as to what exactly he did in the back room. With measured steps, he shuffled toward the very same alleged den of iniquity to a chorus of gasps. "What I have in my storeroom will directly benefit you, my most *valued* customers." Another two steps took him to the doorway. His audience strained forward, each pressing against the counter, their eyes wide.

Ah, the gullible. Ducking into the store room, Tyler pulled a bottle of mineral water from its box. The bells on the door rang again, prompting him to add a second bottle. With any luck, he'd sell the whole box today which would be a good indicator of what he could expect on Sunday at the City Market.

The first woman his gaze fell on after leaving the storeroom was Julia Spencer. His heart slammed into his ribcage while subtle heat sang through his blood stream. What was she doing here? Could he go through the farce with the journalist watching? Since their meeting earlier that morning, he hadn't been able to shake her from his mind. Having made some of his money on the power of observation, he'd easily memorized her features and recalled them several times throughout the day.

Not beautiful in the docile style men of the day seemed to favor, Julia's blonde hair and blue eyes tugged at a deep down protective instinct in him, except on closer examination, she appeared anything but helpless or even submissive. She had strength of will and an integrity he lacked. He'd feel envious of that had he not been preoccupied in further committing the enticement of her curves and narrow waist to memory. Something about the would-be journalist held him captive, and he'd bet everything he owned she held secrets of her own behind that false front of bravado. But what? And how could he worm it out of her to use to his advantage?

As she stood staring back, with a pencil stuck into her perfectly coifed hair and her blue eyes radiating disapproval, he confirmed his next course of action. If he could convince the press—and her—he was legitimate, they'd have no choice but to print a retraction. If all went well, perhaps he could finagle a kind write-up on the front page or even a public nod of approval.

His grin widened until he thought his jaws would crack. And how else did a man convince a woman to do what he wanted? Flatter her, lavish on the compliments, and wine and dine her until she capitulated. Julia represented a challenge, and he intended to conquer her resistance. If none of the former worked, he wasn't above throwing a little seduction into the mix.

"Miss Spencer. How kind of you to drop by my humble establishment." Tyler deposited the two bottles on the countertop. "Ladies, you're in for a treat. Miss Spencer works for the *Indianapolis Sentinel*. She's a crack reporter and she's here," he winked and edged closer to the group, "to write a column about this." He gestured to the bottles of water.

A unison gasp nearly sucked the air from the room.

"What is it?" Mrs. Samuels stretched out a hand, touching a finger to the proffered bottles. "Is it liquor?"

Tyler gave her an indulgent chuckle. He ignored Mrs. Samuels in favor of holding Julia's gaze. "*This* is what I've named my Marvelous Mystery Tonic." He plucked one bottle from the counter and slowly came around until he stood in the midst of the women. Their combined body heat added to the close feeling in the store. Body odor mingled with the scents of powder and perfume to clog his throat. He pushed down his aversion to the circumstances in favor of making a sale. "Have you ever been plagued by phantom pains you cannot explain? Do little niggling aches bother you, but you cannot clarify where they originate? Do you suffer from insomnia when all you want to do is sleep?"

Five pairs of eyes followed his every movement. Five pairs of eyes stared between him and the bottle of clear liquid he held up to the light, but only one of those sets of eyes held a huge dose of skepticism. Time to localize his pitch.

"Just think of it, Miss Spencer." He gently pushed through the cluster of women to stand before the reporter. "Every time those pesky female complaints come calling, take a few sips of the tonic and you'll never need to worry about them again. You'll wake up rejuvenated and wondering if you imagined the problem." Uncorking the bottle, he held it out to her. "One taste. You can be the one to tell these women how refreshing my mystery tonic is."

"I have no need to swallow any of your vile concoction. I'll tell you exactly what I think it is right now." A frown graced Julia's lips. "Most likely, it has no healing properties."

"Ah, but that's where you're wrong." His pulse increased. Somehow, he needed to convince the woman to play into his act. "This mystery tonic has been known to clear away skin blemishes, quiet an upset stomach and even restore patience." Conscious of his audience, he lifted the bottle to his lips and took a deep drink. As he lowered the vessel, he let his eyes drift close for a few seconds. When he opened them and caught Julia's gaze, he smiled. "There's nothing quite like the feel of the elixir as it moves down my throat. It warms my belly. I can feel it coursing through my veins, searching for something to heal."

Julia emitted an unladylike snort. "That's ridiculous."

"Is it?" He'd seen the flash of disbelief in her eyes, but behind it was a sparkle of curiosity and hunger to trust. When a customer teetered, it was only a matter of time until they fell on his side. "Try it and see." Tyler edged closer to her. The sweet scent of her perfume or soap provided a welcome reprieve from the foul air around them. "I'm certain there are hidden hurts you would do almost anything to soothe away, to forget."

"I rather doubt—"

"Let me finish." He dropped his voice to a mere whisper. "My mystery tonic has been known to ease the mind's torment as well."

The four other women pressed forward. Everything hinged on what Julia would do. Breaths were held, conversations stilled and the atmosphere itself tingled on the brink. Shadows swirled in the darker depths of her eyes as an internal debate raged.

Finally, due to curiosity or the pressure inherent in the room, Julia took the bottle from him. Her fingers brushed his and a jolt of energy akin to lightning shot up his arm. Her eyes widened as if she felt it too, then she lifted the tonic to her lips and took a mere sip.

Tyler's breath shuddered from his throat. He hadn't been aware he held it. "Why limit yourself to such a tiny taste? This bottle is but a sample. Please, indulge yourself." She narrowed her eyes but did as he instructed. The muscles in her neck constricted with every delicate swallow, and when she pulled the bottle away, a lone drop of water clung to her luscious bottom lip. He stifled a groan as the urge to kiss away the moisture grew strong.

"I won't deny it has a sweet, crisp taste." Julia handed the container back to him, careful not to linger. She darted out her tongue and whisked the water droplet from her lip. "However, as to its healing properties, I'm afraid more research is needed." She frowned and cocked her head to one side, considering. "Yet, I'd be remiss if I didn't mention that I do seem to *feel* it in my body, which is quite preposterous."

That was as good an endorsement as any. Tyler grinned and turned to the other women. "You see? If I were you, I wouldn't wait too long to purchase this marvelous tonic for yourselves. Once I take it to the Market this weekend, the demand should be strong. Who knows when you might need it? Dig deep into those pocketbooks and sacrifice the mere one dollar per bottle." He plunked the half-empty bottle on the counter. "Please, have a sample if you're unsure."

A flurry of activity commenced as the newly fleeced women scrambled to procure the cash and fight over the water. Tyler gently grasped Julia's elbow and drew her from the fray. "While I appreciate your preliminary endorsement, I'm troubled you don't fully believe."

"How can I when I'm still firmly convinced you're out to scam these poor people? You ought to be ashamed."

"Shame is only for much worse crimes." His groin hardened as his mind fixated on her lips. "To show you I'm not the criminal you believe, come on a picnic with me this Saturday. Bring your friend if you like. I'll convince my friend to accompany us if you require a chaperone. Spend time in my company, and you'll eventually see I'm not out to deceive."

She nodded curtly. "Let me think on your invitation. I promise to give you an answer by week's end." She turned and left the shop.

Tyler frowned. Julia was a mystery to be sure. What was it she was so eager to purge from her soul, and why did gaining her regard and good opinion weigh so heavily on him?

Chapter Four

The scent of gunpowder filled the air. All around him, buildings burned. The orange glow of the flames tinged the cloudy sky pink then red, a reminder that war took no prisoners, had no favorites. Death claimed whoever was weak—the man who was loved as well as the man who had everything before him.

"Fall back! Damn it, Tyler, we need to move! The cavalry's advancing." Victor clasped his shoulder. As captain of the small outfit, his word was law when it came to position on the field. Their platoon had lost more than a few members over the last few days. They couldn't afford to lose any more. "Come on."

"Right behind you." Tyler gripped his pistol tighter and jammed his wide-brimmed hat onto his head. "Joshua, we're moving out!" He glanced over his shoulder, making sure the youngest member of their platoon followed.

They called Josh "the kid" even though he'd celebrated his twenty-first birthday on the field the day before. Under his hat, the kid's springy flame-red curls gleamed. Fear reflected in his huge green eyes. "Doin' my best, sir."

"Stay close and low. Our goal is the foxhole up ahead, just behind that rise. At best, the mounted patrol will race right by us." Tyler focused on Victor's shoulders as his friend performed a strange sort of duck walk and crouch.

All around them, shouts from both sides of the conflict rang out. Heavy Spanish accents identified the enemy while the twang of the Americans reminded him of home. He could almost taste the sweet, sour lemonade his mother made or hear the buzz of bees in her rosebushes.

Longing filled his chest, but he had no time to linger in fond memories.

The ground trembled, a forewarning of the impending horse-mounted charge. Several of the Americans passed them in the retreat, and judging from their determined expressions, they were none too happy about the prospect.

Ahead of him, Victor stumbled, his left foot twisting when it caught on a clump of tangled weeds. His friend fell heavily to his knees. His rifle flew out of his hands. "You all right?" Somewhere close by, rifle reports accompanied the bark of orders.

"Twisted ankle I think." Victor staggered to his feet, limping heavily. "Go on. Get the kid to safety." He waved Tyler off.

As Tyler dithered, Joshua joined them. From behind a cluster of shrubs, an enemy soldier in a green uniform popped up with his rifle trained on Victor's heart. No time for hesitation, Tyler took aim and pulled the trigger. Dust rose up when the man hit the dirt. "Damn it, Victor, you can't walk." He jammed the pistol into his waistband then ducked under Victor's arm. "Lean on me. It's not far now." He grunted as Victor leaned his weight against him. "Keep close, Josh, I'm not in the mood to save your ass, too."

Minutes seemed like hours as the trio slowly covered the uphill ground. Bodies littered the area, some dying and some already dead. They couldn't spare the time to help. Tyler vowed to save all he could once the threat passed. Seconds later, they collapsed into the trench as sand and loose dirt fell on top of them.

Other soldiers crowded the space, making the air close and stagnant. His heart raced, almost shooting out of his chest from the exertion of the forced march and hauling Victor to safety. He yanked off his hat and fanned his face. Sweat poured down his back, soaking his khaki uniform. *God, this damn island is sweltering.*

Beside him, Victor propped his foot on the earthen wall of the trench, his face blanched beneath its tan. On Tyler's other side, Joshua crouched. His eyes were still wide and Tyler smelled the young man's terror. He laid a gloved hand on the kid's knee. "Take it easy. The snipers will get most of the mounted. After that, we'll fall back and join the rest of our fellows. We'll have a good night's sleep then beat the bastards tomorrow."

"I need to know what's happening. I can't sit here and not know." Joshua's eyes went wild, a sure sign of exhaustion. He staggered up.

Tyler grabbed the boy's pant leg and yanked him downward. "You'll keep your fucking ass down unless you want your head blown off." He dropped a hand to Joshua's shoulder. "Keep it together. We'll get through this. I promise."

The boy nodded. "I got a wife back home, ya know? My baby girl just turned two. On my birthday." A weak grin lit his face. "We share the date."

"All the more reason to stay alive, don't you think?"

Joshua drew a deep breath and let it out. "It's hard."

Tyler squeezed his friend's shoulder. "Stay down." He turned his attention to Victor for a mere second when movement from Joshua caught his attention. The boy stood, leaving his torso exposed, and then it was as if the seconds turned to hours. "No!"

The snap of a rifle exploded in the air. A dull thud of the bullet lodged in human tissue. Joshua's body jerked backward and slid down into the trench. The red bloom of blood stained his shirtfront, growing increasingly larger, darker.

"Damn it!" Tyler scrambled to the fallen man. "Can you hear me? Don't die on me, buddy." But it was too late. Joshua's eyes dimmed. He clutched Tyler's jacket with one hand while pressing against his wound. Blood oozed through his fingers, staining them, too.

"I had to know…" His breath rattled wetly and grew labored. "Take care of my girls. Make sure they have the life I wanted for them." A pain-filled groan gurgled from his throat. "I should've listened…" Uttering a tiny sigh, he slumped into the trench, his eyes sad and locked onto Tyler's face.

A heavy wash of guilt crashed into Tyler's chest. He cursed the heavens for the futility of war and shot to his feet, determined to avenge the death of his innocent friend. Despite Victor's call of warning, Tyler drew his pistol and jumped from the trench.

Before he could take more than a step, agonizing pain ripped through his knee. Another vein of hot torment shot through his thigh as shrapnel carved open his flesh. He cried out, angry at the world. The force of the hit sent him tumbling backward into the trench, consumed by blackness.

Tyler sat bolt upright in bed. Sweat drenched his body. The taste of dirt and sulphur coated his tongue, so real he could almost feel the grit of it on his teeth. With his pulse frantically pounding, his lungs heaving as if he'd spent the last minutes fleeing from encroaching enemy armies, he swung his legs over the side then toppled to the mattress, awash in a wave of white-hot pain.

He'd had the dream again. And once more, he'd been unable to save Joshua's life. It never changed; never offered him a different glimpse than the one he'd seen played out in his mind every week since he'd come back from Cuba five years before.

Struggling upright, he massaged his knee. The pain didn't recede, so he yanked the soft trousers from his limbs to examine the wound. Of course, the actual injury was gone. Left behind was the network of scars marring his thigh and the rows of angry, twisted flesh. Some days, bone ground against bone since most of the cartilage had been obliterated by the bullet.

The pain subsided, but the memories raged as if he'd just lived through them. The first shot had shattered the side of his kneecap. The doctors stateside had performed what he called "miracle" surgery, so he now retained almost full use of the socket joint. The second shot had furrowed his thigh. Even now, bits of shrapnel lay still embedded somewhere within his flesh. At times, a tiny piece would work its way to the surface and the pain was unbearable, a constant reminder of what he'd done—or hadn't done.

Rolling onto his back, Tyler stared at the ceiling. He didn't live in the past, couldn't change it no matter how hard he wanted to. There was only the future—except for the damn nightmares that wouldn't cut him loose. He needed to think about something else, wedge goodness into the gaping maw of violence and death until the light shone into his heart again.

An image of Julia Spencer slid through his consciousness.

Tyler grinned and closed his eyes. He'd been in her presence twice, the last being two days prior, but he craved another meeting. Her blonde hair tempted him and he wanted to see it unbound, free about her shoulders. Perhaps it would flow to the middle of her back, maybe long enough to cover her breasts as she lay naked against his pillows. That thought brought a chuckle. As if the prim and proper Miss Spencer would ever consent to that sort of relationship, with him least of all.

He'd bet a year's pay she was a virgin beneath those very business-like gowns, button-up jackets and hideous hat. What else could she be under all that strict attire? His groin ached and grew hard as he mentally stripped her down to her underclothes. Would they be serviceable garments or did she let her personality shine through embroidery, lace and ribbons? What if he was wrong about her altogether? Tyler opened his eyes and considered the ceiling once more.

Cracks crisscrossed the plaster, and in one corner of the room, a brown water stain marred the crown molding. Most likely she came from old money. Being from the near-south himself, he'd heard the faint Southern accent in her voice. What part of the country did she come from?

She was too forthright and distrustful to be a pampered miss. Just the fact she'd become a journalist spoke volumes about her belief in herself and the issues of the world she lived in. Yet he couldn't forget the secrets lurking in her blue eyes or the haunted expression that stole over her face when she thought no one was looking.

Julia Spencer had a past, he was sure of it. And he was exactly the man to uncover it. He absently rubbed his knee again, but the phantom pain had gone. Interesting that spending time in her company, albeit only in his thoughts, made him temporarily forget the horrors he'd seen. If only she could take away his guilt as well.

Glancing at his pocket watch later that evening, Tyler heaved a sigh of relief. Seven o'clock meant time to close the shop and head for home through the shadows. Even though he was exhausted from the restless sleep of the night before, he had no intention of succumbing to dreamland quite so soon.

A bottle of brandy would be his companion, perhaps he'd unearth a box of cigars and invite Victor and some other friends over for a few hands of good-natured poker. The conversation and convivial ribbing would clear the cobwebs from his mind and the alcohol would ensure he wouldn't remember his dreams when he finally dropped into slumber.

It would also relieve the crushing guilt every Thursday brought.

If it wasn't for the one last errand he needed to make before gaining his own home, he could look forward to the evening. Refusing to think about the task ahead, he ducked into the back room, gathered the empty box for his mineral water and returned to the main shop room. The wooden container fell from his suddenly lifeless fingers as his gaze met that of Julia.

The bells hadn't rung to alert him to her arrival. He darted a glance at the door, propped open with a brick to catch the cool night breeze. Damn it! He'd forgotten about that.

"Ah, good evening, Miss Spencer. How fortuitous you've chosen to visit me, but may I inquire as to why?" He didn't trust her speculative expression or the way she regarded him as if he were a criminal.

"My walk to the cab stands and the interurban takes me directly past your shop. I saw your door open and wanted to give my regards in person." She moved farther into the shop, looking around at the bottles and tubes that lined his shelves. "How did business go today?"

"Should I be honored or flattered you remembered me?" When she didn't answer, Tyler chuckled and grinned. "Let's try a different question. Are you asking about my apothecary or my side business? For that matter, do you wish to know for yourself or for the newspaper?"

A hint of a blush infused her cheeks. "Both."

"I see." Stowing the wooden box beneath the counter, he gripped his cane and joined her in the center of the store. Burning interest consumed him to know what motivated the visit. "I'm proud to say both ventures are quite successful, thank you for your inquiry." Uncomfortable under her steady stare, he wracked his brain for a way to knock her from the lofty pedestal she'd placed herself on. "Tell me, Miss Spencer, have you always wanted to be a reporter? Surely a beautiful woman such as you has had other hobbies, other pursuits that have interested you in the past."

"You don't know me well enough for me to answer that question." She captured her bottom lip between her teeth. It was an endearing habit, that gesture. "Or to comment on my looks." A frown followed the words.

What did she wish to hide? And why?

He sneaked another quick peek at his watch. Damn it all to hell. If he lingered much more, he'd be late, and already, these Thursday appointments were long enough. "Let me walk you to the nearest cab stand. I'll even pay your way home." Hobbling to the door, he procured a ring of keys from his pocket and slid the brick away. "After you."

"Do you think I'm incapable of reaching my home without being molested?" She swept past him, waiting on the wooden walkway outside.

Her haughty attitude stuck in his craw like rancid meat. "No, but I intend to do the honorable thing and relieve my own conscience. Why don't you pretend you have a fluttering, womanly heart beneath that tough exterior and let someone take care of you?" He ignored her while he locked the apothecary door. Once the bolt rang home, he pocketed the keys and turned to her, offering his arm. "Walk with me." It was an order that dared her to defy him.

The steady *clip-clop* of horse hooves against the cobblestones rang between the buildings, drowned out occasionally by the roar of an automobile engine and the ebb and flow of pedestrian conversation.

"Thank you for the escort." She slipped her hand through his crooked elbow and matched his stride.

Mollified by her compliant change, Tyler nodded. "You're welcome." He acknowledged an acquaintance as they passed. "If you intend to pursue me for a newspaper article, please do so during business hours. However, if your interest is of a personal nature, you'll be welcome anytime. I have a business to protect, so do your worst. My reputation is already damaged beyond repair."

"You're a rude man, Mr. Browning, but I appreciate your honesty. However, a reputation is a fickle thing. You'd be better off to make sure your actions match your words." A fleeting smile graced her lips. "Let's say my interest in you lies in both camps and leave it there."

That didn't make this meeting any less of an annoyance. Did she not have an inkling of how to flirt while in a man's company, or was she simply not attracted to him?

Damnation, the woman was a bitter pill. Mentally, he shrugged. It meant he'd need to work more diligently at wooing her into revealing her own secrets as well as firmly securing her paper's endorsement. Too bad he couldn't postpone his appointment this evening to start on the subject. The taxi stand loomed ahead. A handful of people milled about, waiting their turn at a conveyance.

"To get what you want from a subject, you must remember the age old game of tit for tat, Miss Spencer." He drew her close enough to see the indigo ring around her irises, shining in the faint light of a street lamp. "If I reveal a tidbit about my life, then you must do the same for me. We'll continue the game until we're both satisfied." He grinned as outrage and denial warred for dominance on her face. "I believe there's a free cab just there."

"Fine. Thank you, Mr. Browning."

Interesting. The blonde reporter became front page news in his interests.

As soon as Julia entered the cab, she glanced out the window, making sure Tyler had continued on his way. Once she'd secured his direction, she exited the cab on the other side and followed him, keeping close to the shadows. He'd ushered her up the walkway too fast, and aside from his last, blatant comment, he hadn't lingered to talk or spend time lathering on his consummate charm.

That alone sent up a red flag of warning that he hadn't been quite honest.

Uncle George had given her this man to her as an assignment simply to keep her out of the newspaper office. That didn't mean there wasn't something shady going on with Tyler Browning outside of selling his ridiculous miracle tonic. Once she found out what he hid, she'd write the piece and convince her uncle she had the instinct to handle articles about issues that mattered instead of a fluff column people would wrap fish in.

Had Tyler not said that one little line about letting someone take care of her, she'd have left him alone until the weekend picnic. It worried her he thought of her as unbending and cold. This wasn't the image she wished to portray to the world. Yet, if she kept people at arm's length, she wouldn't be hurt again. Anything else was too dangerous, too wicked …too disappointing.

Lost in her musings, she didn't see the alleyway Tyler turned down and wasted five minutes backtracking. She stepped in a puddle, silently cursing as water seeped into the leather of her boot, wetting the stocking as well as the hem of her skirt. The steady tap-tap of his cane against the cobblestones gave away his position. She followed the sound. How had he come by the injury?

After a series of twists and turns through the damp warrens of tight streets and dark alleyways, they reached a dead end. Julia glanced over her shoulder as the hair on the back of her neck prickled. If she were to be accosted in this unknown section of town, she'd have no idea how to return to the safer, well-lit central streets of the city.

A run-down tenement building loomed in the lowering darkness. Few windows were lit from within, and the ones that were held the shadows of the occupants who lived there. Julia ducked behind an unruly line of shrubbery as Tyler stepped furtively to one of the doors on the ground floor and knocked quietly. When the door opened, the faint illumination revealed the figure of a woman.

Pretty enough, her brown hair hanging in disorganized waves around her shoulders and a drab gray dress enclosing her slim figure, the woman appeared pleased to see him. A healthy blush stained the young woman's cheeks as she chatted with Tyler and invited him inside.

A gentle thump sounded as the door closed, leaving Julia alone.

Who was she? A wife, a lover, a sister perhaps? Heat infused her cheeks. Bored, nerves fluttering in her stomach, she crept closer, leaving the safety of the hedge. Surely he wasn't making a house call to hawk the miracle tonic, and he certainly didn't carry a parcel which would necessitate a delivery.

Her breath caught as a new thought occurred. Were the articles in the paper correct when they stated he provided the female population relaxation by way of illicit sexual practices? Did he conduct an affair even now, warming the unknown woman's bed? Was this a regular assignation or a new relationship?

Her stomach clenched at the unconfirmed knowledge. What difference did it make to her how Mr. Browning used his time or his affections? He was nothing more than an acquaintance to her, a business associate at best, yet everything she'd seen of him made her burn with a thousand questions. The unfortunate side-effect of her body's reaction to his nearness could easily be ignored. It had been much too long since she'd cultivated a connection to a man.

As if any of her prior associations regarding the male of the species had been cultivated by her. She shook her head in disgust, desperate to clear the memories.

She needed hard facts—not wasted energy in an emotional connection to someone who wouldn't care for her once he'd gotten his pleasure. No, she intended to keep their association to the business of the press, and she refused to march into the *Sentinel's* office without a well-researched article.

A barking dog in the distance caused her to shrink back into the shadows afforded by the building's façade. Gentle rain had begun to fall, adding to the general miserable conditions as she dithered. Should she wait until Tyler exited the apartment or should she take a chance at finding her way back to polite civilization in the rapidly gathering darkness? Or worse, what if he indeed was engaging in sexual pleasures behind that door and wouldn't be through until dawn? She could hardly skulk around in the bushes like a thief or a voyeur.

Her cheeks burned. What right did she have to mentally disparage his after-dark rendezvous when she herself was hardly pure? Luckily for her, no one knew the truth; no one in her social circles had an inkling of her past—otherwise, her name would be splashed across the papers the same as Tyler's. Of course, there was one huge exception. The general public would turn a blind eye to a man's indiscretions under the guise of sowing wild oats while her secrets would be scandal fodder for months. Not to mention the anguish and embarrassment that tidbit would have on her family or the future of her own prospects.

God, she'd really botched her life. It wouldn't be fair to drag those she loved through the dirt of her past. It was her nasty little secret, and she'd carry it around for the rest of her life. With any luck, she wouldn't need to share. No one knew what she'd done, and she intended to keep it that way.

Which meant pouring all her energy into unmasking Tyler Browning and resisting his efforts to pry into her life despite his tantalizing assurances of tit for tat.

"What have we here? A prowler or a nosy journalist, or perhaps stalking is your game of choice, Miss Spencer?"

The sound of Tyler's voice so close at hand cut into her wandering thoughts. She jumped but couldn't mistake the anger in his statement. She wasn't given a chance to defend her reasoning for he roughly grabbed her upper arm and yanked her from her hiding spot.

"Did you hope to catch me doing something illegal, perhaps scandalous?"

Julia shook her head. She needed to get herself together and gain control of the situation. "I intend to do an article on you. Logic dictates I follow wherever you happen to go in order to determine what you're doing, to learn your habits." Her attempt to wrench away from him failed since his grip didn't slack. His hair gleamed nearly blue in the failing light, but she couldn't gauge his expression.

"I warned you earlier to ask whatever questions you liked. I must tell you I draw the line at creeping around." He halted them in one of the shadowy streets then captured her gaze. "Becoming part of the criminal element is easy once you make the decision to act like them."

"You'd certainly know about that." When he didn't answer, only pressed his lips into a tight line, her anger grew. "You consider me a criminal simply for performing my job?"

"Why not? You basically accused me of the same, several times."

"That's what you are if you insist on selling everyday water as a miracle tonic." She touched her tongue to a corner of her mouth as if she could taste the slightly sweet, clean water. "What of your meeting with that woman?" She gestured toward the tenement building. "Is she part of the scheme, or are you running a separate scam using her?"

Barely contained rage flashed in his eyes. "If I told you the truth, said I wasn't a bad person and had legitimate reasons for what I do, would you believe me, or have you already formed an opinion and will abide by it regardless?"

"I—" Julia broke off on an outraged squeak when he shook her arm.

"The press has a habit of presenting the public with their version of the truth. Suffice it to say, you can never begin to try and fathom my actions. Don't patronize me by pretending you're interested in finding out the real motivation when you have no intentions of printing it."

"Are you done?" His grip loosened. As she pulled back, she planted her hands on her hips. "Though you have every reason to mistrust the press, you can be assured I'll do your story the justice it deserves. I can do no less." She stared him down, daring him to look away first. "You have my word." In an effort to repair a convivial air, Julia extended a hand.

To her great relief, he clasped it, his warm fingers closing smoothly around hers. "I'll hold you to your promise." Grinning, he eased her hand to his lips and placed a feather-weighted kiss on her knuckles. "May I ask you a question?"

A host of shivers crept down her spine as much from his whispered query as the touch of his lips. "Yes." A one-word answer? What kind of a wordsmith was she?

Tyler turned her hand over and plied a kiss to the sensitive underside of her wrist. "Do you consider me the same man the reporter from the *Sentinel* wrote about? The one doing depraved acts in my apothecary shop?"

Flutters tickled her stomach, and their wings caressed her womb with sensation she thought had long been banished. "I haven't been given evidence to convince me otherwise." A few drops of rain accumulated on her lashes. She blinked to remove them.

"Ah, then allow me to rectify that problem." His dark eyes glittered in the dim illumination as he tugged her into an alley.

Black as pitch between brick buildings, puddles dotted the pavement. She and Tyler splashed through the wetness in silence. Her heart pounded, slightly in fear, but more from anticipation and excitement. Tyler Browning lit her curiosity and captured her imagination. The need for facts slid from her brain in the face of exploring such tumultuous undercurrents.

"Mr. Browning, have you taken leave of your senses?" Her mouth went dry as he whirled around, grasped her hips and wedged her between the brick wall and the harder, more interesting wall of his chest.

"Actually, Miss Spencer, I'm very aware of what I'm doing." His warm, moist breath danced across her cheeks.

"And that would be?" She could hardly force the words past her tight throat.

"Showing you the man you believe I am."

His lips descended on hers, imparting the energy of a small lightning bolt. Firm yet pliable, he moved over her mouth as if he were comfortable kissing strange women all the time.

Perhaps he did.

She put up a struggle, for what sort of woman would she be if she didn't try to fight? Then, her common sense fled when he didn't attempt to restrain her. Perhaps he wasn't like the men of her previous acquaintance. A sigh escaped from deep at the back of her throat as she slid her hands around his neck and pressed closer to him. She'd been kissed numerous times before, but none of those embraces made her feel as if she were floating and burning from within at the same time.

He skated his tongue along her bottom lip then he repeated the action on her top one. She gasped at the exquisite spirals of pleasure exploding low in her belly. She burrowed her fingers into his soft, thick curls, knocking his bowler hat slightly askew, and sighed again when he slipped his tongue into her mouth and flirted with hers.

Liquid warmth eased between her thighs. Heat prickled through her body from every point they touched. His kiss invoked images of what a woman should feel, everything wholesome and good that could occur between a male and a female, and then a wave of crippling ugliness spilled across the visions, marring their beauty, leaving dark stains, obliterating them as if they never occurred.

She could never have a normal life. Not with Tyler. Not with anyone.

Not anymore.

Emitting an anguished cry, she angled her palms against his chest and pushed, using all her might. "Enough. You've made your point, Mr. Browning, and I must say my opinion of you still stands." She hoped the alley was too dark for him to see the tears in her eyes or the trauma that must surely reflect in her face.

Tyler drew a deep breath and blew it out. He clenched his hands into fists, frustration evident in his stance. "You could be a pleasant person if you'd just let yourself relax for a man to become acquainted with the softer side you hide from the world."

She attempted to laugh, but the sound came out a sad, strangled sort of noise. "The last time I let down my guard, people took advantage, men used me and I lost control of my life for a time." Lifting her gaze to his, Julia shook her head. "Never again. Now I live for myself."

"Do you, or are you so hell bent on attention you'd lap it up from anyone?" The words were soft with no hint of censure.

"I...that isn't your business." How could she explain, even if she wished to?

"I can help you work through the pain." He reached for her. She sidestepped his effort. "I understand how guilt can own your soul."

"How, by telling me to drink your tonic? What a lark." She wrapped her arms around her middle, suddenly cold. "Don't assume you can preach to me when your life is as damaged as mine. I see it in your eyes." She drew in a shaky breath and let it out in a whoosh. "I'm doing fine on my own." But was she? Her uncle's words of the morning came back to haunt her and she wondered how long before the past found her.

"No, by finding a friend you can trust. Right now, I think that's exactly what you need." Gently, he grasped her hand and drew it through his crooked elbow. "Allow me to hail you a cab and see you home. You have had a trying day."

Surreptitiously, she blinked away moisture from her eyes. It would be an even longer one tomorrow, for she'd continue to hound Tyler and try to unravel the mystery of his tonic water. If only it really could work miracles, but that, of course, was impossible. The paper was the only thing she needed in her life. Yet, a glimmer of expectation flickered in her chest.

Perhaps she did need to learn how to trust again, but she would advance slowly and work silently to keep the walls around her heart defended.

Chapter Five

Throughout the long afternoon the next day, Julia held her tongue at the newspaper office. Several telegrams had come in from her counterparts in Galveston, Texas describing complete devastation from the hurricane. The city had virtually been wiped off the map. Thousands were dead and missing. One hurried report chronicled the masses of corpses and whether they should be sent out to sea or burned to prevent disease. Another excited statement gushed about how an assistant to the inventor Thomas Edison had smuggled a moving picture camera to the scene. The reporters couldn't wait to see the film.

Julia gritted her teeth and continued to write preliminary details regarding Tyler Browning, but she couldn't concentrate on anything except the big story in Texas. How unfair that she was stuck in Indianapolis working on the con artist story instead of real news.

After breaking her pencil lead for the second time, she threw the writing utensil down in frustration. It was impossible. Between the field reports and her mind constantly remembering last evening's embrace, she hadn't written more than five words in the last few minutes. So Tyler had kissed her. It wasn't her first, and most assuredly it wouldn't be her last. Why then did her traitorous body heat and prickle just at the mere recollection of the episode? Why did she crave a more intimate relationship?

She jabbed at the "a" key on her typewriter, sending a line of the same letter across a piece of paper until the hammer stuck from her vehement pounding. He was nothing more than the subject of a newspaper article.

Heaving a sigh, she stood just as Uncle George entered his office. Julia smoothed a hand over her shirt, lightly touching the pearl buttons down the front, and took a deep breath. "Uncle George."

"Ah, Julia." An eye roll accompanied the salutation as he maneuvered around her and then claimed his chair. "I can only imagine what question you'll bother me with today." He folded his hands upon the desktop and lifted an eyebrow. "Well?"

"Why do you and Mr. Hayes not get along?"

"Why do you expect? If he's a spy from the *Indianapolis Star*, he'll yank our livelihoods from us."

"No, it's more than that. There's a different sort of tension between you two now." She edged around his desk, leaning close. "You mentioned he'd partaken in ugly gossip. You of all people should know not to believe idle gossip without proof." She kept her voice low so the others wouldn't hear. "You can tell me. I'm discreet."

Uncle George stood to his imposing height as a rush of angry, mottled color crept over his face. "I told you before; you don't need to concern yourself. I've taken care of it, and that's all for the moment." He engulfed her in a hug. "Your parents are comin' home tonight. I'm throwin' my dear brother a welcome home dinner at y'all's house. Why don't you take the rest of the afternoon off and go beautify yourself? In fact, let me give you some money." He delved his free hand into a pants pocket and brought out a money clip containing a slim wad of bills. "Go buy a new hat or some other geegaw you women lust after these days."

"You never mentioned a party to me. Who's doing the decorating, the food, or any of it, and why didn't you ask me to help?" She bit the inside of her bottom lip. Honestly, she'd forgotten about her parents' return, what with worrying over Tyler. They'd been gone on their trip for weeks, and she hadn't given them a thought. Not only would she need to learn how to tolerate their presence again, she'd need to suffer through a social event that hinged on everyone adoring them. "Keep your money," she added as he attempted to shove it at her.

"Didn't occur to me you would want to participate in such things. You're always had your nose to the typewriter, which is surprisin' since I thought you'd throw the chance at the apothecary article back in my face." He chuckled and when she didn't respond, he let his arm drop from her shoulders while replacing the money clip in his pocket. "Damn, Julia darlin', don't get in a snit. I sent my Rose over to help Bess. Besides, both of Bess's daughters are doin' the cookin' and what not. There was no cause to worry your pretty little head, and now you can enjoy it without bein' exhausted. I'm tryin' to care for you despite what you may think."

She'd rather do anything except make the rounds at a party for her parents where she'd have to talk about innate subjects and field asinine comments about her single state. Not to mention dote on the two people in the world she had nothing in common with except blood and ancestry. Her stomach clenched. Would it be so bad if she forgot about her irritation with her parents and forgave them? "I have too much work to do, so I probably won't be there—"

"Nonsense." Uncle George tweaked her nose as if she were a five-year-old. "In fact, no more work for you today or this weekend." He sent her a significant glance. "Enjoy yourself like a normal young woman. Mingle among the guests and have a nice conversation with a gentleman, perhaps snag a beau, but I don't want to see you playin' at work."

Playing. That's what he thought she was doing. As if she could never settle down and be serious about the job. Julia groaned. At this rate, she'd never finish her article. Yet, he appeared so anxious, so worried, that she softened toward him, wanting to set his mind at ease. "Yes, Uncle. I'll try my best." If she did become the good, doting daughter, would her parents finally see her as someone worthy of their love?

Her uncle beamed. "Good girl. I expect to brag about you after dinner. Do me proud so your daddy won't think I didn't take care of you. Too bad Frank's on assignment. I'd have him escort you."

"Too bad." She'd rather pluck out her eyes than go anywhere with Frank. Her head started to pound and she took a few steps backward. "I really need to, well..." She gestured to the door with her chin.

"Wear somethin' pretty." Uncle George winked.

Julia's stomach rolled in protest. She did *not* want to attract attention—specifically from men. Perhaps her headache would blossom into a debilitating pain and she could stay in her room without resorting to dishonesty. She gathered her belongings and stormed out of the newspaper office. Her dramatic exit lost some of its staying power when her skirt caught in the outer door as she slammed it shut. Uttering an oath, she yanked it free and slammed the door a second time to be sure her point was made.

Why did her uncle persist in treating her as if she still wore her hair in braids? Shaking in rage, she longed for the day when the world at large saw her as something other than who she was—or what she had done.

The sharp report of her boot heels rang against the walkway. With each step, her temples throbbed. Her shoulders drooped and her stomach clenched again. She should try to be more grateful toward her uncle. Courtly gentility was all he knew, and if he thought she couldn't make it in the newspaper profession, he'd try to make sure he circulated her around to all the available men in his circle.

He wanted her to be taken care of, just as he'd said. But she couldn't even let herself trust him. Perhaps that was the more terrible crime, that she'd been unable to forget her past and it bled through to her present.

The thought stretched her nerves taut as far as they would go. Society is a very different place now, and she could take care of herself — she had no choice.

So intense were her musings, Julia hadn't realized she was two doors away from Tyler's pharmacy. A slow smile spread over her face. What a heaven-sent opportunity to keep an eye on Tyler as well as keep her uncle's machinations in check and manufacture a red herring.

Like the day before, a brick propped the door open. She entered with determined steps and almost plowed right into Tyler. A group of women headed toward the door from inside. Their bodies and overpowering fragrances filled the tiny shop. All of that flew out of her head when Tyler gripped her waist as he led her to the far side of the shop.

"To what do I owe the honor?" A teasing grin lifted the corners of his lips, and mischief twinkled in his deep brown eyes. "Two days in a row. If the trend continues, I'll grow too big an ego to fit on your front page."

For the love of all that was holy, she'd never seen eyes of such a rich, intriguing color. She felt as if she were falling from a great distance and considered letting herself go merely to see what it would be like to drown in such warm depths. His knowing chuckle yanked her out of the silly thought. Julia stepped away and banged her elbow painfully into one of the shelves behind her. A few bottles rattled together but none toppled.

"Thank you, Mr. Browning. I'm not here in a business capacity." She nodded impatiently at the herd of matronly women as they exited the shop with slow steps and more than a few coquettish glances Tyler's way. Once they left, she continued. "I wish to extend an invitation to a party at my home this evening."

If she'd hoped to shock him into abject silence, that statement did the trick. His eyes widened and his jaw went slack, then he pulled himself together and the ever-present charm slipped over his person.

"Ah, do you think that's wise, Miss Spencer? We hardly know each other well enough for you to invite me home." He darted his gaze over her shoulder before focusing on her once more. "But if you don't mind this little peccadillo..."

"It's a dinner, not asking my father for my hand." A shiver tripped down her spine as he moved a tiny bit closer, backing her into the shelf. In this proximity, the gold flecks in his eyes glowed. "It's a party, given by my uncle to welcome my parents home from weeks of traveling through the southern Americas. If you'd rather not come—"

He put a hand on either side of her head, leaning so close his body brushed hers. "Oh, there's no doubt I want to come. The question is: when do you want me?"

Heat flamed her cheeks at his double meaning. Answering warmth unfurled in languid precision through her belly, and for one insane moment, she considered kissing the slight cleft in his chin merely to see what he would do. She wanted to feel the rasp of his stubble on her tongue, taste the salty sweat on his skin. "Mr. Browning, I..." Her breath stalled. A crisp, clean scent wafted to her nose, reminding her of freshly laundered clothes with a hint of citrus. His presence filled the small space, being everywhere at once, the breadth of his shoulders blocked the brilliance of the sunset through the front windows, allowing enough light to escape to turn his black curls into a wondrous, molten halo.

Her eyelids lowered of their own accord as she rose on tiptoe, moistening her lips. Anticipation made her mouth water. So close, the kiss was almost hers...

The forceful clearing of a masculine throat nearby broke the magical tension and the moment was lost.

Tyler sprang a few feet away as if she'd suddenly caught fire. They both looked at the intruder. "Miss Spencer, please allow me to introduce my friend, Victor Archer. We served together in the military years ago." He moved his head slightly in silent communication with his friend. When the man didn't budge, a glint of anger touched Tyler's face. "Victor, this is Miss Julia Spencer, the journalist I told you about."

The other man inclined his head a fraction of an inch. "Pleased to make your acquaintance." He narrowed his eyes. "Have we met before? You look familiar."

"I cannot place you." The feeling of unease sneaked into her being once more as she scanned her memory, trying to remember him in the flood of faces she'd seen during that horrible time. "No, I don't think so." Why now? Why did everyone appear vaguely as if she'd known them but couldn't definitively recall?

Had she been wrong, keeping her past indiscretions to herself? Was this God's way of punishing her, forever tormenting her, mocking her?

"Mmmhmm." His steely blue gaze drilled into Tyler's, obviously dismissing her. "May I talk with you for one moment?"

"Once I finish." Tyler's firm tone brooked no argument. The blond man retreated to the far side of the shop but never took his gaze from her.

Julia shivered. He acted as if he'd like nothing better than to break her in half, stuff her body in a shipping crate and send her to a deserted island. Why? She'd never met him before. And why did Tyler need a watchdog?

Pushing the imposing man to the back of her mind, she focused on Tyler. Regardless of the frantic beating of her heart, she smiled as if she were conversing with President Roosevelt. "If you should decide to join me for dinner, service starts at seven o'clock at this address." She dug into the small bag hanging from her wrist and took out a calling card. As his fingers brushed hers, her breath shuddered from her body and the same heat from before shot up her spine. "And please, feel free to call me Julia."

She darted out of the shop before her legs could turn to mashed potatoes. Once she'd gained a bit of distance, she sagged against a sign post. That had been the most intense few moments of her life, and all because of one simple glance from the dratted man. Had she learned nothing from her past? Hadn't it been ingrained into her very pores that the touch of a man brought no happiness?

Such feelings were the beginning of the end. Away from Tyler's overwhelming charisma, her head resumed its pounding. If she managed to make it into dinner this evening, she had no idea how she'd be able to sit near him, let alone talk to him.

After that foolish bit of girlish insanity, she would *not* allow herself to feel anything remotely similar again. It was imperative she keep her wits. She'd remain businesslike at all times.

Tyler glanced at the embossed card in his hand, tracing his thumb over the border of stenciled flowers. He recognized the address. It was one of the well-to-do neighborhoods around Brookside Park. Lifting the bit of stationery to his nose, he smiled. Lilies of the valley. The same, elusive scent he'd noticed when he met her in the woods. Subtle and different than the florals most women wore, and compared to roses or lavender, it was non-assuming, delicate but could hold its own in a flower bed.

Much like he imagined Julia would be in a bed of a different sort.

"Will you be spending much more time mooning, or do you want to hear what I need to tell you?" Victor's voice grated over his nerves.

"Jealousy doesn't become you, Victor." Slipping the card into his jacket pocket, Tyler moved behind the counter. "I'm not mooning. Why should I? I barely know her, and from all I've seen, she's harmless. If she manages to write an article about me, it's all to the good. Free publicity will keep the curiosity seekers coming."

If nothing else, Julia would be a shallow flirtation, nothing more. Keeping her close meant being able to direct her attention away from his mineral water scam. If she knew for certain it was bunk, the extra money would dry up and then what would happen to Joshua's widow and child?

"I'm most certainly not jealous." Victor leaned a shoulder against a shelf and crossed his arms over his chest. "Miss Spencer has too much opinion for me, but she may be just the thing to keep you in line, or at least on your toes."

"Why do you say that?"

"She won't rest until she digs into the heart of your ill-advised tonic. I imagine along the way she'll stumble upon a few things you're desperate to keep hidden. You forget I've known you your whole life. Some of your secrets are beginning to rot your brain."

"I suppose I'll need to keep her discombobulated." The ever present knot of self-loathing tightened. What would she do when she discovered how many scams he'd run in the past? Worse yet, how would she react when she found out he'd essentially killed Joshua in that trench? He couldn't think about that right now. Instead, he focused on what else Victor had said. "Why do you think she looks familiar?"

Victor's scowl didn't lesson. "You know the exclusive gentleman's club north of Meridian Street? The one with no name that has a carving of the stallion on the door?"

"Yes, what of it? I haven't visited for months, ever since I—"

"Sold the owner cheap cigars that made him and everyone else sick, not to mention they were laced with hashish and gave them hallucinations?"

A hot flush crept up Tyler's neck. He averted his gaze to the cash register. "That wasn't my fault. Not directly."

"It never is." Victor pushed off the wall to rap his knuckles on the scarred, wooden counter. "Since I still retain my membership, I happened into the establishment not a week past. Above the bar, in a prominent spot, is an oil painting of Miss Spencer, except she's posing in an evocative manner, clad in risqué undergarments."

"That's impossible." Anger steeped in the pit of his stomach, rising through his innards until it heated his chest. "Julia would never consent to do anything of the sort. She's too classy a woman. Hell, I doubt she'd let anyone see her less than fully clothed. I demand you apologize."

"Oh, and you know this because you're so intimately acquainted with her?" Victor's glare shot cold, blue darts. "Now who's acting jealous?"

"I'm not. Perhaps in the near future." Tyler's mind reeled from the implications. "Take back what you said."

"If you don't believe me, drop into the bar and see for yourself. I have no designs on her." His eyes glittered. "Besides, what difference does it make? You have no claim to this woman. Hell, it doesn't appear you have an interest in her other than using her ties on the paper to your advantage."

"True, yet think of the benefits. She moves in a part of society I don't currently have access to. The more well-off folks. People with money. People with substance and roots." He rubbed his hands together. "If I befriend her, maybe she'll tell her acquaintances about my tonic. Imagine the cash flow."

"Why not instead imagine the potential jail time? If you manage to get anywhere close to her, chances are she has enough male relatives to run you out of town once they figure out your motives. Knowing you, you'll use that charm to get her into bed and leave. Unless..." Victor moved into Tyler's personal space and poked him in the shoulder. "Unless she's a con the same as you."

A red wave of anger crashed over him. He shoved at Victor's chest. "How dare you besmirch her reputation?"

"Her *reputation*? If that image is truly hers in the saloon, then we both know what sort of woman she is." Victor pushed back. "I find it fascinating you rush to defend her when you have no idea what the real story is, let alone the one she's chosen to portray to the world. Did you ever stop to think why she's potentially lying?"

"You're right." Tyler drew a deep breath and let it ease out between his lips as he stared at his best and most loyal friend. "I'm sorry. I have no excuse." He grabbed his hat, jammed it on his head and took up his cane. "Do you wish to attend the Spencers' dinner as my guest? She made no restrictions to my bringing a friend."

Victor gave a curt nod. "Perhaps I should. This way I can monitor you, or provide a chaperone as the case may be, only if you promise to stop in at the club in the next few days and take a look at the painting. You can go as my guest. Question the owner. Hell, I'll even let you rough him up a bit, but the matter of Julia's purity and character needs to be settled before you go further with her — in whatever direction."

That gave Tyler pause. "Why are you taking an intense interest in this?"

"Life has kicked you in the teeth a few times. I don't want this woman to hurt you, and I'll stop it if I can. Call it trying to repay my debt." A ghost of a smile touched his lips. "A piece of tail isn't worth it for the long haul if she's playing fast and loose. You deserve better."

"I suppose I should say thank you." Tyler's throat constricted. He'd be damned if he'd let Victor see his weakness. "I have a feeling Julia is an ordinary woman who simply has an excess of bravery and opinions who just happened to be the subject to an artist's fanciful imagination."

At least he hoped so because anything else had the potential to set his blood on fire and land him even further in the mire.

23 Woodbury Lane was everything Tyler expected of an address on this side of town. As he and Victor alighted from the cab, he stared at the two-story Georgian-style home. Soft, golden illumination glowed from every window, the sashes thrown open to usher in the cooler night air. Laughter and sounds of gaiety spilled into the street, compelling him forward through the wrought iron gate and up the pebbled walkway. Before he and Victor gained the three front steps, the white-paneled door opened and Julia stood in the frame.

Tyler stumbled to an awkward halt. Victor was obliged to spring off the path and onto the manicured lawn. He couldn't remove his gaze from her person, so different did she look from how he'd seen her at their previous meetings.

Her gown of robin's egg blue silk hugged her body with the care of a lover. The neckline was low enough to tantalize without giving too much away, but it was her golden-red hair that caused Tyler's breath to still in his throat. Sparkling combs caught up the sides while the rest curled loose about her shoulders and down her back. He wanted to tug her into a shadowy corner and tangle his fingers in those heavy tresses, pulling ever so gently that her face would tip up, her soft, full lips waiting for his kiss.

"Pace yourself, soldier."

When Victor clapped a hand on his shoulder, Tyler's heart slammed into his chest. The fantasy was broken. "Thanks."

"I believe it's quite gauche to gawk at your hostess. You'll have time enough to gaze at her like a sick puppy over dinner—provided you actually enter her house." The amusement in Victor's voice was unmistakable.

"Laugh all you want. I intend to enjoy myself." Mustering every ounce of charm he could summon, Tyler pasted a grin on his lips and strode to the door. "Good evening, Miss Spencer." Her pulse beat beneath the black velvet ribbon around her neck. A silver locket dangled from the scrap of fabric. He'd give up his good leg to catch a glimpse of Julia wearing only that... He cleared his throat, conscious he had to say something into the silence. "Careful or else you'll outshine every other lady in attendance."

Victor snorted behind him. Both Tyler and Julia ignored him.

"Blatant flattery won't gain you any more favor, Mr. Browning." Julia's eyes twinkled. "Won't you and your friend come in?"

No sooner did he do exactly that when a tall, barrel-chested man blocked his path. "I don't remember invitin' you." A heavy Southern accent clung to the deep voice.

"Oh, that's my fault, Uncle George." Julia bustled between them, laying gloved fingertips on Tyler's forearm. "This is Tyler Browning. He owns the apothecary recently featured in the *Sentinel*." She sent her relative a significant look. "I invited him to dinner figuring it would be a nice way to become acquainted."

An indulgent expression crossed the tall man's face. "Always thinkin', darlin'." He tapped his temple and winked. "Good girl. You young people go and jaw with the others. I'll find your daddy and call everyone into dinner."

Almost as fascinated with her relative as he was of Julia's appearance, Tyler patted her hand that still rested on his arm. "What are we celebrating?"

"I told you before." She stared at him then continued after a sigh. "My parents have returned from their grand tour of Panama. I half-suspect they visit such locales to feel better about themselves as they spread random acts of charity throughout the poor villages. And, of course, they brought a photographer with them, as much to forever capture the plight of the poor as to save for posterity them shaking hands and giving their time." A touch of bitterness wove through her voice. "They're home now. Therefore, the rest of us can do nothing but dance attention upon them."

This time when Victor's attempt to stifle laughter resulted in a series of snorts and coughs, Tyler glared at him over his shoulder. "Perhaps you should seek out some spirits. It would help your breathing issues."

"It's unfortunate you didn't bring your tonic. That could have healed me in a flash." Victor ambled off through the house in the direction Julia's uncle vanished.

Groupings of settees and chairs sporting delicate legs were interspersed throughout the room. Bone china teacups and saucers as well as half-filled crystal wine glasses decorated occasional tables and shelves. The enticing aroma of roasting chicken perfumed the air. Heavy mauve drapes were held back by golden tasseled ties, displaying the front window while the faint sound of music drifted over the ebb of conversation. Did they own a phonograph? That'd be interesting to see.

By the time Tyler turned his attention back to his hostess, she'd recovered from her laughter. He was used to Victor deriding his life choices. It didn't sit well when Julia did the same. "Why exactly did you invite me this evening?"

"Honestly? I'm curious about you, Mr. Browning. I suspect you're trying to pull the wool over the eyes of the people in this city. That alone warrants further scrutiny." They advanced through the room a few steps before he stopped them.

"Is that the only reason, Julia? And please, my name is Tyler. Mr. Browning reminds me of my father, which serves to recall sad memories." He squeezed her fingers and, leaning close, he put his lips to her ear. "You wouldn't want to be the cause of my mental distress, would you?"

"If you're in the grips of a mental disturbance, I somehow doubt anyone but you are the cause." Julia pushed him away, albeit half-heartedly. She held his gaze, her eyes sparkling. "I will admit to inviting you to vex my uncle and parents."

"Why would meeting me cause a stir? I found your uncle amiable enough." With slow, purposeful intent, he swept his gaze along the bodice of her gown, devouring the tops of her creamy breasts. When he met her eyes again, there was no doubt she'd seen the action.

The muscles in Julia's neck worked as she swallowed. A slight shiver followed and gooseflesh covered her exposed skin. "He'll lure you into a false sense of security, and then he'll pounce. Besides, he's aware of who you are. He authorized the article in the paper, you know."

"Ah, then I'll try to put on a good show for him. Now," he steered her toward a group of chatting people. "Suppose you tell me where your parents are? I'd love to make their acquaintance and thank them for creating such a divine creature as you." Pleased when a rosy blush graced her cheeks, he grinned.

Were Victor's words true? No woman who colored from a few well-chosen words of flattery could be a loose female. It was on the tip of his tongue to ask her if she'd ever done a portrait when she stiffened beside him.

"What is it?" Tyler glanced about the room but didn't see anything out of the ordinary. Of course, not being familiar with her peers, he had no idea who set off the reaction. "Julia?"

"Oh, my God." Shock or fear widened her eyes. Tyler couldn't determine which.

The next moment, she slumped against him in a dead faint.

Chapter Six

Julia's faith in Tyler's reaction never wavered. It didn't matter he was a con artist and a snake in the grass—at least he possessed some manners. She'd heard the Southern drawl buried deep in his voice and assumed he must have been raised with a modicum of gentility or perhaps it was merely what she chose to believe. As soon as she crumpled against him, he draped an arm around her waist, but when he didn't immediately catch on to her pretend swoon, she went pliant. Tyler, true to *his* pretend concern for her well-being, shoved an arm beneath her legs and lifted her in his arms. She laid her head on his shoulder and hoped the company at large, as well as Tyler, believed in her act.

She opened her eyes to slits. Tyler carried her through the gasping, gawking assembly until he reached Uncle George.

"Um, sir, excuse me." Tyler's request rumbled in her ear.

Not able to see the massive man clearly, she focused on Tyler's face in profile. A faint shadow clung to his jaw. It evoked erotic thoughts and sent prickles of heat through her body—the kind of sensations she'd told herself she could never invite again yet persisted in plaguing her every time Tyler came near.

While she studied him, he told Uncle George of her alleged plight. The low, deep murmur of her uncle's voice directing him to the small back parlor washed over her, calming her frazzled nerves, much like it had when she was a child. If only he could soothe her problems now. He'd be so disappointed in her if he knew. She shut her eyes, swallowing down the rising hysteria in her throat as Tyler carried her down a short hallway away from the bulk of the party goers.

The relative quiet of the new venue was more jarring than the constant noise. He set her down none too gently on a crushed velvet fainting couch. She frowned.

"Fess up, Julia. I know you're faking. You might as well give me the explanation before your uncle and a host of well-meaning family members stream in."

She opened her eyes. Tyler loomed over her, his expression full of anger and a hint of amusement. "What makes you think I'm not seriously ill or suffering from what you call a female complaint?" When she caught him glancing at her exposed stocking-covered legs, she righted herself on the couch, moving her skirt to cover her lower limbs.

"Your heart rate is too fast for someone who supposedly just passed out from a fright or illness. Secondly, this dire 'disease' only occurred when you spotted someone in the entryway." He sank down on the sofa at her feet. "Now, suppose you tell me who that person was and why you felt the need to make a not-so-subtle getaway. Why you are afraid of whomever you saw?"

Her mind jumped to the moment Jackson Hayes entered the house. Clad in the same dark evening clothes as the other men, only one touch set him apart, something so unique it jogged other memories from deep in her past—ones she tried nightly to forget. Pinned to his lapel, he wore a white rose. The middle of the flower was a startling, blood red. Julia had no idea if the flower naturally grew like that or if he dabbled in gardening or paint, but she'd seen that same type of flower before—at least twice when she'd made a living in a less than honorable profession.

He never wore a flower in his lapel while in the newspaper office, which wasn't odd. The fact he wore it to social functions was far more ominous and niggled something hidden in her mind. Of course, she hadn't really been in his close proximity while in the office before. Was he attempting to make an unspoken statement?

Even more unsettling, a spark of recognition had lit in his eyes. He *knew*. He'd remembered what she had done — and with him. The thrill of the hunt had briefly illuminated his expression. That terrified her. The past and her present had caught up to her at last.

Dread chilled her blood until she felt numb to her fingertips and toes. As she stared into Tyler's soulful brown eyes, the compulsion to tell him the whole, sordid story overwhelmed her. How could she when she hadn't even revealed the truth to her parents or her uncle? Worse yet, what did Mr. Hayes plan to do now? It had to be the only reason he'd attended, for she doubted her uncle had invited him. She sucked in a breath. Was that why Uncle George and he had argued that day? Bile climbed into her throat at the implications.

"I'm sorry. I can't do that." She needed time to think, to formulate a plan and possibly damage control. Disappointment and anger fueled the flash in his eyes and she averted her gaze. Why should she feel bad? He was a mere stranger. Yes, they had shared a kiss, but that didn't mean she owed him anything.

Long ago, she vowed not to make decisions from the heart or while mired in emotion because heartache was the result. She operated solely on facts, proof and smarts — never feelings.

"I see." He opened his mouth to say more, but the arrival of Bess, her housekeeper, appeared in the doorway, interrupted further speech.

"Miss Spencer, your father suggested you rest in here until you're able to join them in a proper, composed state." Her thin lips turned down in a frown as she stared at Tyler. She patted at her gray hair, returning an imaginary escaped strand to the fold. "He and your mother are telling stories of their travels and good deeds. They don't wish to abandon the guests if you're merely indulging in a temper tantrum."

Tyler cleared his throat. "I beg your pardon, ma'am. Who are you?"

"I'm the housekeeper, sir." She drew herself up as if an iron pole was bound to her back.

"Ah." Tyler shot to his feet, his face as tumultuous as a thunderstorm. "That is no way to address anyone, sick or otherwise. Miss Spencer has just received a rather large shock."

"Tyler, it's fine —" Julia began but a sharp shake of his head cut her off.

"No. Regardless of this woman's station in your household, she has no right to belittle you, whether your parents do or not."

"Thank you." A flush warmed Julia's face at this quick defense. No one, not even her parents, had defended her or feigned an interest in what happened to her before. She rather liked having a champion, albeit from a con artist. It spoke of a person's character more than silence did.

Bess inclined her chin. "I've helped raise Julia since she was a babe. Who would know, better than me, the antics of the girl?"

Tyler cocked his head to one side. "Enlighten me."

"Every time Mr. and Mrs. Spencer return from a trip, she pulls a stunt to divert attention, and they're understandably vexed by it. They deserve all the adoration given to them from their peers. Why would their only child be exempt?" She leveled a harsh glance first at Tyler then at Julia. "When you're done sulking, you may join the assembly for dinner, but I refuse to hold it back. I also refuse to close the parlor door. I care for your reputation even if you have long since left it behind."

Disappointment sank in her stomach. Her terrible secret wasn't at all well-kept if Bess knew, or perhaps only alluded to it. "Thank you, Bess." Julia let her head fall against the sofa back and closed her eyes as the housekeeper retreated. Was what she said true? *Did* she cause a stir every time her parents returned? Some of her issues had been legitimate over the years and, of course, she demanded parental attention after being left to her own devices for so long.

Shame heated her cheeks. Tears clogged her throat, yet she couldn't shed them. *Never again.* Feeling sorry for herself didn't help. Tears didn't change the situation or make her a new person.

Nothing ever would.

When she opened her eyes, the intensity of Tyler's gaze almost burned through to her soul. Golden flecks flared in his murky depths while he held his mouth in a tight line. She wasn't comfortable under his scrutiny. "Don't judge me. You cannot fathom what my life is like or how I came to this pass."

"I know better than to offer comment on the alleged sins of your past. Like you, I have my fair share of indiscretions and regrets." He paced the carpet, his hands clasped behind his back. "However, nothing gets my dander up faster than watching someone brought low by another's barbed words." Tyler stopped abruptly and captured her gaze once more. "Only you have the authority to judge yourself, Julia. No one else. The key is to learn from the mistakes, not define yourself by them."

"Yes, that's all well and good except some mistakes are too big to fix by an apology or the telling of them.

Sometimes, once a person's reputation and innocence are lost, no amount of wishing can repair the damage." She hoped he wouldn't ask any more questions. As much as she wanted to unburden herself, she couldn't trust him. "Too bad you didn't bring any of that mystery tonic. The chance to wash away my sins, as it were, would be welcome."

"God, you sound like Victor. Sadly, I didn't think the tonic would prove useful this evening. I shall endeavor to bring you some when next we meet."

"Ah, not a very good salesman if you're not prepared."

"Don't try to change the original subject." Tyler grunted and threw himself onto the end of the sofa. "We're only given a certain amount of time in this life. Best to make the most of your days and not wallow in the might-have-beens."

"Is that what you're doing?"

He hung his head. "Not even close," he whispered.

Words refused to leave her throat. She'd kept her disgrace to herself for so long, it had almost become a part of her, an ugly, cancerous growth that would remain fixed on her soul until she died. Instead, she shook her head. "Is that what makes you a good con? You conveniently forget those you leave behind in order to scam the next batch?"

"That could be the truth unless there's no one to leave behind." Ragged pain wavered in his voice, resonating in her chest to mingle with her own agony. He lurched to his feet. His eyes, now hooded and hard, didn't retain any of the lively emotion of before. "At least the con is mine until I'm ready to move on. It never disappoints or leaves me."

Julia bit her bottom lip to keep from blurting out her history to him, beg him to understand why she did what she did, but she fought the urge. What was he, really? Once he tired of the mystery tonic gig, he'd leave town, just like he said. Better to be selfish and keep the pain now and not give it a chance to grow any larger.

No way did she want to drag him down into her agony. "Please leave. I'm not feeling well and would like to lie down." She struggled to her feet, swaying slightly as a real headache beat at her temples. "Thank you for coming. Feel free to join the rest for dinner before you go."

"A dismissal. How original of you." He gave her a mocking bow. "I didn't expect you to shed all your secrets so soon after meeting me. However, there will come a time when you'll be so eaten up inside you'll have no other recourse but to unburden yourself. I hope you choose to trust me at that time. Only a man who has secrets of his own could understand and help."

"I'll bear that in mind." She clasped her trembling hands at her waist.

Tyler snorted. "I'll let you escape for now." As if considering his next option, a slow grin curved his lips. "Be warned. Our stroll through the park will still occur tomorrow."

She'd forgotten about the arrangement. "Perhaps it would be best if we cancelled —"

"Oh, no. You selfishly cut my dinner engagement short this evening, cheating me out of my time with you. I intend to become your friend, one way or another, so tomorrow it is. Broad daylight, in the full accompaniment of our two pals. How much of a threat can I possibly be?" He stalked to the door and was gone.

A trace of anger crept over the top of her earlier sadness. If that man thought he could march into her house and order her about, he was sadly mistaken. She clenched her hands into fists until her nails bit into the palms. If he wanted to spend time, fine. She'd use it to her advantage and find out exactly what his scam was and what others he had in mind. At least then, that would keep him from testing the walls around her heart.

An hour later Tyler sat at the highly polished bar counter of the gentleman's club, waiting for the owner to make an appearance. It had taken some convincing, but Victor had a sterling reputation, and he clung to that flimsy thread to respectability. Entrance was given, but only for the evening and on the assumption Victor would arrive soon. His friend had been correct. There was a painting of Julia above the bar, and from all accounts, it was a highly popular rendering. More often than not, appreciative glances from the men would drift to the piece.

He hated every one of them.

Like he'd done nearly every moment since he'd entered the bar, Tyler lifted his gaze to the portrait. How could he not? The painting measured a good four feet across and two feet in height. The owner had placed it dead center on the wall behind the bar, high enough that any patron in the establishment could see it from all corners of the large, smoke-shrouded room.

Julia lounged on a black velvet chaise, but not the woman he'd met. Aside from being a good several years or so younger, *this* woman held an expression of knowledge well beyond her years. Mystery, daring and sexual innuendo lit her blue eyes. A soft, sensual smile played about her full, pink lips while long, blonde waves of hair spilled loose over her shoulders, a stark contrast against the velvet. Yet, the beauty of her young face couldn't hold a candle to the artist's rendering of the rest of Julia's body.

Tyler swallowed in an effort to force moisture into his throat. He couldn't tear his gaze away. A stiff-boned corset covered in light pink satin pushed her breasts nearly out and over the garment. Granted, she wasn't as well-endowed as she was now, but she still had a great figure. She reclined, one leg bent at the knee while the other was stretched along the length of the chaise. Her stockings and garters in full view of prying eyes. And what was more, it appeared the corset and stockings were the only item of clothing the woman had on, if the smooth rounded flare of her naked hip was any indication.

He had trouble telling since she'd draped the hand not flung behind her head over the apex of her thighs, effectively covering any forbidden bits. Knowing they were one flutter of her hand away from being exposed sent the blood rushing straight to his cock. Tyler shifted on the padded barstool he occupied and tried for a more comfortable position. There was none to be found, not while Julia was laid out for full erotic view.

He motioned to the bartender to refill his glass. Only drinking copious amounts of alcohol could prevent him from thinking about her motivation behind posing for such a scandalous portrait—or perhaps it would aggravate the problem. What had she been thinking? What did her family say after she revealed the less than noble act? In one swift move, Tyler downed the whiskey, welcoming the burn of it in his throat. It wasn't as if the Spencer family needed the substantial sum of cash the painting undoubtedly brought.

Why, then, had she done it?

He moved his gaze back to her face as he studied it again. Now, instead of the blatant come-hither glint in her eyes, he imagined a light of uncertainty. He sat up straighter. Something didn't ring true. The woman in the portrait still had a purity and innocence about her. Even though her pose and outfit stated the contrary, he'd bet money the Julia in that painting had never known the delights of sexual pleasure.

He nodded when the bartender asked to refill his shot glass. Concentrating through the slight alcohol-induced haze, Tyler recalled the Julia he'd left more than an hour before as she'd lain prostrate on a similar couch. With solid conviction, he'd bet a month's salary *that* Julia had been introduced to bed sport. The fluidness of her movements, the way she held herself, the lush curves, the way she'd matched every movement of his lips and tongue during their fleeting kiss in the alley all indicated a level of experience the portrait lacked.

Damn it all to hell!

The amber liquid in the shot glass taunted him. He left it waiting on the smooth oak bar. Had she flown too close to the flame and gotten burned, destined to carry the shame of the act for the rest of her life? As he reached for the glass, wanting to drown out his unanswered questions, a hand clamped on his wrist while another drew the shot down the counter.

"Victor. I wondered how long it would be before you tracked me down." He shook off his friend's grip and turned slightly to regard him. His black suit jacket gaped open and his black tie hung about his neck like a dead snake. "You look like you've been to hell and back."

"Trying to get out of that insane asylum of the Spencer household was pretty much hell. Her parents love to hear the sound of their own voices, not to mention the stir your lady's exit caused." He yanked Tyler from his stool. "Let's move to a more comfortable venue."

Tyler had no choice but to follow his friend through the groupings of leather chairs and ottomans until they'd secured a couple well away from any of the card games or conversations playing out around the room. "What can relocating possibly gain us?" He didn't argue when Victor shoved him into one of the soft chairs while he sank into the one opposite him.

"For one, having your back to that infamous portrait will go a long way to clearing your mind." Victor crossed his long legs at the ankles, appearing every inch the southern gentleman. "For another, you had no control over said painting, so it's best to forget it altogether."

"I can't." Even now, though he wasn't facing it, he felt compelled to turn around and stare, but he quelled the urge. "The image is seared onto my brain, etched into my mind's eye, and it bothers me."

"Why? Is it because she did something so scandalous, or that perhaps she gained a monetary reward for it?" Victor cocked a blond eyebrow. "Or is it due to the fact she might have done something much worse than pose for the painting?"

"Julia has more scruples than that!" Tyler half-launched himself from the chair. "Apologize." Several men looked in their direction.

Victor's laidback expression turned into a glare. "Lower your voice and sit down." Controlled anger underscored his voice. The voice of a leader in a theatre of war. His eyes were like icy flint as he stared.

"I'm sorry." Tyler sank into his chair. His stomach clenched as nerves took over when Victor remained silent. This was the man who'd led his battalion into battle, became surrogate parent, head shrink, mentor and friend to more than a dozen men. His word was law in combat; not much else had changed since he'd become a civilian. "I suppose it's not out of the realm of possibility Julia could have been involved in something seedy."

"Indeed it's not." Victor steepled his fingers beneath his chin. "Consider your own life. You found a vehicle to con the public, make them believe they're getting something more. Perhaps Julia's con is on a more personal level for whatever reason."

"We don't know that yet."

"No, we don't, which is why you're going to stop going off half-cocked every time I mention the woman's name. In case you've had occasion to notice, half the world's population is male, and she'll need to interact with a fair portion of them." He chuckled. "You'll charm her and, given time, maybe she'll share her secrets. She's a woman who needs trust first. Until then, you have no claim to her. You must simply pretend it doesn't matter."

Tyler inwardly reeled. Why did he care how Julia spent her life, past or present? What difference did it make that she'd already given herself to a man? Did that tainted reputation sully her personality or her soul? Not to his way of thinking, so then why did he care? When he realized Victor waited for a reply, he cleared his throat, feeling very much like he did in the field of combat.

"Why are you interested in me furthering her acquaintance?" He gripped the armrests of his chair so hard he left impressions in the leather.

"For too long you've been ungrounded. You deserve a chance at happiness. Why not attempt to find it in Miss Spencer?" A slight grin graced his face. "It would seem, at least from what I've witnessed, you two are well matched."

"Except she's only interested in me from a press perspective." The thought brought on another bout of depression.

"Ah, but then you're interested in her for her newspaper skills as well. It's a match made from above." Victor lifted his eyes heavenward.

"Touché. I still think it's nothing except fancy from your imagination. Banking has given you too much time to daydream." A reluctant grin tugged at Tyler's lips then vanished altogether as a tallish man with graying hair and a goatee approached them. "May I help you?" He rose to his feet, aware that Victor did the same.

"Mr. Browning? I'm Abel Camden, owner of this establishment." The man extended a hand which Tyler shook. "I was told you're interested in talking about my painting."

"Yes, indeed." Tyler curled his right hand into a fist. Concentrating on keeping his temper in check, he nodded. "I'd like to know where you purchased the piece."

"Oh, I'm sorry. I hesitate to reveal the source of my art." He made a superior sound in his throat. "Once I find a subject as, ah, thought provoking as the one here, I like to try and secure more pieces."

"Bastard." Tyler drew back his hand but Victor caught him before the punch could be thrown. "Who painted that portrait?"

Abel's chuckle nearly sent Tyler into the ceiling. "Does it matter? From everything the man told me, he created my piece from a photograph and I'm told there are others of the same subject, less clothed. I'm anxious to inspect them, though no contact has been made between the dealer and me."

"Like hell you will." Regardless of Victor's restraint, Tyler lunged at the club owner, pinning him to an oak-paneled wall, rumpling the lapels of his pin-striped suit. "Now listen to me, you ass. I want the name and location of this man, or else I cannot be responsible for my actions."

Both of Abel's eyebrows hit his hairline. "Are you threatening me, Mr. Browning? If so, I must warn you I have two security experts waiting for my signal. These gentlemen don't care if they happen to break a couple of your bones in the process of throwing you out of this establishment, which, by the way, I believe you were not allowed back into anyway."

Tyler saw through a film of red for several seconds as the atmosphere of the room dropped into chilly animosity. Conversation died and money was exchanged as the occupants seemed to hold their breath for the next round.

"Perhaps now is not the time for violence, Tyler." Victor's cautious tone sank into Tyler's brain and took the edge off his anger.

"Fine." He crushed Abel's lapels further before releasing him. "Don't bother to call your goons. I'm leaving and I won't return."

"Make sure you don't."

Without a word or a glance, Tyler stalked through the lounge and out the door. Once Victor joined him in front of the building, he rounded on his former commanding officer. "What the hell was that? I thought you'd at least help me muscle the information out of the smug son-of-a-bitch."

"There are many ways to the same result. Why not simply ask Julia about the photographs? Why must you make an ass out of yourself?" Victor clapped a hand on Tyler's shoulder. "The scuttlebutt around the Spencer house was she went white as a sheet before succumbing to a faint. Perhaps you should inquire as to the source of her fright."

"I tried, but she's not talking."

"Not yet. Give her space and understanding."

"Once again, your level-headedness is much appreciated. I'll endeavor to question her tomorrow morning."

Surprise reflected on his friend's face. "You still intend to squire her around the park?"

"Why not? Besides, this will keep the events fresh in her mind and maybe weaken her guard. Whatever secrets Julia keeps are bound to be eating her alive by now." He frowned, shaking his head. "I honestly think she's terrified of someone. I'm duty-bound to help."

Victor heaved a sigh. "Your good nature will land you into trouble before long. Guilt is just as strong a prison as sins."

"I am aware." As much as he wanted to know what Julia was hiding, he'd need to give up part of his past as well. She wasn't the type of person to willingly offer a piece of her soul without a sacrifice from him. Trouble was, what could he reveal that wouldn't reflect badly on him for future reference or harden her heart further from him?

Chapter Seven

Julia tossed and turned until the bedclothes twisted about her legs. She shoved the hair from her face and stared at the ceiling as light and shadows played on the plaster.

It was a hopeless cause to try to forget her past. With every beat of her heart, a different memory would surface, a different horror, and they chased around in her brain like a demented carousel. She'd been sentenced to relive certain memories, yet there was little enjoyment associated in them. Forced into prostitution under the guise of a finishing school, her life had been essentially taken from her.

She closed her eyes, pleading to a God she wasn't sure she believed in that sleep would come and it would be dreamless.

She was back in her hot bedroom at the school, waiting for her next assignment. Glancing at the decanter of brandy on the dresser, she considered pouring a hefty dose and drinking it to further numb the well of pain her life had become.

Before she could definitively make up her mind, the door opened and admitted a man she'd serviced a couple of times during her career with Madame at the Ladies' School of Advanced Etiquette—a younger version of Mr. Hayes, though she'd not known his name at that time. Another shiver careened down her spine. He never spoke more than a few sentences on any visit, and both times he'd come, he was rough in his handling, brutal when he conducted intercourse. She hadn't known his name then;

never knew the names of any of the men who visited unless they were one of the male instructors at the school. Perhaps more comforting, they didn't know her real name either. To them, she was Veronica Peterson, a stage name taken for her protection—if a name could do such a thing after they made use of her body.

"Take off the robe." He didn't look her way, merely removed his suit, tie and shoes. As he carefully folded the jacket and pants, he draped them over the back of her vanity chair. A white rose, scarlet in the center, fell from his lapel and rolled beneath the corner of Julia's bed. He always wore that flower. "I said strip, girl." Clad in a white button-down shirt and short pants, he stalked around the edge of the bed, his erection evident behind the thin fabric of his drawers.

For the first time since she began the bizarre odyssey at the school, a spark of spirit burned in the pit of Julia's stomach. She hated the way his beady eyes bore into hers, searing with malicious intent, the way his gaze slithered over her person as if she was nothing more than an object to be conquered and defiled—used then thrown out. "I don't think I will, thank you. I'm sure one of the other girls would be willing to have you in their beds."

Jackson traced his thin, black mustache with a thumb and forefinger. "I don't doubt that, but I plan to sink my cock into you, and I've paid lavishly for that pleasure. Now, take off the robe. I won't ask again."

Julia shook her head. "No. This is not the life I want anymore." The urge to go home and confess all to her parents and uncle grew strong. She longed for the comfort of a warm embrace or hug and to hear them tell her they were glad she was back. She wanted to be safe. "Get out."

"You listen to me, whore." He closed the distance between them so quickly she didn't have time to defend herself when he delivered a sharp backhand smack across her face. "You have no rights, no voice. You trade your body for basic services, thus you gave up privilege for a different life as soon as you took your first client into your bed. You chose this, and every time your spread your legs, you keep yourself here."

"I won't accept that." Her cheek stung as much as the truth of his word. She was certain her lip bled, yet she firmly stood her ground. "Get out." Dread chilled her blood. "I'll scream until someone comes." She backed away, pausing only when the mattress bumped against her legs.

"All to the better. I like it when the girls fight." He shot out a hand and she cringed. Instead of hitting her, he ripped the delicate robe from her shoulders, exposing her body. "It makes the conquest more rewarding."

She pushed him away. He grabbed her and threw her onto the bed. As she crawled to the opposite side, Jackson yanked off his drawers, clamped a hand around her ankle and reeled her toward him. "Let me go." When he used one of his large hands to pin her wrists above her head, fear tried to paralyze her. She continued to struggle, determined to escape. "Please."

"One of these days, girl, I'll own this town, and then you really will beg me to spare you. I intend to remember exactly who you are and make certain you remember me too."

"Life is long. You'll forget."

"No. I have a specific photograph. In it, you're sitting on a chair, legs splayed, pussy on display."

"Bastard." She spit the word at him while her mind reeled at the vulgarity he'd used.

He gripped her face with his free hand, squeezing hard, as he used his knees to spread her legs painfully wide. "That pussy belongs to me, understand?" He cupped her womanhood then squeezed it as hard as he'd done her chin. "No other man will ever want you after your time here. You might as well enjoy your profession. It's all you have—all you will ever have. And I will always remember you no matter where you go."

Silent tears slid over Julia's cheeks, and sobs shook her shoulders while he used her body as a plaything. She closed her eyes and went pliant, not even able to summon the energy for a fight as he pumped into her with animal lust. She'd murdered her life before it had a chance to begin.

She woke up, gasping for air through tears she couldn't control. Julia wiped her nose on the sleeve of her nightgown as she cried for wasted time and the stupid decisions in her youth.

Never again would she allow anyone to lure her into doing something based on fast words and a too-good-to-be-true story. Never again would she give her trust to anyone. Without facts and concrete proof, nothing was worth the risk.

Her body may be abused and unwanted, but no one would ever have access to her heart or soul. Those were hers alone, and they weren't for sale. Not even to a charming, brown-eyed man who made her feel needed and put silly little dreams in her head.

"You had another nightmare, didn't you?" The concern in Gretchen's voice later that morning nearly set off another round of waterworks.

Julia dropped a sugar cube into her tea and swirled a spoon through the amber depths. She didn't care if the sweetener dissolved. Nothing mattered at the moment except concentrating on her morning. "Yes. I think my past means to haunt me until I scream surrender or consign myself to an asylum." She glanced at her friend. "Why are you here so early?"

"Mr. Browning and Mr. Archer are taking us on an outing today, silly." A stain of rosy color eased into Gretchen's full cheeks. "I'm glad you invited me. I think both of them are handsome."

"I couldn't very well go about the park with two unmarried men by myself, now could I?" She dropped in another sugar cube, this time letting it sit on the bottom of the teacup, then plunked her spoon onto the tablecloth. "I don't know why I'm worried. My reputation is already ruined, as well as my body. No man will have me." Tears again threatened, but she blinked them back. She couldn't change the past.

Gretchen frowned and patted a linen napkin against her lips. "I don't understand why. You're never seen in the company of a gentleman, you live a structured, aloof life, plus you never do anything that would call the least little attention to yourself outside of haranguing your parents every once in a while."

Julia eyed Gretchen as she bit her bottom lip. She'd known the other woman since secondary school. Luck had continued to shine upon her when Julia's family moved into a house two doors down from Gretchen's. Fate had been sealed, even more so when they shared secrets over the years—except the one currently rotting the edges of Julia's soul. It had been too embarrassing and disgusting, but perhaps it was time to let someone help carry the burden.

"I haven't been completely honest, Gretchen." She pushed her teacup away as her stomach protested the scant sips she'd already taken. "I wanted to tell you, so many times, but I couldn't do it, didn't know how you would respond." She traced the pattern on the lace tablecloth. "I didn't want to lose your friendship because of my stubborn stupidity."

"I doubt I'd abandon you." Gretchen moved to the other side of the dining room table and plopped into the chair next to her.

"You're too inherently *innocent*." She wiped away an errant tear. "I cannot explain you better than that."

"Tell me." Gretchen grasped one of Julia's hands. "If it bothers you, it bothers me." Her soulful gaze softened. "What happened?"

The urge for redemption burned too hot to ignore. "It started ten years ago. I attended what I thought was a finishing school but was, instead, an institution that taught girls how to sell their bodies for money." Tears flowed freely down her cheeks. "I wanted my parents to come for me, rescue me, tell me they loved me no matter what. When they didn't, I stayed there and did all those vile things." At the end, she drew a deep breath and let it out. "Now my life is ruined beyond repair."

"Sweetie, what happened in the past is done. You made what you thought were the right choices at the time. They didn't work, but you learned from the mistake. It doesn't mean you're a bad person or unlovable." Gretchen squeezed her hand. "It's not as if you continued on that path."

"No, but nothing changed between my parents and me." Julia fixed her gaze on her skirt, moving it up and down the lavender and white stripes. "When I'm alone, at night, I cannot help but think I'm a terrible person. My parents and Uncle George have no idea—no one does except for you. It's trapped inside me, refusing to leave. The point I attempted to make while being essentially a whore was never made."

"Julia, you have to let it go."

Her admission didn't bring any relief. "What if I meet a man and fall in love? What if he learns of it and refuses to go forward into a relationship because I'm not a virgin or even a good person anymore or he considers me used?" Fluttering waves of panic rose in her chest. "I'll live here forever and perhaps not even then if my parents find out."

"No." Gretchen shifted in her seat until Julia looked at her. "You need to forgive yourself. Give yourself permission to be a woman and to enjoy your life now." She smiled and released Julia's hand. "I believe there's someone out there who'll love you in spite of your past. It only takes one gentleman to say yes. That's all. You just need to find him."

"Oh, how I want to believe you." She wiped the last of her tears away. "Now that I remember who Mr. Hayes is, what do I do? When I met his gaze at the party, I know he recognized me. I'm afraid." Which wasn't a lie. She had a permanent rock of worry sitting in the pit of her stomach. "Back then he said he'd never forget who I was and that he'd make sure I remembered him."

"Be the woman I know you can be. If there's trouble, stand up to it and fight. It's the only way. If you deny it, the problem will fester until it has power over you. Once that happens, you might as well call defeat."

Julia managed a small laugh. "How did you get so wise?" She pulled the teapot toward her and poured a fresh cup of tea. Too bad the problem of Jackson Hayes couldn't be dismissed as easily as her concerns.

"I'm not wise, just jealous of you. Imagine, all those years I thought you were at a finishing school and you were merely across town, having relations."

"It wasn't so glamorous."

"Maybe, but still." Gretchen moved back to her own chair and reached for a slice of toast. "Would you like to know why I'm jealous?"

"Of course. If you had a brain in your head, you'd sever our friendship and never darken my door again." She sipped the tea, welcoming the comforting warmth as the liquid slid down her throat.

"Hardly." A sly grin parted Gretchen's lips. To Julia's way of thinking, her friend resembled a prettier version of a fairytale princess, one who hovered on the verge of great and wonderful things. She had a whole, unblemished future before her. She'd make a wonderful match and have beautiful babies and a family. A tiny pang of envy bloomed in her gut, but she banished it in her next breath. Gretchen deserved every good thing that came to her.

"You have been with a man in intimate ways and are so...worldly. Please tell me what it's like." Gretchen leaned forward, eager anticipation shining in her eyes. "Is it wonderful? I've heard stories that the sex act can defy imagination."

"Honestly, the first few times are not pleasant. There is a bit of pain involved, some tearing and blood. You'll need some time to adjust to the newness of it, but for me, I never experienced that sought after bliss some women talk about." Julia frowned as a new wash of tears threatened. "After a while, it became something I hated. A man does his business and leaves. I felt...nothing, as if I was dead inside, as if the *act* wasn't happening to me. At times, it seemed I was watching myself but was simply numb." She bit her lower lip. "Afterward, I cried. I always cried and hated myself. But then, my circumstances were rather different than a normal woman's experience."

Gretchen's happy expression fell. "I'm sorry, Julia."

"So am I."

"No one should ever go through what you did."

"In different circumstances, I imagine there's a certain closeness, a feeling of communion with another person that only lovemaking can bring." She shrugged, dousing her bitterness by a gulp of tea. "I'll never know."

"You cannot foretell the future." Calmly, as if they discussed intercourse and bed partners over breakfast every day, Gretchen spread marmalade on her toast. "What you need is a man who'll brave that thorny wall you've erected around your heart. He'll hack his way through, vowing to love you because you're wonderful, not broken. Only then you will realize you weren't fucking the right person."

"Gretchen!" In shock, Julia dropped her teacup, which clattered against the china plate and broke into three pieces. Amber liquid spread in a puddle over the white, lacy tablecloth. "I'm surprised you can even say that word." She mopped at the spill with her napkin, but the damage to the cloth had already been done.

"Sometimes I whisper dirty words in my room where my mama can't hear. And sometimes, I practice kissing on my pillow." Gretchen's smile lit her face. "You aren't the only woman in this city who has secrets."

Julia's mouth fell open. "I pity the poor man you finally select. You'll have him so fooled into believing you're a good girl, he'll be liable to faint dead away on your wedding night."

"In that case, it's best to coerce him into bed before that time comes." When she grinned, a dimple appeared in each cheek, a testament to her perpetual good humor. "After that, once the wedding night happens, we can really indulge."

"Thanks for being such a great friend." Julia balled her napkin and threw it onto her plate. "I could never make it through without you." She sprang from her chair so quickly it tumbled to the floor. Leaving it, she darted around the table and engulfed Gretchen in a hug. "I'm glad to have you for a sister, even if it's not by blood."

"Miss Julia?" Bess's arrival into the dining room interrupted the tender moment. "There are two gentlemen in the front parlor." The slight inflection in her voice over the word "gentlemen" made no doubt as to her belief they were not. "They claim you have promised them the entire day."

"Thank you, Bess. Gretchen and I most certainly do have an appointment with them." Julia crossed her arms over her chest as she held the housekeeper's gaze. "We may or may not be home in time for dinner. I'm sure you'll understand since you dislike holding a meal back for reprehensible me."

Bess sailed through the door and into the butler's pantry, her nose stuck in the air. "Far be it for me to attempt to impart morals..." The rest of her speech died away as she slammed into the kitchen beyond.

Julia rolled her eyes. "Do you think she'll ever realize it's a hopeless cause?"

"Who knows?" Gretchen stood. "Let me find Fitzwilliam, and then we can go."

Nodding, Julia left the dining room and joined the men in the parlor. They both scrambled to their feet as she entered. "Good morning." She nodded to Victor but held Tyler's dark gaze. Both were impeccably dressed in suits and hats, yet Tyler's dark curls were much more appealing than Victor's blond locks. "I must apologize for my abrupt departure last evening."

"There's no need." Tyler flashed the smile she glimpsed during their first meeting. "Consider today a new opportunity to make another impression."

Heat tumbled through her belly, and she nearly melted under the force of his charm. "What a delightful way to look at the situation." By willpower alone, she broke eye contact to glance at a scowling Victor. "As soon as Gretchen retrieves her dog, we can head out."

"She's bringing a dog?" Victor turned a little green around the edges at the prospect.

"Oh yes. She never goes anywhere without Fitzwilliam. In fact," Julia turned to the door as Gretchen arrived, "Fitzwilliam has the right to fully inspect each one of Gretchen's beaus, and if you don't pass muster, well, we have sent more than a few, and their wet shoes, home."

"I'll bear that in mind." He warily eyed the furry monitor.

Julia laughed. She grabbed her gloves and hat from a nearby table. Hopefully, she'd just given a potential match between Victor and her friend a gentle shove. Gretchen deserved to be married and happy. "Come Gretchen, I believe the men are anxious to start."

If nothing else, she could make Tyler and Victor so uncomfortable, they'd think twice before buzzing around her again. At least that way, she could keep her secrets while maybe delving for Tyler's because at the end of the day, she had a job to do.

Chapter Eight

Tyler flexed his fingers around the rough-hewn fishing pole. Not having access to the more advanced equipment, and because he hadn't thought ahead for the outing, he and Victor had simply tied line to the pole and hooks, content to make do with the makeshift tackle. Unfortunately, the White River was a harsh mistress. With the breeze and warm temperatures, the fish weren't biting. After two hours, and though Victor managed to pull in a couple bluegills, the only thing Tyler caught was a boot, which had seen better days.

"The women are restless. Perhaps we should let them attempt fishing." He shot a glance to a small copse of pines and a few maples where Gretchen and Julia teased Fitzwilliam with a ball. When they'd all arrived at the quaint spot, they left a picnic basket and other supplies in the shade for later use.

Victor followed his line of vision. "We could, or perhaps joining them would be the more advisable course." He chucked his pole and line onto the bank beside him. "Since your plan to seduce the fair reporter went down in flames last evening, I would think you'd want to make up for lost time."

"What makes you think I'm out to seduce her?"

Victor's expression proclaimed him the village idiot. "You can't help it. Your charm has gotten you into too many beds and out of too much trouble over the years. Why should Julia be any different?" A smirk passed over his lips. "And how convenient you've forgotten the near-seduction in your shop yesterday afternoon, in front of me no less."

How could he forget when he'd thought of nothing except the feel of her lips against his? Given another chance, he would have conducted matters exactly the same. "I admire her form, this is true, and I wouldn't mind stealing another kiss, but I do mean to befriend her as well." He placed his pole next to Victor's. "I think she's a lonely and unhappy woman." He shrugged. "I guess growing up with every luxury doesn't necessarily bring joy."

"Luxury according to your perceptions." He shot Tyler a speaking glance. "Is it you who's disenfranchised or her?" Victor stood, dusting off his pants. "A person's story is told in their eyes. Odds have it Julia has quite a history."

"You see it too, huh?" Tyler followed, leaning heavily on his cane as his knee protested the movement. "Does it matter if I'm disenchanted? I have obligations that prevent me—"

"Of your own making due to misguided guilt." He held Tyler's gaze with concern evident in his. "Look, Joshua's death wasn't your fault. You need to accept this. Death during war can be blamed on many people, but you are not one of them. Let his memory free so you can live *your* life. He is no longer alive for his."

"What about his family? I need—"

"What?"

The time had come for disclosure. "I run the miracle tonic con to bring in money for Anna's support and that of her child." He didn't feel the relief from telling Victor.

"It's worse than I suspected." Victor shook his head. "You need to let the widow go. Allow her to find her own way. If not, and you marry her out of guilt, you'll find yourself a prisoner after the first week."

"God, Anna's nice, and I'll admit to warming her bed months ago when we were both missing Joshua, but I have no intentions of marrying her."

Victor's jaw clenched. "Then there is no problem."

Did he regret sleeping with Anna? Not at the time. They'd both been lonely and looking for comfort. Why did his friend's annoyed silence bother him? "You think I was wrong to bed her." He'd always felt Victor's censure, even in the military, which was fine since he often considered his friend a moral compass.

Now, it was nothing more than an annoyance and added to the mounting pile of guilt building inside.

"How you conduct your life is not my concern unless your actions harm yourself or the people you're trying to protect." His gaze wandered to their female companions. "Are we done discussing your problems or did you have more angst to reveal?"

"What's *your* angle, Victor?" He looked between his friend and the ladies then back again. "Don't tell me you're interested in the other one?"

"Gretchen, not the other one. She has a name. I would caution you to remember this in the future."

"Damn, Captain Archer." Tyler slapped a hand to his thigh and stared at his friend. "You fancy her."

Dusky color crept over Victor's face. "It's early days but," he fixed his attention to the lady in question, "those eyes of hers do something to me. It's more terrifying than staring down a cavalry charge." He gave a wry smile and a shrug. "If she just didn't have that stupid dog. I feel as if it's a furry chaperone, always watching me."

For the first time in a long while, genuine mirth escaped Tyler's throat, a deep belly laugh, which cleansed the anxiety and stress from his insides. He clapped Victor on the shoulder. "My best advice to you? Better start

learning to like animals. I can almost hear the pitter patter
of little furry paws around your bachelor lodgings."

"Heaven help me. May I repeat, it's early yet? I have
no idea if we'll suit." He cleared his throat. "I wouldn't
laugh too hard, my friend. The day is coming when you're
felled by a simple glance. Strip away your charm and
flirting and you're merely a man looking for the same
thing everyone else is—love and acceptance in a cruel
world. Somehow, I'd bet Julia will be the one who gives it
to you."

Tyler held his tongue as Victor walked across the grass
and interrupted the interaction between the females and
the dog. All turned bright gazes on him, and the ladies
nodded at a question he'd apparently asked. The dog ran
excited circles around the three as if he sensed a new
adventure was about to begin, and then Julia shook her
head and glanced Tyler's way. Victor touched a finger to
his bowler brim, offered his arm to Gretchen, who slipped
her hand into the crook of his elbow, and they leisurely
strolled along the bank of the creek with the dog trotting
behind.

Tyler forgot they existed as Julia moved toward him.
A slight smile curved her lips, yet it didn't light her eyes—
at least the one he could see as the brim of her lavender
hat sat at a rakish angle, partially obscuring her face. Her
striped skirt rippled in the gentle late summer breeze, and
he swore he smelled her faint floral scent on the air
seconds before she joined him.

"Why did you not join Gretchen and Victor? He's a
great conversationalist." Anxious shivers ran down his
spine while she continued to regard him with an assessing
stare. He wanted to throw himself on her mercy and
confess the darkest secrets of his soul if only to soften her
gaze or provoke a smile.

"Strolling along the river with the two of them, while idyllic and somewhat romantic, is not exactly what I had in mind for the day." A frown played at her mouth. "I suppose I'm not quite in the mood for that sort of thing right now. I had a restless night."

"I'm sorry to hear that." Tyler deliberately let his gaze linger on her cream-colored blouse, the silk so thin a lacy camisole beneath showed through. Admiring her figure brought back the image he'd seen in the painting. Desire burned through his gut, and he transferred his attention to the river. Too many thoughts like this and he'd have her on her back in the grass, seeking out the evidence he wanted on a very organic level. "Do you want to tell me about it?"

"Not really." Silence followed the statement.

"Fair enough. Let's talk about our friends. Do you feel they won't suit?"

Julia's tinkling laugh was unexpected but wrapped around him. He very much wished to do something that would have her laughing again. "Gretchen has an excess of energy and a sunny disposition, not to mention her parents are well off. All of these attributes will land her a husband before too long."

"Ah, but you never answered my question." *Or any of my others for that matter.* Time to press the advantage. He drew her hand through the crook of his elbow and, gripping his cane with the other hand, set them walking in the opposite direction of Gretchen and Victor. "Do you think they're a good match?" Cursing the brim of her hat hiding her expression, he waited for her reply.

"I want to say they would be perfect for each other, but in my experience, even when the best of men appear perfect, inside they're merely rogues, liars, cheaters...or worse." Her voice dropped low enough he nearly missed the last words. She grew so silent Tyler thought she'd finished talking. Just as he took a breath, preparing to jump into the void, she continued. "However, because I want the best for Gretchen and her happiness, I'll keep an open mind and pray your friend doesn't upset her."

"Victor is everything honorable. Take my word for it."

"The word of a con. How charming."

Finally, he had an excuse to lodge an inquiry. "What happened in your life to make you so cynical toward men? The acid coming from you does you no favors and will shorten your natural life."

A slight bark of laughter escaped her. "My memories will do that for me."

Interesting, but how to coax her to share? "Luckily, I have a tincture for such a problem." He internally groaned when she didn't laugh at his pathetic joke. As he glanced at her, the brim of her hat once more prevented him from looking into her face. He halted, staying her movement. "Please remove the damn hat. I feel as if I'm talking to the milliner's wall and would much rather see you."

"How refreshing to know I'm not the only one who detests this thing." Julia removed a long hat pin, then lifted the lavender, flower-and-ribbon-covered confection from her hair. She threaded the pin through the hat's brim and flung the head gear toward the river. It skimmed the surface before settling on the gently moving waterway. "Is that better? I do hate remembering to wear the things." She turned toward him, and Tyler became rooted to the spot.

Blue fire danced in her eyes while the breeze caressed a line of baby fine curls framing her face. A tentative smile parted her soft, rosy lips. She was every bit as bewitching as the first time he'd seen her — perhaps more so.

"Yes." He gripped the cane handle so hard the carved brass pressed into his palm. He concentrated on the pain, anything to take away from his body's growing reaction to her. The angelic vision next to him would *not* distract him from drawing out her secrets. "I'm surprised you bow to conventions. I can imagine you going about town, head uncovered, like your hands."

A light blush rose in her cheeks. "Forgetting the gloves is a chronic problem, but the hat is much harder to ignore, especially when Bess practically jams it on my head as I leave." She sighed and walked beside him. "I do hate them, though. Nothing but trouble on a windy day, and yet another reason women need to make a stand against the social injustices imposed on them."

The passion in her voice sank into his chest until he, too, felt sympathetic to her cause. "It's fascinating you have a community conscience. Perhaps you should write about the issue."

"Maybe I will, after I expose you for a fraud." She never slowed her determined stride.

"Except that will never happen because I, my dear, am not a fraud; however, I think you might be." When she didn't look his way, vexation lodged in his chest.

"Then you'd be wrong because I'm not hawking a fictional tonic." Faint amusement lingered in her voice.

"True, yet I think you've sold something much more valuable." For a moment, she slowed and her shoulders slumped. He'd won a small victory and pressed on, determined to chip away at her guarded confidence. "Julia, something has come to my attention regarding you that I'd like to discuss." Instead of wasting precious time in worthless flirtation, he'd be forthright and ask her about the painting.

"Ah, but remember your tit for tat rule." She stopped, glancing over her shoulder. This time, all laughter vanished from her eyes. Instead, icy coldness emanated from the depths, palpable enough to chill his skin. "I'll answer your question then you answer one of mine."

"I haven't forgotten." The desire plaguing him since he'd walked into the Spencer house intensified with enough force to singe his blood. Not only did she remain fully in control of herself, the very fact she did so made her more attractive. "In fact, it's the only fair way to exchange information." How far would she let him push before she pushed back?

"So, Mr. Browning, what is this burning question?"

He took a deep breath and released it in a rush. "I happened to visit a local bar recently, and imagine my shock to find an oil painting of you clad in your unmentionables." She remained quiet. Tyler cleared his throat. "Why the hell did you pose for that photographer, and are there other prints?"

"That's none of your business." She stalked to the copse of trees. By the time he reached her, she'd yanked a quit from one of the baskets and unfurled it with such force, the ends snapped like angry turtles. "I'd appreciate you dropping the subject."

"And I'd appreciate you answering the damn question." He had her on the run, literally and figuratively. Taking one edge of the quilt, he helped her spread it on the ground. "Per accordance to our deal, I gave you an inquiry. Now, I expect an answer."

Julia dropped onto the quilt and raised pain-filled eyes to his face. "Please respect my privacy and don't pry into my past. I'd rather not relive those days. They're all too difficult to forget as it is."

The agony in her tone sliced straight through his heart. A protective instinct rose up and no matter what, he vowed to keep her from further harm. Tyler carefully lowered himself before her, holding her gaze. "You can trust me. Let me take your burden and carry it for a while. Tell me your story."

Julia fell headlong into the molten chocolate warmth of his eyes. The concern in his voice wrapped her in its softness, tugging at her secrets. As much as she wanted to tell him everything, she couldn't trust anyone, let alone him.

Old habits died hard when it came to encouraging another person close—no matter how much she wished to explore the option with him. Despite his being a con, he was different than other men, had already treated her as such.

As she shook her head, she kept her hands, and her brain, busy by pulling the picnic basket toward her and rummaging around its interior. "I'm afraid I cannot do that." Remnants of her dream swirled through her mind, draping a black net over everything she felt.

Though she wanted to escape the past, it persisted in following her around like a haunted pet. It was only a matter of time before it pounced.

"Julia—"

"Hush." She held up a hand. "Spare me the rhetoric. If I told you, you'd hate me. You'd want to distance yourself from me as fast as if I had the measles." Mentally, she berated herself for not swearing Gretchen to secrecy. One string of kind words out of Victor's mouth, coupled with a well-placed caress, and the girl would sing about every story she'd ever been told.

"Why don't you let me decide?" Tyler scooted closer until he sat at her feet. He took one boot into his lap and ran his fingers lightly along her ankle, moving a tiny bit higher on her calf beneath the hem of her skirt. "You forget I've seen the horrors of war. Whatever it is you think is so terrible couldn't possibly compare to death and destruction at the hands of men."

"The problem is not that simple though it does stem with destruction at the hands of men." When she attempted to break free of his grasp, he tightened his grip, his hand warm upon her skin. To distract herself from the shivery sensations crawling up her leg, she pulled a bottle of the miracle tonic from the basket, frowning at it to avoid looking at him. "I answered your question by declining to share information. Now it's my turn to ask you one." Hoping he took her explanation at face value, she met his gaze and almost melted into a puddle at the heat emanating from him.

Concern battled with desire in his expression, which made her all the more wary. Men who let their cocks lead them were definitely not to be trusted. Hadn't she learned the lesson?

He lifted an eyebrow and nodded. "I'll let you avoid the issue for now, but don't think we're done discussing it." His grin sent tingles cascading down her spine and tripping through her stomach. "Sooner or later, I *will* get what I want from you."

The low words, fraught with teasing and innuendo, provoked an opposite reaction in her. Memories of her time at the school, letting too many men take what she didn't want to give, rushed through her mind, obscuring the comforting warmth Tyler created. Julia shivered, pushing away the unsavory images and stood, wanting nothing more than to run far from this man who caused such havoc in her body — the man who made her feel like a real woman instead of a whore — a woman worthy of love.

She didn't need any of it, didn't deserve to have urges of an erotic nature after what she'd done, let alone expect him to continue to want her once he knew…

No. If luck was on her side, he'd never find out. In order to spare his feelings, he could never, ever find out. It was imperative their relationship stay on a business level.

She had a job to do, and that was what she needed to concentrate on. Being given a spot at the paper was the beginning step into building the life she wanted. But first, she needed to separate from him, put distance between them and break the intimate connection. Gripping the bottle of water tight in her hand, she ran into the trees.

"Julia, wait!"

If it hadn't been for an exposed root, she could have escaped. Tyler caught her and, grabbing her elbow, turned her around to face him. She wrenched away. "I refuse to talk about this. Do you understand? And if you persist in pestering me, I'll walk home without you."

"I doubt it very much."

"Why?" She bit her lower lip. Why did he sound so confident yet didn't appear to be threatening in any other way like most men of her acquaintance? "Don't presume you know me."

"Oh, but I do. I know people. I make my living on it." He looked her up and down. "The one thing you want in this life is to be taken seriously by those you love and respect. I'll even go farther and say, at this point, you want to find your place—and the truth—in this terrible world." He drew the back of his hand over her cheek, his grin widening as she trembled. "In order to do that, you must continue to investigate me and my tonic, is this not correct?"

"Yes." She retreated, pulling away. "I intend to prove this," she held up the bottle, "is nothing more than regular water and has no healing properties whatsoever."

"How can you be so sure, but you refuse to allow me a tiny bit of trust when it comes to your past?" He took the bottle from her and popped the cork. "What makes the difference?"

"You're a con, a liar. Why should I trust you?" Her back connected with a huge maple tree. Tyler's eyes sparkled. He held his ground a foot away.

"I could ask you the same thing, yet I think you relate to me more than you want to admit." He took a deep drink. The cords and tendons in his neck worked as he swallowed. "Somewhere along the line, you too have used people to your advantage. Quite frankly, I doubt you're done."

She kept her gaze focused on the bottle. "You have no right to make assumptions about my life."

"Then give me the correct foundation. Explain why you're so driven to succeed. You're skittish around people you don't know but refuse to give them a chance." He pressed the bottle into her hand. "Not everyone is as unscrupulous as the men who exploited you for those pictures. I wish you could see this."

"I..." Julia had no idea what to say. Oh, he was a smooth talker, but so were they all. Not one of them had cared about her. Best to move the conversation away from her and back to him. She glanced at the bottle and held it up to the light. "Intrinsically, the tonic has no value."

"Perhaps not to you because you have a strong will. Others have no imagination. To them, this tonic is their savior, a last chance, if you will, to make things right."

"That's ridiculous. Why do people clamor for it when it has no capacity to heal?"

"Why do folks look for answers already in their control?" Tyler moved closer and rested a palm against the tree trunk near her head. "Sometimes, people want to believe so badly in an object they'll give it whatever properties they think they need." He held her gaze. "Is the mystery tonic useless? It depends. When you drink it, do you feel the liquid coursing through your body, touching disease, reversing damage, soothing pain, or do you desperately need it to do so, and in your mind, you believe it does just that?"

She shook her head. "If it doesn't work—"

"How do you *know*? If you believe it does, which prevents your mind from dwelling on whatever terrible thing is haunting you, isn't that the point of the elixir? What's the harm if I give people hope? In the end, that's what I'm peddling." He nudged her hand. Shockwaves skittered to her elbow. "Drink it, Julia. Let your troubles wash away. Affix your hurts to the water and swallow it down. Heal yourself."

He was so convincing. "Why haven't you done the same?"

A flicker of pain passed over his face, vanishing like a breeze. "My troubles aren't up for discussion." He nudged her again. "Drink it. It's my gift to you."

The soothing timbre of his voice wrapped around her like the softest blanket. She wanted to believe. Oh, how much she wanted to forget what she'd done and finally live again. Slowly, she lifted the bottle to her lips, closing her eyes. Taking first one tiny sip, she tipped the bottle back for a bigger swallow, and for one insane second, she thought the ordinary liquid could touch her soul, wipe away the black stains there and make her new, deserving, worthy of love.

Please God...

Common sense kicked in, much more tactile than believing in the healing properties of Tyler's scam or even of an unseen deity who'd hidden the lighted path from her years ago. Her eyes flew open. She focused on Tyler and his knowing expression. "My first impression of the tonic still stands. It's total bunk, and you, sir, are a liar." Disappointment pinged through her chest at the knowledge. "It does *not* work."

"I'm sorry you think so." He moved into her personal space, trapping her between the tree and his body. "Apparently, I'll need to work doubly hard on convincing you."

Julia's heart raced like a wild horse. Her pulse thundered through her veins, pounding in her temples until she feared he would hear. "It would be a waste of time. I'm unconvinced about you as well." His citrusy scent teased her nostrils. She couldn't breathe properly, couldn't do anything except stare at his jawline, drink in the way his hair curled beneath his hat and his eyes darkened with desire.

"Perhaps I need try different options to sway you." He slid a hand around her nape, cupping her head. "Maybe this will convince you."

There was no time to think, no chance to move, before Tyler's lips were on hers, questing with insistent, gentle pressure. She stood immobile. If she didn't return his advance, he'd give up and move on. That's how men worked. The problem was she craved his touch more than she cared to admit.

Tyler lifted his head. Questions churned in his brown eyes. "I apologize. I apparently overstepped the boundary. I thought perhaps you wanted the kiss."

"Wait." Threads of panic slid over her spin as he pulled away. Where was the harm in letting the man embrace her? Lord knew she'd never had the luxury before. One kiss, she promised herself. Only one. There was a chance it would be as different as he.

A host of conflicting emotions played across his face— curiosity, annoyance, need. "The others will return soon. I'd rather not waste the moment—"

"Please kiss me again." Appalled that her penchant for interrupting plagued her now, she rushed to cover her confusion. "I meant to say I wouldn't be opposed to another — "

Tyler cut off her babble by taking her into his arms and claiming her mouth. Still gentle, the new embrace held an urgency the first one lacked. The bottle fell from her hand as she twined both around his neck and encouraged him closer. He took the hint as well as the control. Julia was never so glad as to give it to him.

He played his fingers along her spine until Julia wanted to scream with the frustration of not being able to feel his touch on her skin due to the layers of clothing and corset. The warm firmness of his lips demanded her attention as he worked her mouth, nibbling at her lips, urging them open then tangling their tongues. As she gave into the mystery of his kiss, experienced the silky heat of the intimate caress, a low moan escaped her throat.

The simple act of kissing was much more desirable than engaging in intercourse. It was extremely personal and encouraged bonding. Julia's mind reeled at being cheated out of such wonderment all those years ago. She removed Tyler's hat, throwing it to the ground in order to furrow her fingers through his curls. So soft and thick. Was the hair on the rest of his body as nice?

Just when she thought he'd end the embrace, he trailed a line of kisses along the underside of her jaw, then paid lavish attention to the hollow of her throat, teasing her collarbone with his tongue. Small fires erupted everywhere he'd touched. Heated wetness tickled between her legs.

Heaven help her, but she needed more.

After sliding her hands over the hard expanse of his chest, she plucked at the buttons of his waistcoat. The natty tweed scraped her knuckles. "Help me undo..."

"Patience." He captured her hands in his. "I refuse to take you like an animal in the forest." Tyler brushed a kiss over her lips, so light it awoke the butterflies in her stomach. "This is a flirtation, nothing more at this time."

She broke away as if she'd been doused by a bucket of water. "What does that mean?" Shame washed all other emotions aside. Julia fixed her gaze on the grass, sure he'd felt her need, her hunger, recognized her less-than-virginal response.

"I don't intend to bed you until we're more comfortable in each other's company. Whatever else you think I am, I'm not a cad." He raked his fingers through his hair leaving haphazard curls behind. "It's perfectly acceptable to kiss without heading directly for the bedroom. The chase is half the enjoyment."

Tears crowded her throat, both from his sentiment and the realization she could never know a real courtship. "I... I'm sorry." She risked a glance at him, terrified of what he'd do. "I assumed men only wanted..."

Silence stretched between them, and with each beat of her heart, she wanted to tell him, confess the truth, plead her case, beg his understanding.

"My God." Incredulity lit his eyes, followed quickly by shock. "Those pictures weren't the worst thing you've done, were they? *That* is your big secret."

Chills flooded her skin. He'd guessed it, but it didn't mean she needed to confirm. She didn't want his pity, didn't want to see his disgust or contempt. Instead, she shoved past him and ran.

No matter that she barely knew him, Tyler Browning had gotten through a crack in her defenses. He couldn't be allowed to continue into to her heart because then they'd both be destroyed by her mistakes, and she suspected she favored him too much for that.

Chapter Nine

The next morning, Julia prowled the quiet house, alone. She'd gotten up with the sun knowing her parents wouldn't rise until noon. Bess wasn't in attendance since she had Sundays off. The household would fend for itself, which meant an early dinner at a restaurant mid-afternoon and perhaps a visit to the park and bandstand later. Her mother didn't cook and rarely did she pass through the kitchen if she could help it. It was just as well. Sitting at the large dining room table staring at her parents in silence held no appeal.

A walk, however, did, and was exactly the thing needed to clear her mind. Thankfully, she hadn't dreamed last night. She didn't think she could survive another haunting so soon on the heels of the latest.

After dressing in a dove-gray skirt and serviceable white shirt, she did up the buttons on a matching gray jacket, jammed a plain black hat on her head out of necessity and left the house. Immediately, the cool air of the morning enveloped her, the trailing tendrils of mist from a light fog kissing her face.

The rapidly approaching season change, coupled with the warmer ground temperatures often produced the low-lying clouds in the morning. In the fog she could well imagine her past hidden, and she could emerge in a different part of town a new woman who had everything to offer life — or a man should the opportunity arise.

Or should Tyler...

Julia shook her head. She'd all but destroyed any hope of *that* since she'd opted to run yesterday. Even if he forgave her inexcusable departure, he'd never forgive her past. In the same situation, would she have the fortitude and courage to overlook a similar indiscretion?

Minutes ticked past as she traversed the silent streets. Occasionally, a shop owner would cry out a greeting. She returned many of them. A boy selling newspapers tried to lure readers with his shouted headlines. She smiled but declined. By the time she'd read the paper, the article that was talk-worthy wouldn't be the same as the one when she arrived home again later that morning. The fickle world would move on to something else.

Ironically, the news wasn't worth the nickel cost unless it was heartfelt and emotional—unless it grabbed the reader and made them think beyond their prejudices and perceptions.

She hoped to do just that at Tyler's expense. She only needed proof he was the fraud she thought, and she couldn't do it while beset by his overwhelming charm or her budding attraction for him. She needed a quiet place to gather her thoughts.

Julia paused on the street before Holy Cross Catholic Church. Its spires rose into the sky, partially obscured by the fog, yet there was no mistaking the peal of the bells, their mournful sound eerie in the silence. Not particularly religious, she considered churches neutral territory, fine for folks who needed a physical connection to the Almighty, yet equally calming for those merely searching for peace from whoever would give it.

And it was perfect. In the time between services, the church would be empty and provide an appropriate hideaway to scribble a few notes, reset her mental priorities.

She made short work of the stairs, then pulled open the heavy oak door. An enormous creak ushered her into a dark entryway. The door banged shut behind her. As her eyes adjusted to the dim light, she edged down the center aisle and slipped into a pew located three-quarters of the way through the sanctuary.

Candle flames danced on the altar while the whispered prayers and the litany of the rosary floated to her ears from a cluster of nuns at the front. Stained glass windows glowed in the rising sun, dappling the worn wooden floors and pews. Julia sighed and let her eyes drift closed. For one moment, she prayed, not in coherent thoughts or sentences, but more with hopes and dreams.

And if onlys...

The pew creaked as someone sat down beside her. "To truly be forgiven, you must first believe that you *can* be forgiven. It starts inside you."

She didn't need to open her eyes to identify the speaker. His spicy, citrusy scent and genteel drawl slid along her skin and sent a shower of tingles throughout her body. She remained silent. When Tyler offered nothing else, she opened her eyes.

"If someone asked me if you were a religious man, I'd probably answer in the negative. Do you come here often, perhaps to visit the confessional to clear your conscience?" She kept her gaze on the group of nuns several pews ahead of them, all sitting in a row like so many misshapen, black chess pieces.

His laughter sounded foreign in the cavernous holy place. A few murmurs of annoyance came from the nuns. "You mean so I can start my week with a clean slate?" When Julia kept her own counsel, he laughed again. "No, my dear. Whatever sins I've committed in my life, I still carry. Consider them pieces of my character."

"Then this church isn't on your list of sights to see?" The warmth from his body licked at her, so much so she could barely sit still. She wanted to burrow her face in his shoulder and feel his solid body pressed against hers, to revel in the weight of his arms around her and take solace in the comfort.

"No. While religion has its place in the world, I believe we can reach our goals through hard work, dedication and a bit of luck, not wholly relying on help from the divine."

"Interesting." She ran her tongue over her bottom lip. "If you're not a regular parishioner, you must be after something else. Why did you follow me?" While part of her wished to be flattered from the attention, a tiny niggle of fear pushed her common sense to the forefront. She finally glanced at him and was obliged to stifle a gasp.

A dark shadow of stubble clung to his cheeks, defining his strong jaw. Black curls ran riot over his head, unruly since he wore no hat. His suit, though cut in the latest style, appeared a bit rumpled as though he'd slept in them.

"I didn't follow you." When a couple of the nuns turned and gave him angry looks, he lowered his voice. "My agenda this morning contained a call on you. After you left in haste yesterday, I worried."

She snorted her surprise. "Somehow, I doubt you could summon sympathy for anyone except yourself." Yet, the part of her untainted by bitterness thrilled with the knowledge. He cared that she might still be upset. Not even her parents had ventured a comment when she'd returned to the house early the day before.

"Ah, Julia, give me the benefit of the doubt." He leaned forward and, resting his arms on the pew in front of him, clasped his hands as if in supplication. He kept his gaze fixed on a statue of the Virgin Mary near the altar. "You have no idea why I do what I do. Sometimes, the con is only a means to an end and more weighty matters are at play."

The raw emotion in the whispered explanation gave her pause. "Suppose you tell me what it *is* about? The truth, preferably."

"Why should I when you aren't willing to do the same?"

"Because..." Annoyance half-heartedly rose in her chest then died. He was right. Too long had she carried around the burden, yet in him she sensed a bigger story lurking beneath the guise of the tonic. That would be the real article. Now to draw it out of him while considering her own tangled web. "Don't lecture me about forgiveness until you practice the same on yourself."

His jaw clenched. He turned dark, tortured eyes on her. "I don't know if I can."

"Oh." Could it be there was actually a human under the layers of scheming flirtation? Curiosity raged in her breast. "Do you want to talk about it? Maybe telling a neutral party will help." *Or at least give me the courage to do the same.* She laid a gentle hand on his knee, snatching it back when he gave her a wolfish grin.

"I hardly consider you a disinterested observer. Truth be told, I consider you the most dangerous person I know at present." Tyler grabbed her hand and placed a kiss upon the back. "In fact, I'll bet against all the profits I intend to make today you're fairly bursting to ascertain my past."

She didn't pull her hand away, even when one of the nuns turned around and shushed them, shaking rosary beads in her fist. "Is that a challenge?" A smile curled her lips despite every effort she spent attempting to hold it back.

"Do you want it to be?" He drew his fingers up the inside of her arm and chuckled softly as she shivered. "Accompany me to the City Market. Listen to my pitch. If I sell all three dozen bottles of tonic, I promise I'll reveal why I need the money." Tyler lifted an eyebrow.

"Done." Excitement pinwheeled through her stomach. "And if you don't?"

The dazzling grin returned, accompanied by a predatory light in his eyes. "If I don't, you must talk frankly to me about those photos."

Bitter bile coated her tongue. He could do nothing else but hate her for what happened, yet there was a chance, however small... "Agreed. What time are you scheduled to be there?"

Tugging a watch from his waistcoat pocket, he frowned. "Not for a couple of hours. Would you care to walk about the city to pass the time? I'll even buy you a cup of coffee at the Market and perhaps a pastry if you wish."

Her stomach growled at the mention of food. She'd skipped dinner last night due to her ire regarding Tyler. "I..." She glanced around the dim interior of the church. The candle flames flickered as they caught the draft, then finally rested her gaze on the serene face of the Virgin Mary statue. In the grand scheme, did her sins really matter? Did his? Hadn't everyone garnered a few stains on their soul?

Was it time to loosen her grasp on her past in order to chase future happiness?

"Julia," Tyler moved his hand to her cheek and gently turned her face so she met his gaze. "It's a non-threatening walk and breakfast. I won't harm you in any way. I'd rather die." Honesty shone in his eyes mixed with a much stronger emotion she couldn't identify. "If at any time you feel uncomfortable, I'll put you in a carriage and send you home. No questions asked."

A shuddering breath left her body and she nodded. When he grinned, her stomach dropped. It felt as if she were falling, scary and exhilarating all at once. As incongruous as it sounded, she knew Tyler would catch her before she hurt herself, before her past could chase her down. "I'd be delighted to accompany you." Not since she was a small child at Christmas had she experienced anything as gut-wrenching yet fraught with happy potential. Maybe, just maybe, learning to trust wouldn't be that bad.

Tyler uttered a loud whoop, and this time, one of the church elders materialized from the shadows demanding to escort them from the church.

"Since we have an interesting wager, I'm anxiously waiting to see what you'll do today." Julia gave him a grin that sent a rush of heat through his veins.

Damn. At times, the woman's flirting drove him batty as it seemed to trip effortlessly off her tongue—a direct contrast to her other persona of the unyielding, common sense reporter. If women were complicated, Julia was truly one of the world's greatest mysteries, and one he couldn't wait to solve. Still, his stomach churned with unease.

"Perfection takes a fair amount of preparation." Tyler attempted to ignore his sudden attack of nerves. He'd made pitches in front of crowds many times before, yet now, it was different. This time Julia was in attendance. He sneaked another glance at her. She stood a few feet from him, holding a small, leather-bound notebook, scribbling with a pencil, and undoubtedly adding thoughts for her article. Every now and again, she looked at him and her sharp gaze roved over his face.

Her intense regard didn't bother him. Hell, in the past he'd run a con knowing the authorities were nearby. The difference was the constantly changing emotions in her blue eyes. Yes, she still regarded him with a skeptic's coat, but it faded beneath a quiet yearning, almost a hunger. He desperately wondered what she wanted from life.

And if he could be the one to fill that need.

Shaking his head to clear his thoughts, Tyler scanned the gathering crowd in front of his assigned area. Not having enough clout to actually reserve a space for his tonic inside the City Market building, he'd been consigned a makeshift stall on the sidewalk outside. Fruit sellers jockeyed for position in the mishmash as vegetable hawkers, milliners, leather workers, poultry men, women selling bakery items and hand-knitted mittens all vied in competition. Shoe shine boys, young women with flowers, and many others too numerous to comprehend joined the throng that painted the background of the city.

He had no time to waste on jealousy for the others as he arranged bottles of tonic on stacked wooden packing crates. The noise level of the crowd swelled as conversation mingled with shouts from the vendors and cries from bored children. A whiff of sweet pastry made his mouth water. He could still taste sugar and cinnamon on his tongue. A smile curled his lips. An hour earlier, he and Julia had shared a piece of crumb cake while discussing banal topics like the weather around the country and the future of politics.

Yet underlying their casual conversation, invisible threads had pulled at him, drawing him closer to her, and binding them together. They'd shared secrets and guilt. He wished to understand what drove her, and above everything he wanted to track down the bastard photographer who took the pictures she wouldn't own up to.

More than that, he wanted to repeatedly pound his fists into every man who'd hurt her, every man who'd looked upon those photos, every man who sought his pleasure thinking about her curves, or worse, every man who had touched her body if his suspicions turned out to be true.

In short, he wanted to protect Julia—if only from herself. He wanted the chance to love—no, he refused to think about *that*, especially if he needed to leave town in a hurry if things went wrong.

The less connection he had, the less likely she'd be hurt again. Yet, in the knowing of her, the urge to flee like usual lessened. She was different. She'd be worth the consequences.

Feeling her eyes upon him, he glanced up, meeting her gaze and unconsciously shivered at the disapproval he found there. For the first time in his life, he disliked being a con artist, but it was a necessary evil. Tyler stood a little straighter and grinned, which she did not return.

What would it take to make the woman see him for more than a grifter or a crook? What would it take to have her look at him as a genuine man who could give her a normal life and everything she could ever desire?

Honesty. The answer slammed into his stomach like a physical blow.

Unpacking the last bottle and placing it on the crate, he cleared his throat. First, sell the tonic, hand over the money, and then he'd think about coming clean with Julia.

"Is this the extent of your pitch, Mr. Browning?" Her husky voice jarred all common sense from his brain and made his groin stir. "If so, I must say, I rather doubt you'll sell your inventory."

"Ah, impatience doesn't become you. Perhaps it should if you want that story." He pulled a tin cow bell from one of the crates and, holding it aloft, rang it several times. "Attention please! May I have your attention?"

The general din around him died slightly. Not good enough. He wanted a small group interested in his act. "If you've ever wanted to be lucky, today is that day. Why?" He grinned and stowed the bell in a crate. He beckoned the crowd closer until they stood tightly clustered about him. "My marvelous, mystery tonic has been reputed to leave your mind so clear and uncluttered you can make business decisions without wavering." A few titters erupted. "Do I have any unmarried ladies in the crowd?"

Several hands tentatively rose into the air, accompanied by shifting gazes and blushing cheeks.

"Excellent! Welcome ladies, and may I say what a lovely bunch you are." He beamed the grin that had won him countless arguments and sales. "After drinking my tonic, you'll be able to discern the man of your dreams in one conversation."

A general buzz of interest rose from the group and a few more cheeks flushed.

At the outskirts of the knot of people, Julia rolled her eyes. Tyler winked. It wasn't necessarily an untruth. Usually, when a woman talked to a man long enough, she knew if he was marriage worthy.

Yet there were too many skeptics in the assemblage for him to be effective. A con thrived on the energy of a crowd and this one needed help.

"Ah, you're unconvinced." He grabbed a bottle and held it aloft so everyone could look upon it. "Let me talk to you on more personal matters." *God, I love my job.* Waves of excitement raised the hair on his nape. Tyler met the gazes of those nearest to him, ignoring Julia completely. "Do you ever wake up in the morning exhausted? Do mysterious aches and pains plague you until you're simply run raw not knowing how to treat them?"

Murmurs swept through the crowd like wildfire.

"Do you ever worry if your man will be healthy enough to provide for you years into the future?" He beckoned them closer until he and his packing crates were an island in a sea of humanity. "Do you ever wish, and this is just for the married ladies in the crowd," he lowered his voice and had the crowd straining on baited breath, "your man had a bit more stamina in the bedroom in order to satisfy your needs?"

When a few shocked expressions sprang up, he assumed a sad posture. "Ladies, I know it's a scandalous subject, but I'm only asking out of concern for your well-being." He frowned as if the weight of the world had descended around his shoulders—a classic ploy in his arsenal. "A healthy life between the sheets means a happy home life, am I correct? If you're unsatisfied, you'll find every little thing wrong with the family."

He let the masses digest that for a few moments and risked a glance at Julia. She looked as if she'd just had a large revelation. What the hell had he'd said to spark such a reaction?

"Now, folks, before I go further, let me tell you the price of this fantastic product." Tyler once again lifted the bottle. He felt quite smug as the sunlight hit the clear glass and shone through the pristine water. "I know money is tight in these times. Trust me when I say I wouldn't be doing this if I didn't need it as much as you. I'd hoard my stash of tonic and laugh myself silly for being twenty ways of good."

Time to endear himself to the buying public. Slowly, using deliberate care, he met each wondering, doubtful, expectant gaze, making a personal connection.

"I can't keep such a fantastic thing for myself. I'm compelled to share and help you be healthy, happy people." He studied the bottle in his hand making a show as to whether to part with it or not. "No, I'm offering it you my fellow city mates. I must. You deserve a better way of life, and if I can make that possible, I will, all for one dollar a bottle."

Several gasps of surprise went up. A couple of people shook their heads, grumbling about the cost.

"I know the price is steep in today's marketplace, but consider what it'll do for you in the long run. My marvelous, mystery tonic has the capacity to obliterate aches and pains in your joints, heads and unmentionable regions. If you dab it on your skin, it can reduce the appearance of freckles. Why, the other day, I received a letter from a customer who said she used it to clear diaper rash."

He supposed if he *did* have a customer with a baby, she *might* have used it thusly, so it wasn't that much of a lie.

The crowd grew restless. He was about to lose them. "All right, as much as it pains me to do this, I'll let this tonic go for eighty cents, but only today, and only if you buy it right here. Please," he lowered his voice again, "don't tell anyone else. I don't want folks to get the wrong idea that I'll offer this kind of deal every day. I feel the need emanating from this audience. I'd hate myself if I didn't offer you a break."

Change jingled in pockets and coin purses. Ah, he had them hooked. Inflate the price on an everyday item, then reduce the cost and people will run to buy it. "Just think how much better your lives will be after drinking a few bottles. Consider, after consuming a whole case, how great your outlook will be." *Because everyone could do well to drink more water in any event.*

The life of a con man was its own reward.

Accidentally, he caught Julia's eye and nearly dropped the bottle he held at the censure spitting from her gaze.

Except on days like today when he seemed to live and die by the barometer of the budding reporter who owned the most luscious lips he'd ever seen. Too bad the overwhelming need for cash conflicted with giving it up in order to explore Julia Spencer.

Tyler thrust thoughts of her from his mind. He had an obligation, damn it, and no tempting siren was going to get in the way. "Don't dither too long in your decision, folks. I brought three dozen bottles of the tonic today. Once it's gone, I won't have more for another week. Who knows what will befall you in seven days. Wouldn't you rather be prepared?"

Then, as if the flood gates sprang open, the crowd shifted and everyone clamored their need at once. Money exchanged hands at a furious pace. Change for a dollar was broken down and bottles of tonic were snatched up as though the apocalypse loomed on Indianapolis. Tyler calmly took their cash and gave them the water, silently chuckling in his head.

Foolish people. Too bad simple mineral water really couldn't heal what ailed them. His stomach clenched in irony. At times he wished it would because he'd drink enough water until the never-ending guilt eating at him went away.

The buying frenzy died eventually and the happy new owners of the tonic went about their business. They melted into the bigger crowds swarming the Market. A few folks remained, apparently undecided. Tyler spared a glance to his inventory. Three bottles left. He looked at Julia and hated the dread in her expression. Did her past haunt her so much she loathed the thought of sharing it with him?

One elderly woman toddled forward. She offered him the change in her shaking hand. For one second, Tyler considered giving her the bottle for free. Chances were she probably needed that money for something else. An image of Joshua floated into his mind's eye as the boy implored Tyler to take care of his family.

He locked the memory away and pocketed the woman's cash. Such was life. He had no choice. He sent the woman on her way. Having two bottles left, he wouldn't be the one baring his soul—at least not on this day, yet the victory felt hollow since his winning would cause Julia additional pain.

A deal was a deal.

Now that the crowd disbanded, she stepped forward, tucking her pencil and notebook into her handbag. "You put on quite a show. Perhaps you missed your calling and should try a career on the stage." Her eyes twinkled, and for a moment the world existed only in shades of blue. "I hope your voice holds out because you'll need it to tell me your story." Julia's lush lips parted with her grin.

Tyler swallowed heavily. He was glad for the packing crates that hid his body's reaction to the mere sound of her voice. "Actually, it'll be you who'll do the talking, my dear. I still have two bottles remaining."

Thank the Lord for small miracles.

"Think again." Using all the speed and panache of a slight of hand magician, Julia slapped two bills onto the packing crate. "I'm buying those." The throaty sound of her laugh spiked chills down his spine. "Shall we adjourn to someplace more private or would you rather meet me for dinner this evening?"

He gaped, moved his mouth open and closed like a fish and stared, astounded. *I lost the bet.* "Uh, dinner would be fine. I'll come 'round to collect you and we'll go to the Carlisle."

"Most acceptable." Julia placed both winning bottles of tonic in her bag. "Until tonight, Mr. Browning."

As his mind reeled at the abrupt change in fortunes, Tyler smiled at the soft swish of her hips. Damn. The woman had as many facets as the rarest diamond, and he couldn't wait to study them all.

Chapter Ten

By the time Julia arrived home, she'd already downed the contents of one of the tonic bottles. As much as she wished the miracle water could heal her hidden hurts, she felt absolutely no different than she did while in the Market. Yes, Tyler hawked a useless product, but the part of her brain that still believed in fantasy and miracles and happy endings thought perhaps, just once, he told the truth.

Of course he didn't, so why did he need to sell the tonic?

Her mind raced as she entered her house. She'd ferret out the answers during dinner. Hopefully, if all went well, she could write her article and demand her uncle treat her as he did the male reporters. Finally, her future was in her grasp. Only one thing marred the shimmering prospect of moving forward. Once she wrote the article, she'd have no reason to see Tyler unless she wanted to encourage his advances, which brought her brain skittering into another direction. Did Tyler view her as a woman suitable to be wooed or had his opinion changed since he'd spied the alleged painting he mentioned?

Pausing, Julia pressed a hand to her heart as if that alone could quell the vague ache. This is what happened when she allowed anyone past her defenses. She wished for things that would never happen. For whatever reason, Tyler's charm had wormed its way in and she thought of him as more than merely her break into serious journalism. She laid her handbag on one of the chairs in the front parlor, and Bess appeared at the door, a full-blown frown darkening her features.

"Miss Spencer, your uncle wishes to speak with you."

"Uncle George is here?"

"Yes. I don't know why this is a shock to you." Frost formed on the backside of her words.

"I simply wasn't expecting him today. What a happy surprise your presence is also, Bess. I thought this was your day off." As much as she wished to say exactly what she thought of the gossipy housekeeper, Julia held her tongue. Some things were best unspoken — for now.

"I promised your mother I'd drop by and leave a poultice for her headache. She usually complains of one after being out on the town. Afterward, I stayed to see to the week's menu."

Julia snorted. *Perhaps if mother wouldn't be so chummy with the free-flowing alcohol at her precious social functions, she wouldn't suffer the hangover's ache.* "Maybe next time you should inquire to Browning's Apothecary for a cure." A rush of giggles threatened to pour from her throat at the thought of the straight-laced Bess frequenting the shop.

"He's nothing but a charlatan. There are rumors he offers more than headache powders and ointments to his female patrons, but instead, he does dark, illicit, *ungodly* things."

"Mmmhmm." Julia couldn't stop the warmth spreading in her cheeks. Even though she'd questioned that part of his racket herself, right now, in this moment, it sounded wonderful...

Bess cleared her throat. "Daydreaming is the devil's playground, Miss Spencer." The older woman crossed her arms over her drooping bosom as her eyes narrowed. "You've been in *that man's* company again."

Immediately, Julia's anger ratcheted up, heating her blood. "Yes, I did spend the morning with Mr. Browning, and if you must know, we were among the huge crowds at the City Market. No cause for scandal was had. If my parents aren't concerned over my whereabouts, neither should you be."

"Your parents worry daily over your future."

"I rather doubt it. They couldn't be bothered when I needed them the most. Why should they try now?"

"One day you'll reap your comeuppance, Miss Spencer."

"What makes you assume I haven't already? I've lived many lifetimes in my existence." When the housekeeper lifted an eyebrow, Julia's tenuous hold on control snapped. "Not that it's any of your business, Bess, but Mr. Browning didn't kiss me, nor did he molest me in any way. If I were you, I'd be comfortable with the idea of having him underfoot. I intend to invite him over at the next opportunity." A tremor of shock moved through Julia as she realized she meant it. She wanted to encourage his affection.

The housekeeper's expression didn't change. "You'll excuse me if I don't set out the good china or silver. The man is nothing more than a thief." Her dark eyes emanated dislike. "Your parents have gone visiting friends for the remainder of the afternoon and most likely will be out to dinner. Your uncle is waiting in your father's study. Good day." Bess pivoted so quickly her skirts flared about her ankles.

Julia clapped a hand over her mouth to keep from laughing out loud. If Bess had her way, Julia would be locked into a convent, never to come into contact with members of the male persuasion ever again. Some of her good humor vanished as the undeniable memories of her past came rushing to the forefront of her mind.

Perhaps being locked away would be a good idea—for everyone's peace.

Winding through rooms that held no fond memories of family or home, she slipped down the hall and into the study. "Uncle George? Bess told me you wanted to..." Her words died as she caught sight of her relative's saddened, pensive expression. "What happened?"

"Come and sit, Julia." He gestured to one of the two leather chairs in front of the desk he sat behind. "Close the door, if you please."

Her stomach tightened. After gently shutting the heavy paneled door, she slipped into the chair. Uncle George rubbed a hand over his jaw. "Why the need for secrecy? Should I be concerned?" Never had she seen him so upset.

"Somethin's been weighin' on my mind for a few days now. I'd appreciate you tellin' me the truth, you hear?" He smoothed a fingertip over his mustache. "I've always taught you to be honest, and that's the most important thing."

She waited in silence. When several agonizingly slow minutes ticked by, she couldn't stand being pinned by his gaze anymore. "Whatever it is, I can take it Uncle George. I'm not a weak female. You know this." Gripping the padded leather armrests on the chair until her nails bit into the fabric, she swallowed.

He knows!

Her heart beat in double time as her mouth went dry. As bad as it would be for her parents to find out what she'd done, it was two times worse that Uncle George knew. His respect and admiration meant everything. He'd essentially raised her. If he guessed, he'd treat her differently...

"Julia." He folded his hands together on the desktop. "Jackson Hayes apparently recognizes you and has made...crude remarks about certain things that may have occurred in your past." Uncle George held her gaze with his unblinking blue one. "Tell me true, girl. Have you met him before comin' to work for the paper? He's got the ear of many important folks in town, and if you've done somethin' to antagonize the bastard, I want to know it. We need to do damage control or even get you out of the office."

"Why do you assume I did something to him?" *I need to go slow and mind my steps.* "Before I say anything, do I have your word you'll believe *me*? And no matter what, you won't judge?" She bit her bottom lip as her pulse continued to flutter too fast.

"I'm a journalist. It's my job to be impartial." His gaze softened, and he gave her a tiny smile. "First and foremost, I'm your uncle. Love trumps any sin. Remember it, girl. Take those words to heart and believe in them."

Tears crowded her throat. She worked them down, yet they fell to her cheeks anyway. Now that the truth was on the verge of coming out, she'd have to confess to the man who held her future in his hands, the man she thought of as a surrogate father, the man who meant the world to her. No matter how hard she'd tried to overcome her history, to avoid this very moment, both life and fate had caught her.

Julia pressed a hand against her heart. Pain tightened her chest as if her soul wept at this crossroad. When she realized she couldn't remain silent a second longer, she sighed. "Oh, Uncle George, I did a terrible thing. Well, many terrible things I suppose." Between tearful torrents she told the bones of the story as best she could without going into too much graphic detail. She couldn't bring herself to admit some of the men beat her because they could, didn't reveal the abject hopelessness she'd felt at times when she thought her family had abandoned her, had never cared to inquire about her life. She refused to mention she'd known Jackson Hayes as a client, seen him naked, suffered indignities at his hands. It was enough

Uncle George knew of her sins. Let him piece together her omissions. "What should I do?"

A pregnant silence fell between them, broken only by Uncle George's occasional grunts and the tapping of his finger against his chin. "Well, that explains a couple of my contacts telling me about some painting or another at a gentleman's club." He shook his big head. "I'm not a member and refused to pay for a membership just to see if they told tales." He pinned her with his gaze. "If I can, I'll buy that damn painting and destroy it."

Oh God. He knew about that? Of course the photographs were still in circulation, but knowing at least one of them had been fashioned into a painting on display for the men of the city? Hot mortification burned through her. When would the folly of her youth end?

"It won't matter. Someone will merely commission another." Never would she be free of the past. She mopped her face using the handkerchief he'd handed her while her stomach churned. What would he do? Why wouldn't he say something? She peered at her relative from beneath wet lashes. He stroked his mustache and frowned, staring at the desktop as if the piece of furniture would have all the answers. Finally, he cleared his throat, planted both palms on the desk and stood. The chair springs creaked in relief.

"Come here, girl." He opened his arms. "A woman shouldn't have to go through somethin' like that alone, not when there's still a man in her family to defend her."

She sprang off the chair. "Oh, Uncle George!" Relief surged through her body like a cooling rain. Julia rushed into his embrace, crying harder as he closed his arms around her, holding her safe and secure as he used to do. She buried her face in his shirt and inhaled the tobacco-and-peppermint scent while her tears wet the fabric. Throughout her childhood, Uncle George had been the anchor, the one permanent fixture in her life she counted on and depended to keep the dragons at bay.

Every time her parents had trotted off to a new party or left for exotic ports of call — all on the back of journalism and creating ties to the community— her uncle moved in for the duration, keeping her company, fending off Bess's barbed and poorly-veiled criticisms. He'd been the one person she truly missed while away at the school; losing his respect and knowing she hadn't lived up to his expectations had prevented her from dragging her aching body across town and home. She'd held off because she couldn't bear to see disappointment in his eyes.

"I'm as much to blame for this situation as you. If I hadn't been caught up in the newspaper during those years, trying to get it off the ground, I'd have seen what was goin' on under my own nose. For that, I'll never forgive myself."

"No, I was too stubborn and so angry at Mother and Father." His shirt muffled her words. "I wanted to hurt them, make them see me as someone of value. I wanted them to notice." She was hardly that now. "And that stunt didn't even change their views anyway."

"In the end, it doesn't matter. Julia, darlin', I think the time for cryin' has passed. What they've tossed out, I've picked up and value all the more." He patted her back a few times then set her away. "Nothin' more to do except clean up the mess. Once you put things in order, you'll have a new lease on life."

She nodded, and as much as it pained her, she lifted her gaze to his. No trace of the expected disappointment lingered there. Instead, humor twinkled amidst steely determination. The weight around her heart eased slightly. "I'm so sorry. If I'd have known you wouldn't judge me..."

"Never mind. Did you learn somethin' from the experience?" His voice rumbled in a soothing timbre.

"God, yes." Julia stumbled to her chair and sank into the smooth leather. "I'm stronger now, more determined to fight and give voice to those who cannot be heard. People will always be exploited. I think it's my destiny to ferret out their abusers and put a stop to them." She twisted the handkerchief in her fingers. "I want to be a reporter, use journalism as my voice, but carrying around this guilt and shame is dragging on me."

Uncle George came around and perched on the edge of the desk. "If you became a better person in that place, then I wouldn't call the time wasted. Honestly, I feared you'd do somethin' rash to punish your parents for their neglect. You always were an outspoken tyke. They didn't deserve you." He stroked his mustache. "My brother is truly daft if he can't see what a wonderful woman you've grown into, full of integrity, drive and a real heart for the truth." His eyes looked suspiciously moist. "I like to think you learned those things from me.

"Absolutely, and I appreciate your belief in me." Now that some of the burden had lifted, she didn't feel quite so haunted. Sure, the shame remained. It probably would for a long time. She had to battle that demon herself. Every time she met the knowing eyes of a man in the city, she'd always wonder if he'd seen that painting or one of those damning photographs. Each one of those occurrences would strengthen her resolve to never forget and to always do better. "I didn't want to disappoint you most of all, couldn't bear it if you'd leave too."

"Never. You make me proud, girl." Uncle George ran a hand through his hair, leaving it in haphazard rows.

All the warm feelings drained away. Julia raised her chin. Something still worried him. "Did Mr. Hayes mention *how* he knew me the other day in his office? Did you two argue about that?"

"Jackson is very skilled in couchin' his words, always dancin' around the subject." Uncle George narrowed his eyes. "He hinted, said he'd seen you in town years ago and knew you intimately at one time." He curled a hand into a fist as enlightenment lit his eyes. "Bastard! I should have put two and two together. He's a snake, though, and I wondered what he was tryin' to get at. You'll not find a bigger idiot than me, my girl."

She shook her head. "At least you know now. Did he threaten you?" The thought of the sneaky man causing havoc for her uncle made her anger rise. "Is that why you don't want me in the office?" Now that she understood, her heart softened toward her relative. He wanted to protect her after all. He hadn't been treating her differently at the paper.

A flush mottled Uncle George's cheeks. "Ah, no darlin', he didn't say such a thing to me, but if or when he does, I'll fight my own battles. I don't want you in the office because you're a distraction to some of the pups."

Liar! Her uncle was never good at falsehoods. "Listen to me, Uncle." She slid out of the chair and laid a hand on his shoulder. "I can hold my own with the reporters. None of them interest me, and they're little better than mosquitoes." Julia grinned as he chuckled. "I'll work on my article tomorrow. If Mr. Hayes is in, he can intimidate all he wants, but you've trained me too well to be rattled. I'll be fine, tucked away at your desk."

"I believe you." He grasped her hand in his. "For my peace of mind, promise you'll stay well away from him. I'm convinced he's not layin' all his cards on the table. I don't trust him, and now that I know..." He cleared his throat. "Well, things have changed."

"I promise." She smiled as he released her hand. The want to lighten the somber mood grew strong. "Do I need to stay for a speech on maintaining morality or attempting not to cause scandal in the city?"

"Would it do any good?" His eyes twinkled.

"I think we both know the answer to the question." She patted his cheek. "Anything else?" The affection in his expression nearly sent her into tears again. Why had she never revealed everything to him before?

"Ah, my darlin' girl, do you think you can fool your old uncle?"

"About?" She truly had no idea what else he meant.

"Tyler Brownin' has captured your imagination, and it's more than a passin' interest for the article, not that you won't do justice to unearthin' his scam."

Flutters filled her stomach at the mention of Tyler's name. She fixed her gaze on the silver chain of Uncle George's pocket watch. "I'd rather not say. My mind is too confused where he's concerned." *Please don't ask more questions!*

"Fair enough." He chuckled and patted the top of her head. "Remember though, sometimes folks have good reasons for doin' the things we think are questionable. Just look at yourself if you don't believe me. Go for the facts, dig to the heart, and don't mind the surface stains." He glanced away, discomfiture in his expression. He cleared his throat again. "I hope your experiences didn't sour you from male attention. There are some good ones out there, and I would hate for you to miss out on a part of life that can be quite enjoyable."

His embarrassment transferred to her and caused her stomach to cartwheel. "It's something I'm working on. Trust is slow in coming."

"Julia?"

"Yes?" Sharing the secret had exhausted her, and she rubbed her eye. All she wanted to do was sleep. This day had already taken an emotional toll.

His expression reflected nothing but paternal love. "Remember a man, no matter how honorable and good he is deep down, won't be able to love you if you cannot love yourself. No one can heal you but *you*, girl. Give it some effort. I believe you're worth every good thing."

How uncanny her uncle echoed Tyler's words from earlier. "I promise to try." In a rush, she pressed a kiss to his cheek and fled the room before he could think of something else. Once inside her bedroom with the door closed, Julia slumped against the panel and gave into the warring feelings swirling inside her while she mulled her uncle's words. She had a chance at redemption, and ironically, it waited on Tyler's doorstep. Maybe it was time to forget the sins of the past and chase after the future with a clear conscience. Tyler's face danced into her mind, all mocking eyes and confident smile and tender kisses. Flutters of anticipation pushed the unease out of her stomach.

She still had a dinner engagement with him tonight. Vowing to meet him as a new woman, Julia smiled.

After all, if she didn't take control of her life, who would?

Chapter Eleven

That evening, dinner proceeded with genteel politeness and forced niceties. Afterward, Tyler paid for the meal. Why was Julia so uncharacteristically silent? He'd been prepared for a barrage of questions and demands for his story, but she'd only picked at her food, answering his questions with one-word responses and avoiding his gaze. When her interrogation didn't come, he worried. Had something happened to her that afternoon? What was more, he missed the brash, outspoken woman he'd gotten to know.

"I've given you the benefit of the doubt, assuming you were nervous. Dining in public with a con man can be a daunting endeavor. Yet, looking back over our previous acquaintance, you've never been timid, so my suspicion is unfounded." He escorted her from the dining room, a hand firm on the small of her back. Once on the boardwalk outside, he stared her down. "What bothers you? Your presence at dinner was a mere shell of yourself, which leads me to believe you're either not interested in me as a man or your mind is conflicted. I'd like to understand why, even if that answer goes against my wishes."

For one heartrending moment, he thought she'd found out his secret and had condemned him for it. Now, upon thinking over the course of their silent dinner, he realized she'd withdrawn somewhere deep inside herself long before he'd spoken a word, perhaps reflecting on her misdemeanors as well. Surely if she'd ascertained his lie, she'd have brought attention to it, scribbled the facts in her notebook or left the table in a huff.

"I apologize for not seeming myself. I've had much to mentally digest today." She drew a black shawl tighter about her shoulders and shivered in the slight evening breeze.

"Understandable. Care to share?" Would she trust him now?

"Have you ever realized at times, quite suddenly and with the force of a hurricane, the past has no bearing on what the future can be?" Her eyes, so wide and blue, twinkled in the fading light.

His breath caught, prompting him to physically remember to continue to take in air and expel it. "I think on it occasionally. I like to hope it's true. We're the only people to whom our past matters, and if the folks around us don't feel the same, well then, I don't guess they matter either." What did she hint at? Her expression revealed nothing, only hosted a tiny smile.

"Well said."

Tyler feared he'd collapse to the ground in relief. "We all have skeletons we'd rather not show. This is how we build our lives. Imagine if everyone had no depth that their past allows. We'd be a boring lot."

She nodded, looking into the dining room through a front window. The breeze stirred the baby-fine curls at her nape and temples beneath the brim of a shallow, black hat. "I'd like to hope if the people we care about stumble upon those skeletons, they won't judge us. Instead, they'll think we've gained experience, tried ourselves by fire and came out unscathed or, at the very least, a bit singed." Julia turned her attention to him, holding his gaze. "What say you to that, Mr. Browning?"

"I've never heard acceptance put quite so eloquently." His feet seemed rooted to the planking as he stared. While the gentle colors of twilight settled around them, her features softened. A rosy stain stole into her rounded cheeks. In the lamplight, her upswept hair resembled the halo of the Madonna, and with her face uplifted as she waited for his continued answer, she resembled a veritable artist's rendering of medieval beauty. Tyler cleared his throat, tried to resist her pull, but in the end, he wasn't strong enough, didn't want to be. "I think also, Miss Spencer, you're easily the prettiest girl I've laid eyes on in a long time."

Her eyes sparkled. The smile she bestowed could put the rising moon to shame. "You're too charming for your own good." She laid a hand on his sleeve. "My name, remember, is Julia, and I haven't been a girl for many years."

Heat rushed up his neck, spreading through his body as much from her suddenly lighthearted attitude as her tender touch. He wanted to kiss those delectable lips. "I'm well and truly chastised, but I must insist it's the truth." For the moment, he'd content himself with small talk, while steadily gaining more of her trust.

"Somehow, I rather think it's a bit of fluff and flattery all the same."

"Perhaps, except flattery is mostly a lie." Offering his arm, the familiar skitters of lightning danced over his skin as she slipped her hand into the crook of his elbow. "Shall we walk? I find I'm in no mood to retire so early." How could he when merely having her near set his body on fire until he feared he'd become a funeral pyre right on the street.

"Delightful idea. Besides," she tipped her face up once more and this time there was no mistaking the determined gleam in her eyes. "You owe me a story. Best make it a good one, don't you think?"

Some of his ardor died. Above everything, she couldn't forget the journalistic instinct. His ego deflated. For one tiny second he thought she'd be interested in him as a man, hoped she felt the same sharp desire he had moments before. Almost by accident, his gaze brushed hers. Curiosity brimmed in the blue depths, coupled with the thrill of victory and something else he couldn't identify. It was that bit of the unknown that bolstered hope in his chest. No matter how she saw him, a deal was a deal. He'd promised her the tale, but anything else he chose to share was strictly off the record.

"You're correct." With gentle pressure on her arm, he set them both in motion once more. For long moments, the rhythmic thud of his cane against the walkway marked the passage of time as he gathered his thoughts.

Julia remained quiet. If the warmth from her hand on his elbow hadn't reminded him of her presence, he could have easily forgotten she was there. Her subtle, lilies of the valley scent wafted in the air, teasing him, threading around him like an invisible web that held him to her side. What was it about this intriguing woman he couldn't shake?

Loath to break the companionable silence, but knowing he owed her an explanation, Tyler breathed in deeply then let out an exhale in a slow gust. "I lived in Kentucky as a boy. My folks had a farm and raised thoroughbreds. Some of the horses we shipped to other countries. That's how well-known our business was." The hollow ache in his chest came out of dormancy as he remembered the sweet smell of the grass as it crushed beneath his bare feet on summer days. "I used to think it was the best place in the world."

"You don't now?" She squeezed his arm. "No sudden urges to take the train south and return home, ditch the flim-flam and take up the equine business?"

The constant *clip-clop* of horses' hooves against the cobblestones echoed between the buildings. Pedestrians ebbed and flowed around them, talking and laughing.

Tyler leaned into Julia, hoping she could hear his response over the street commotion. "That place was for another time. When I came home from war, I wasn't the same man I was when I left." Pain slashed through the empty void. He walked on regardless of Julia's soft inhalation of breath. "My family is still down there, but I don't plan on returning."

"It's good you've grown enough to move on." Sympathy flowed smoothly from her soft response, a balm to his wounds.

He shook his head. "That's my luck I suppose." Having Julia look at him with compassion in her gaze lessened the ache inside. "Victor and I were the best of friends and a handful back then. Mom was at her wit's end and practically forced me to join the service. Victor followed, since we'd always looked for adventure together. Soon, we found ourselves in the thick of things and were sent to Cuba of all places. Peacekeepers, they said."

"What about your father? Did he want you to join the service?" She tugged him around a corner and into a grassy area more suitable for quiet conversation. Couples strolled past, locked in their own private thoughts while a few folks walked dogs or rushed toward the interurbans and cab stands.

"Dad died the week before I first joined. He never knew what kind of a man I'd become. On the other hand, he never heard of the cons I ran or the money I fleeced." A tiny wobble cracked his voice. He glanced quickly at Julia, but she didn't appear to notice. "In his memory, I remained his spitting image, both inside and out. A fine man, a man who'd do good things. He never knew the truth."

"Sometimes, kindness can be found in death, even if it does sound strange to say out loud." They walked in silence, and the harsh sounds of the city grew fainter. "The story of losing your family isn't the story you want to tell me."

"No." Tyler unclenched his jaw. He could do nothing about the past, but it still had the power to throw him off-kilter. "My unpardonable secret occurred while in Cuba."

"Were you there before the war officially started?"

"A good two years. That didn't stop a few conflicts from flaring. We were mostly there to keep violence at bay. It didn't quite work out." Spying a wooden bench nearby, he steered her toward it. "I thought perhaps you'd enjoy a rest in order to watch the day go to sleep." He cringed at the overly poetic words. Apparently, being in Julia's company had addled his brain.

A demure smile graced her lips. "If you weren't an inherent scam artist, I'd swear you were meant to be a lyricist." She released his arm and settled on the bench, arranging her midnight blue skirts around her legs. "Tell me why the guilt never leaves your face. Share your secrets with me."

Oh, if only talking about it was that simple. His stomach knotted as he sat beside her, so close their shoulders touched. "It was my fault one of the young men in my unit died." In a low voice, Tyler told her an abbreviated version of the story, not wishing to go into great detail. The horrors of war should be spared whenever possible. He refused to let his nightmares haunt her as well. "He took a bullet in the chest."

"Why do you feel it's your fault?"

Absently, he rubbed his thigh as the phantom pain started. "I could have been clearer when I asked him to stay down. Hell, I should have shoved the boy face first into the dirt to make my point. But, I didn't. It happened too fast..." The faint aroma of gunpowder filled his nostrils.

148

Julia's inquisitive gaze held him steady, kept him in the present. "Except you *did* try to keep him safe, didn't you?" She arched an eyebrow. "Yes, you're a con man, but deep down, I think you want to do the heroic thing, and, in fact, have done it. That last act of kindness gave you the wound, didn't it?"

"Yes." Internally, he reeled. How could she possibly know what sort of man he was when she knew next to nothing about him? "Victor's the man responsible for saving my worthless hide. He shook his head, attempting to shove the memories away. "I'll never forget what happened that day."

"You shouldn't forget. It's part of your history. It's what has formed you into the man you are now." Julia turned toward him and laid a hand against his cheek. "We all have something."

Heat bloomed from her touch even as guilt sank into every pore when he thought of the wife and child Joshua left behind. "Even now, Joshua's death won't release me." He couldn't bring himself to tell Julia about Joshua's family or why he ran the con. For the first time in years, his devil-may-care lifestyle embarrassed him regardless of the altruistic intentions. He wanted to be a better man in order to win Julia's regard, and he couldn't do that by hawking a tonic for questionable motives no matter that they'd originated from a good heart.

She traced a fingertip along his jawline before dropping her hand into her lap. "The stronger memories have a tendency to do that." Moments passed before she spoke again. "Joshua was simply another kill during wartime, and you happened to be there when he died. You can't blame yourself either way. I'm sure many others also lost their lives that you didn't witness. If you had, would you feel guilty for them, too?"

"Joshua was more than a by-product of war, Julia. Why can't you understand that?"

"I feel your pain. It's in your voice as you talk about him, but for all your heroism and his, the war was bigger, and it took his life. It was a risk." She touched his arm. "I'm sorry all the same. He was too young."

"You have no idea what fighting in the military is like." He frowned. How could she be so uncaring? "Haven't you seen something in your life that was so vile, so wrong you can never forget? Do you ever feel guilt for anything?" He hated his quick words, but she needed to understand.

"I'm not a stranger to that emotion, trust me." Her chin trembled and she turned away. "Thank goodness it was you who lost the wager. You handle the raw emotions well. Had it been me confessing, I'd have broken down by now."

"Hardly." To his way of thinking, there was no woman stronger.

"You're a good person."

To hear that praise from her seemed a benediction of sorts, yet he snorted at the incongruity of her statement. "I sell a miracle tonic that has very little healing power."

Julia twisted to face him and a smile tugged at her lips. "Very little?" An eyebrow rose in challenge.

Warmth infused the back of his neck. This was the Julia he'd become accustomed to. "Touché. You were correct before. Intrinsically, the tonic is worthless, but it *is* mineral water, so therefore it has a few properties that are good for you."

"Be that as it may, I suspected you were lying from word one." She drew a small, leather-bound notepad and a pencil from her handbag. "May I quote you?"

"What about this instead?" Tyler removed the items from her fingers, laying them on the seat at his right side.

He slid an arm along the back of the bench and swiveled fully to face her despite the screaming denial in his knee and thigh. "Tell me why you wanted to believe in the tonic so much? What secrets are locked in your soul that need healed?"

"I... I can't tell you." She averted her gaze, only to fix it on the buttons of his waistcoat. "At least not tonight. You're the one who promised to reveal all, not I."

Tyler put a finger beneath her chin and tilted her face. "If you tell me, I promise never to use the information against you. I'll share the burden, tuck it away inside me so you can finally live free." Shock ricocheted through his gut like shrapnel as he realized he truly meant every word. Something kept Julia captive—something dark and ugly that had its roots in the painting.

"I gave up the right to live free a long time ago." Tears welled in her eyes. "But thank you for the concern. I don't have offers of that nature very often."

When she attempted to pull away, Tyler slid his arm around her shoulders, holding her close. "You'd be surprised at what I'll promise to the right woman. If you ask me for a piece of the moon, I'll try my best to procure it for you by any means necessary."

"An impossible endeavor. Why do you find pleasure in giving things to others who can potentially hurt you? Do you seek approval from them or from yourself?"

"I could ask the same of you." He moved a fraction of an inch closer until their lips nearly touched. "Every woman wants a man to be her hero, even if she won't admit it." With a slant of his head, he brushed his mouth against hers before pulling back. "That's the glory of believing, Julia. The more impossible the task, the more improbable a thing is. If you trust in that person or object, it's what makes all the difference."

"Is that what you truly believe?" Her whispered question sent eddies of heat over his skin.

"It's all I have left." He cupped her cheek with his other hand, tracing her lush bottom lip with his thumb. "Have faith, my dear. When you find that one person or thing to believe in despite the odds, despite every doubt, your eyes will finally be opened and you'll give in. Life will indeed be as sweet as you dream." As he continued to sit with her, look at her, he believed it too. Something about Julia made him want to be her hero, to grow as a person for himself as well as for a future.

"Oh, Tyler." Sniffing, she relaxed into him. Her scent, her searching gaze, her pliant mouth all conspired to captivate him. "I've forgotten what it's like to lose control as much as I'd like to."

What held her confined and kept the shadows in her eyes? Why couldn't she trust him enough to unburden her soul? "It's never too late to learn."

"Be patient. It would seem I'm much a work in progress."

"As are we all, but know this. Whatever it is that holds you down, what's in your heart will always win." *Please God, let her see that, especially when I tell her about the family Joshua left behind, and why I can't leave them.* Content to hold her in the gathering twilight, Tyler rested his cheek on her hair. Perhaps his redemption wasn't that unattainable after all. He hoped she would realize the same for herself.

Julia witnessed dawn break the next morning. Her nerves continued in a state of unrest, which hindered sleep. Accompanying that, tremors of anticipation kept her stomach jumping and finally, she'd gotten out of bed. Not wanting to rouse the maid so early, she skipped the corset and dressed in a camisole and drawers. Afterward, she donned a, serviceable gray skirt and mannish white shirt and gray tweed vest. Carrying a pair of lace-up boots, she tiptoed downstairs. Her parents, as well as Bess, were still abed. It made navigating the house relatively easy. Not having to account for her every movement gave a small measure of relief. Attention from Bess was not what she wanted to cultivate.

With her mind still in a tumble concerning her recent revelations to her uncle and her growing feelings for Tyler, Julia decided she'd throw herself into her work. Gain a level head, that's what she needed to do, and the only way to accomplish that was to build her article regarding Tyler's miracle tonic. It was no secret the man scammed the citizens of the city then pocketed the cash. They had a right to know, especially since he was fleecing them blind.

She slipped on her boots and laced them with a frown. Did she have the fortitude to expose him for the fraud he was? Did he deserve it? Julia had no idea. Had he told her his whole story? Probably not. She'd had the distinct feeling the night before he withheld a vital piece to the story. Until he revealed all, she couldn't decide what to do about him. Having watched Uncle George charm information out of people over the years for his own articles, she needed to garner pointers that would let her con the story from the con man.

Regardless of her splintered emotions, she had a duty to her job. The newspaper would be there for her long after Tyler left. His kind always did no matter what they told a woman. Her chest tightened. She needed to remember he'd say anything to earn her compliance and trust. As her thoughts turned to the gentle, companionable evening they'd shared last night watching the world go by, she shook her head. All kisses and lovely words aside, men were crafty. It was best to be careful and keep the heart protected since Tyler was the slickest of the lot.

Still, the urge to believe him, trust him, throbbed in her chest. If she wanted him to accept her and all her faults, shouldn't she do the same for him? She shook her head. *Why does life have to be so confusing?*

Julia tucked a few strands of hair into its updo, then donned a black coat, silently cursing its tight, tapered sleeves, but she left the garment unbuttoned. Though the early hour would be a bit chilly, she had no interest in succumbing to the extreme properness of a dress code. In that vein, she left her hat and gloves behind as she exited the house.

Half an hour later, she alighted from a carriage in front of the newspaper office. The shade on the outer door rested halfway up, which meant someone had already arrived. Julia grinned. Good old Uncle George. He was the most dedicated worker she'd ever seen and always came early to make headway in his massive stack of paperwork. After pushing into the reception area, she strode into the bullpen. At this hour of the morning, quiet filled the room, the desks were unmanned, and the typewriters sat silent. The printer in the back room didn't hum as it was an off-printing day.

Maybe I should work early every day. No annoying journalists jockeying for attention. No posturing men. No heavy cloud of cigar smoke. No breaking news or pedestrians dashing in front of the windows.

Peaceful.

As she moved between the desks, she fixed her gaze on the door to Jackson Haye's office. It stood ajar, which meant he was in residence. A knot tightened in her stomach. "Uncle George?" Her inquiry jarred in the still environment. She glanced toward her uncle's office, but the door yawned and the office remained dark. The knot tightened. The urge to flee grew strong.

The sound of a throat being cleared echoed behind the editor-in-chief's door. Chair springs creaked. Footsteps followed. The door opened inward before Julia could take more than a few steps toward the reception area. Jackson Hayes stood in the frame, his beady eyes glittering with dangerous intent. "Luck is not on your side, Miss Spencer. Had you arrived ten minutes earlier, you would have caught your dear uncle. As it stands, I sent him to cover a fire near the government offices."

Every instinct she possessed screamed to run. She couldn't trust this man, didn't like him by half. She remembered her promise to her uncle. *Time to go.* "Very well, Mr. Hayes. I'll return once he's come back." She'd barely cleared Frank's desk before Jackson spoke again.

"I'd like a moment of your time, Miss Spencer." He intercepted her with a hand around the upper part of her right arm. "Or should I say Veronica Peterson?"

Cold dread dripped down her spine at the false name she used at Madame's school. Jackson Hayes definitely knew her identity. Julia lifted her gaze to his and gasped at the hatred in his dark eyes. "I'm afraid I have no idea who you mean." It was best to play ignorant. She glanced between Jackson and the bullpen door. Ten feet. *If I can just get away —*

"Oh, I think you do." He tightened his grip and propelled her across the floor. Their footfalls echoed in the silence. "All this time you've been right under my nose, and I had no clue until the other day."

"What gave it away?" Despite the fear gnawing at her insides, her curiosity won the war. She squirmed in his hold, but he was just as strong as she remembered.

Jackson slid back the pocket door that led to the printing press and shoved her inside the room. "I'd recognize that ass anywhere, though I've only seen yours naked. I told you I'd never forget. You have put on a few pounds, but the new figure is pleasing."

Old familiar shame heated her face. "How dare you?"

"Because I can." He cornered her between a wall and a wooden file cabinet. "I'd wondered what became of you after Madame closed the school and fled the city. You were the best of the girls I used." He stroked her hair. "Such fire and spirit. I admired the chase."

Her breathing came in quick gasps. *That's what Tyler said earlier. But the two men weren't cut from the same cloth. Were they?* She turned her face away as her pulse raced. In a flash she was back in that horrible room, powerless. *Please let me go.* The air stank from ink, turpentine and the musty odor of paper. Adding the stale cigar and old coffee from Jackson's breath set her stomach roiling. Though she desperately wanted to curse the man to hell, knowing Uncle George depended on the paper for his livelihood curbed her tongue. If she told this man exactly what she thought, would he fire her uncle? She swallowed past the fear clogging her throat. " I'm not that woman anymore." Once the words left her mouth, she stood straighter, realizing they were true. Her past didn't define the rest of her days. *She* did, and she desired that future.

"I doubt that, Miss Spencer." He pressed his body into hers, rubbing against her in a manner that left no doubt of his inflamed arousal. "Once females like you get a taste for sex, that craving never goes away. You've thought about it since those days, haven't you?"

Her tenuous grip on control snapped. She pushed at his chest. "Bastard." When he put space between them, she shot out a hand with the intent to slap him. Perhaps he anticipated her desire, maybe he knew his words would earn him at least that, but he caught her wrist and squeezed. Pain shot up her arm. Memories crowded in of him doing much the same all those years before. "Let me go." Her voice shook.

"Not quite yet." Jackson yanked her hand then swiftly twisted her arm and held it behind her back. His gaze bore into hers, his thick brows slanted downward, his hooked nose even more menacing than she'd remembered. "You and I are at a rather interesting crossroad, wouldn't you agree?"

"No. What we are is done." When she raised her free hand, he captured it too, twisting it behind her back as well. Her breath came in ragged gasps. "I'll scream."

"Go ahead." His smile held no goodwill. "It's early. No one will hear you, and if they do, which of our stories do you think they'll believe?" He jerked upward on one of her wrists. Her eyes watered from the pain. "The way I see it, you sought out a former client, and since I've been nothing except an upstanding member of this community, have even gone so far as to ready this shoddy paper for a buyout, they have no reason to suspect anything else."

"That's not true." She'd worked so hard to put those years behind her, to try and live an ordinary life. Now, this vile man had the power to cancel her efforts. An idea took root in her brain, so vivid and strong the desire to make it happen consumed her. "I have a right to tell my story, accuse you of the vile things you've done to me and the other girls who went to that school." Julia went lax in his hold in an attempt to alleviate the pain. "I'll do it publicly if you don't release me."

"Let me tell you why you won't." Jackson held both her wrists in one of his hands. He grabbed her breast with the other and squeezed hard, laughing as she cried out. "If you breathe a word of what transpired here or back then, your wonderful Uncle George loses his job. I'll implicate him in some of the unsavory things going on in the city at the moment — labor disputes, kidnappings, murder. I have many sources and contacts that will make it happen. They've been the best witnesses and make great copy for stories. A little money here and there helps."

Shaking from fear and anger, Julia struggled against him. His hold didn't break and the close confines left no room for maneuvering. Her fears had come to life. "You have nothing to gain." She stared into his face, taken aback by the dislike reflected there.

"Oh, but I do." Again, he applied pressure to her arms. When she went pliant, he crushed his mouth to hers. The kiss was nothing less than savage. He pulled away. She spat out his taste. "You haven't lost your spirit, Miss Spencer. I appreciate that as much as I'll appreciate having you in my bed, servicing me."

The bitter taste of bile rose in her throat. Anger took hold and shoved out some of the fear paralyzing her body. She wrenched out of his hold only to sag against the wall as her limbs went weak. "That will never happen. I'd rather go public with my story and lose the rest of my reputation than have anything else to do with you." Her heart beat madly. *I need to get out of here. Find Uncle George. Confess everything.*

Jackson's thin lips twisted into a cruel grin. "Let me sweeten the pot for you. Not only will your uncle be at risk, so will your father's position in society. A man in the limelight such as him always has a secret or two lurking about. I'm the man who can unearth those secrets. You wouldn't want to disappoint him yet again, would you?"

In her mind's eye, she saw herself balancing on a slim ledge with steep drop-offs on each side of her. Which way to go? Either way would bring heartache and hurt feelings. *Time to make a stand and put value on myself.*

A swath of shame and embarrassment caught her in the stomach with the force of a blow. All the progress she'd made from Tyler's support and her uncle's kindness teetered on the edge of panic at this new problem, but she remained firm in her new resolve. *I'm better than this.* She raised her eyes to Jackson's and lifted her chin. "Go to hell." As she pivoted then strode into the main room, she heard him say behind her,

"I'll be in touch. You won't win. No one does against me."

Chapter Twelve

Two days later, unwilling to chance visiting the newspaper office and encountering Mr. Hayes, Julia remained tucked away in the back parlor with a mid-morning cup of tea and the remains of dry toast. After the incident with Jackson, she'd pleaded a headache and hid in her bedroom. The forced exile grew boring the following day, especially once Uncle George had inquired about her article over dinner. She'd replied with vague answers, still battling her conscience on exposing Tyler. As much as she'd wanted tips from her uncle before, circumstances had changed. She could make trouble at the paper or concentrate on her own work, but the risk for both grew exponentially. She played a dangerous game, and one not of her own making.

Now, she was wracked with worry and nearly paralyzed with sick fear from Jackson's threat. Not realizing her preoccupation, or perhaps not caring if they did, her parents left her alone. Julia had her work to keep her occupied. Showing Tyler as a fraud might earn her a byline as well as respect in the newspaper world, but how would she feel about that afterward? In a world where reputation meant everything, if someone challenged hers, how would she defend?

Acting on the courage it would take to grasp a new life would apparently not be an easy undertaking. She sighed. If nothing else, she deserved to claim the happiness waiting for her. Fear had no place in that.

"Miss Spencer." Bess cleared her throat at the doorway, yanking Julia from her tumultuous thoughts. When Julia glanced her way, Bess narrowed her eyes.

"There's a gentleman here to speak with you, and I use that term loosely as it is *that man* from the apothecary."

"Tyler is here?" Julia stood. She scrabbled at the items on the secretary's top as her stomach fluttered. "Please tell him I'm indisposed. I don't feel like talking with him." She wasn't prepared to see him again so soon.

"As much I would love to throw him out, he refuses to leave the premises until he speaks to you personally." She'd no sooner stood aside than Tyler swept into the room.

"Thank you, Bess, but let's have Miss Spencer decide my fate in her house." He touched the brim of his bowler hat, his grin at the housekeeper decidedly cool. "Please do us the courtesy of not eavesdropping. I have no issue closing the door. However, in deference to Miss Spencer's reputation or perhaps your prude-like attitude, I'll refrain."

Julia pressed a fist to her mouth in order to stifle hysterical laughter. Oh, she adored it when he put Bess in her place. She admired his confidence. Inwardly, she trembled that he continued to defend her sullied honor, yet how much of it was the real man?

Taking a deep breath, she let it ease out while clasping her hands in front of her as Bess strode away, her heels clacking in the hall. "What are you doing here, Mr. Browning?"

"We're well past formalities, Julia. You know my name. Use it." He closed the distance between them and took her hands in his. "Where have you been?"

"What do you mean?" He'd noticed her absence? Her heart skipped a beat.

"Don't be coy." Annoyance flashed across his face. "For two days I've checked in at the *Sentinel* office only to find your uncle surly and angry if he was there at all. The other reporters said they hadn't seen you."

"I find it hard to believe you called twice over. You must have an ulterior motive." Still, a flash of pleasure warmed her insides.

"I do, and I did." His grin promised dark things. "I worried about you, so my next course of action was to track you down." His gaze intensified, connecting with something deep inside her. "Woman, I think you need a protector."

"I do not." Heat rushed over her skin. Julia bit back the urge to inquire if he felt the need to apply for the job. It might be nice to have someone willing to look after her welfare who wasn't her uncle. "Thank you just the same."

"Not the answer I want. I can smell a con a mile off, so what's wrong?"

She attempted to pull her hands away, but he held tight, stroking her knuckles with his thumbs. "I haven't felt well. Instead of venturing out, I stayed at home, working on the article on you. Feel free to look over my notes if you don't believe me."

"Oh, I believe you." He didn't lower his gaze. Instead, he tugged her against him and moved his hands to hold her waist. "Why are you hiding, Julia? I've been in your company enough to know this sort of behavior isn't normal for you. What, or who, are you afraid of?"

"I..." His citrusy scent teased her nose, his touch sent flutters through her stomach, but his body so near her own caused her pulse to accelerate and her breath to come in tiny gasps. "What makes you think I'm afraid?" Were her emotions that obvious?

"When we last enjoyed dinner together, for the first time the shadows that usually haunt your eyes had fled. I thought you'd made a definitive change at putting the past behind you. Now the fear has returned. I want to know who put it there and why." He cupped her cheek.

"Tyler, I'm not certain—"

"It's time to trust someone. It might as well be me."

They were only words, yet they had enough force behind them to crack the wall around her heart. With that one, tiny blow, he'd breached her barriers. She glanced over his shoulder at the open doorway then snapped her attention to his face. "I have an article to write, you know."

"I do." He waited. So did she, with nothing but the beat of her heart keeping time.

She forced herself to answer his question instead of merely staring at him as if she had no manners. "Will you tell me the rest of your story, the reason you continue to run the con?"

"How do you know I haven't already revealed all?" His grin widened and the dark promise of forbidden delights grew stronger.

Julia smiled and relaxed beneath his touch. When he drew the pad of his thumb over her bottom lip, she shivered. Pleasure skated through her lower belly, coiling need deep inside. "If you see fear in my eyes, I see guilt and pain in yours. It seems we're both skilled in keeping secrets."

"I've had enough of them. I'd like to try new beginnings for once."

"Yes." Perhaps he was the right man. "Trust runs both ways."

"Indeed it does. Who shall make that first step?" His breath warmed her cheek.

"I'd hate to unburden my soul, then have you leave once you hear it." More than anything she wanted him to act the part of the strong protector. "After everything else, I'm not sure I could bear that sort of rejection as I've become accustomed to having you around." She could hardly believe she'd made the admission.

"Ah, Julia. I'm truly sorry for the terrible times you must have experienced." Empathy shone in the brown depths of his eyes as he tucked a wayward tendril of hair behind her ear. "Perhaps we should start with this before you make your decision." He replaced his thumb with his lips.

On the end of a sigh, Julia surrendered to his embrace, the perfect balm to the horrible events her life had become of late. She slid her hands up his chest and locked them around his neck in order to settle more comfortably into the kiss. He moved his mouth over hers with gentle intensity, neither demanding nor seeking. Heat tingled through her body as he stroked his hands along her back, and she marveled anew at how different her response to Tyler was compared to her past experiences. Of their own accord, her fingers threaded through his hair beneath the brim of his hat.

She pressed closer and returned each advance he made. Nibbling at the corners of his mouth, power and euphoria filled her. The chains of her previous indiscretions fell away. Tyler made her feel wanted, desired, for the woman she was, not simply because she could spread her legs. Perhaps she could chase dreams she never knew she'd have. Thrills of excitement brushed through her core. When he prodded the seam of her lips with his tongue, she invited him in. The silky glide of it against hers elicited an extended moan from her. Oh, with Tyler, sexual play would be most definitely different—for her satisfaction as well as his. Hard on the heels of that thought, fear came tripping in to cover her heart with a cold veil. None of it would happen as long as Jackson's threats remained valid. She couldn't let Tyler become unintentional damage.

"No." She planted her palms against his chest and pushed him away. "This cannot happen. There are too many unknowns—"

"Damn it, Julia, I've had enough of innuendo and intrigue." He whipped off his bowler hat and slapped it against his thigh. "Today, you and I will break through that barrier whether you want to or not."

"How can you say that with such conviction?" She pressed her fingers to her burning cheeks. A mixture of awe and fear shadowed his eyes as his expression darkened. His jaw clenched. He crushed the brim of his hat. "You have no idea what I've done. I don't deserve good things." Shame and fear of disclosure clawed in her chest despite the brief feeling of freedom she'd experienced during the kiss.

"This is why you're going to tell me today. Let *me* decide how to react. Allow *me* the honor of helping you overcome the obstacles. You can do the same for me."

She gave in quicker than she'd anticipated. It sounded so nice. As she nodded, he visibly relaxed and jammed his hat on his curls.

"Go upstairs and pack the items you'll need for an overnight stay."

"What? Why?" The abrupt request edged away the doubts plaguing her while tiny tremors raced up her spine.

"I'm taking you to my townhouse."

Julia narrowed her eyes. "For what purpose?" Surely he didn't expect her to perform sexually without permission? Had he discovered her secret and wished to exploit it? Disappointment niggled in. "I cannot believe such of you, even if you do have an equally spotty past."

"Think what you may, but my only thought was for your welfare. I won't be able to keep you safe if I have no idea where you are."

"It's not your job. You have no right." Yet she couldn't stop her smile. He was stubborn and a good match for her.

"That may be so. However, if you aren't in the office where your uncle can keep track of you, I must step in and fill that gap."

"Do you not have an apothecary to run?"

"I do, but as I went in before dawn and dealt with all my patrons through the noon hour, I feel justified in closing early today. Besides, without easy access, the demand for my services goes up exponentially." He moved toward the doorway. "Now, will you pack your own bag or shall I summon Bess? Imagine how amused she'll be to learn of your sudden travel plans and your destination." A twinkle appeared in his eyes.

"I have yet to agree to this insane proposal." She bit her bottom lip. His masculine taste lingered on her tongue.

"I'm well aware of that fact. Let me add one footnote. You have my word I won't touch you or molest you in any way unless *you* desire it. My only motivation is to remove you from this depressing house and its occupants." He crossed his arms over his chest. "Do you, or do you not, wish to finish your article?"

"I do." She shifted from foot to foot. "Where will I sleep?"

"In my bed, of course." Before she had an opportunity for rebuttal, he continued. "I plan to bunk in the front room or parlor if the night is warm." He held her gaze. "Does that set your mind at ease?"

"In a way." While Julia pondered the validity of his offer, she couldn't help but be intrigued. She'd likely not have another chance to interview him in his own home or an informal setting.

"One more thing." He clasped his hands behind his back. "Victor lives directly next door to me. In the event you need someone to vouch for my character or feel ill at ease, he'll be at your service to defend. Then there is my housekeeper, Hilda. She doesn't live-in, but she visits every day at noon. You'll be in highly capable hands."

Who was he trying to convince, her or himself? "Then, I accept your unorthodox invitation with a caveat of my own."

"And that would be?" Lines of stress etched his forehead.

"While entrenched in an interview I find very intriguing, I may resort to desperate measures to procure the answers I want." As she swept out of the parlor, her stomach fluttered with nerves so badly, she quelled the urge to giggle in hysterics. She hadn't been this excited to write a newspaper article since she'd started at the paper. On a whim, Julia glanced back at Tyler. When he grinned, heat rushed between her thighs and she hurried upstairs.

Once behind her closed bedroom door, she sagged against it. If she were honest with herself, the excitement was only partially due to the article. A good portion of it was for the opportunity to be with Tyler. She'd castigated herself long enough. No matter of the threats looming, it was past time to let her dreams free, and at least one of them centered on the miracle tonic man.

It took Julia an hour to assemble her belongings, then an additional hour for both her and Tyler to find a carriage and make their way across town to his lodgings in Fletcher Square. As time consuming as it had been, filled with an argumentative Bess and her sour expression, then reassuring Julia it would be all right, finally having the budding journalist to himself was well worth the slight annoyances. Over and over he'd revisited her parting remark. It still stunned him. The previously cool reporter had flirted and quite blatantly indicated she might resort to… Well, he had no idea what she'd eventually do, but inventing scenarios sent his cock pressing against the front of his trousers.

When the carriage jerked to a halt outside his townhouse, he heaved a relieved sigh. Ensconced in the confines of the vehicle, breathing in her floral scent, knowing she sat not a foot away, had tried his self-control. Above all, he wouldn't take advantage if she didn't seem ready to receive his overtures. The reward would come with patience. For a while, he'd doubted this day would come. Now, Julia's secrets were in his grasp, yet… He glanced at her, grinning as she met his gaze. Acute desire tightened his loins. Despite the burning need to know why she insisted on hiding today, he wanted to coddle her, treat her with gentle respect and quiet friendship in the hopes she'd let down her guard enough to act like the passionate woman he knew lurked beneath that surface control.

He wanted to see her eyes light with need, hear her voice roughen with lust or laugh in delight, anything to banish the ghosts of the past and give her hope and happiness.

I'm the man to do it. Haven't I sold bottles of mineral water on the pretense of working miracles?

Snorting in derision, he opened the door and hopped from the carriage. He sucked in a breath when his knee screamed with pain. Tyler ignored it and snatched his cane from the floor. While his day-to-day life was essentially a lie, it was the last thing he wished to do with Julia. For the first time, he dared entertain hope for *his* future. He limped around the carriage and swung open Julia's door, handing her down to the pavement. "Welcome to my humble lodgings."

She tipped her head, her eyes twinkling beneath the brim of her beribboned and gauze decorated hat. "Or perhaps more to the point, the abode where you plan your immoral scams?"

"Yes."

Her mouth curved with a teasing smile. "I'm honored. The first reporter to see such an intimate portion of your life."

"Indeed, and if all goes well, I might reveal the secrets of my tonic." As surprise gripped him at the admission, he collected her two carpetbags, holding them awkwardly in his free hand then led her up the cobbled walkway to his front door. "I'm afraid my home is a step down in comfort compared to yours. I apologize in advance."

"Tyler." He dropped the bags. She laid a gloved hand on his forearm and stilled his hand in the act of unlocking the door. When he turned his head and met her gaze, heat swept through his insides. "Don't apologize for this place or your position in society. I live in my parents' house. It's theirs, and was designed to *their* tastes, not mine. Given the chance, I'm not certain how I'd choose to live, or where, but I'm am and always will be my own person regardless of where I reside."

"Ah." He twisted the key in the lock then deposited it in his pocket. "I assume from that statement you'd be interested in any unusual offers that might come your way, even if that man's earthly income is not as large as his reputation?" He picked up the bags once more.

Confidence brimmed from her smile and more than a little invitation before she moved her head a fraction of an inch and hid her expression from view. "It would depend on the man, wouldn't it?"

Tyler nodded as his thoughts circled around Joshua's widow and child. *He* could be that man if a good chunk of his income didn't go to a woman he only saw once a month for the sake of a hasty promise given on a bloody battlefield. Frustration clawed at his gut. When he'd made the original deal, he hadn't anticipated being completely captivated by a feisty blonde with secrets in her eyes. Oh, what he wouldn't do for freedom.

She softly cleared her throat, recalling him to the present. "Will you invite me inside or shall I take up residence on your doorstep?"

"By all means, please come in." He stood aside. When she moved over the threshold, her jacket sleeve brushed his chest and sent jolts of awareness through his body. His rash plan had backfired. It wouldn't be Julia who'd be in danger with the overnight accommodations—it was him. Rapidly, and with the alacrity Victor had warned about, Tyler fell deeper under her spell. He shook his head. Time would tell if such a thing would come to pass. Julia was still an enigma. "Would you like me to deposit your bags in the bedroom?" Desire thickened his voice. Could she hear it?

"Well, Tyler, what would you like to do?" Slowly, as if she meant to drag out her movements, she untied the cream-colored bow from beneath her chin and removed the hat. Setting it on a circle-shaped table in the entryway, she stripped off her ivory kid gloves then dropped them, one by one, on top of the hat. The fact she'd attempted to observe society's rules with him heated his blood. She was a walking contradiction. "I imagine if I'll be sleeping in your bed I should have a chance to inspect the premises."

Warm sensation crept through his belly. "Right. It's just upstairs." Renewing his grip on the bags, he led with his cane. They both climbed the wooden staircase, their steps echoing in the small space. Never had he been as nervous as he was now. Women in the past had meant nothing when compared to her. She was inspiring.

At the tiny landing he guided her into the large room on that level and promptly placed her bags on the trunk at the end of his bed. "I apologize for the state of the room. I hadn't expected company." He looked about the area with a mind to how she'd see it.

A massive four-poster bed with rumpled bedclothes occupied the middle. The heavy navy drapes on the windows had yet to be drawn. Dirty shirts and trousers littered the floor and the wingback chair, while a few empty liquor bottles, mineral water bottles and stubs of cigarettes decorated the top of the bureau. Definitely a typical bachelor residence and one a self-respecting lady would want no part of. His shoulders slumped. "Julia, I—"

She held up a hand. "It suits you." She walked around the bed and pulled open the curtains. "Wonderful lighting you get here. With a small desk in the corner there, it would be perfect."

For who and what? He raised an eyebrow as his chest tightened. Why did he have need of a desk? Did she mean to move into this room permanently and use the space? His mind executed a free fall at the implication. By the time he'd gotten a grip on his thoughts, she'd moved around him to inspect the bureau drawers then an old armoire in another corner that contained more clothing as well as mementos from the war.

Abruptly, she pivoted to face him, her expression closed and that of the no nonsense reporter once more. "Yes, this space will be lovely."

Unaccountable relief surged through him. "There's a small water closet across the hall. It's temperamental at best. If you should feel the need to have a bath, there's a tub in the parlor downstairs."

"Why in the parlor?"

"Why not? It doesn't fit up here and besides, heating water on the stove is much more convenient if the tub is close by. I found it when the building was being renovated, and liked it once I saw the lion's feet the tub stands upon." He grinned at her look of astonishment.

"You must remember, after all, I'm an unattached man and have no reason to care much about the placement of such things."

"You're surprising at every turn and refreshing to boot." The smile she bestowed rivaled the dappled sunlight streaming into the room beyond the trees outside. "I'm feeling rather restless. Shall we take a walk? For whatever reason, this room doesn't seem the appropriate place for the exchange of confidences."

"Ah, because of its sexual connotations, or perhaps the mess is off-putting?" He led the way out of the room and down the staircase.

"Not at all. Any place can be used for coitus. The presence of a bed has no bearing on how two bodies come together."

"I see." He tripped on the last step, righting himself just in time to prevent crashing into the opposite wall, yet his cane clattered to the hardwood beyond his reach.

"At the moment, I'd like to be outside." She retrieved his cane, handing it to him with a quick wink. "There's plenty of time to discuss the various uses of a bed later, don't you think? I want a look at that bathtub, if you please, before we head out. I'm curious."

Tyler gaped as she disappeared into the parlor. *This* was the same woman who refused to show any sort of interest in him outside of a journalist capacity unless he'd managed to steal a kiss? He sneaked down the hall and peered into the room, struck again by her shining hair and the change in her demeanor. When she giggled upon finding a pillow and blanket in the tub, which resided partially behind a silk privacy screen, his heart lurched.

Being in the company of a woman he found both fascinating and interesting on a base level had all the components of danger, yet he ignored them all in order to forge ahead. This promised to be the greatest adventure of his life—or else the biggest lesson in stupidity. Either way, after today, his relationship with Julia Spencer will have changed permanently.

Chapter Thirteen

Julia's stomach jumped with nerves as she followed Tyler through the wooded area behind his neighborhood. Though she didn't fear harm from him, the thought of being utterly and completely alone in his presence screamed of stupidity. A wry smile curved her lips. Of course, tucked into such an intimate setting was almost a Godsend. Ever since he'd vowed to protect her, her regard for him had grown. No, it went beyond that. Her awareness of him as a man had risen to point she could no longer hide behind the façade of journalism. She was done with living behind fear, and in him she'd found the man to begin to live again with.

Regardless of what he might be on the outside, she sensed a good and decent person underneath, a caring heart that called to her, promised that with him she'd always be safe and treated with respect. Now, walking through the woods beneath trees whose leaves were just starting to embrace autumn's colors, falling under the spell of the easy timbre of Tyler's voice, watching the rhythmic sway of his cane, the attraction to him took hold and bloomed more intensely.

For the first time, Julia ignored the doubts, the nasty little voice of her conscience that told her she wasn't good enough, and she enjoyed the moment.

"Why are you taking me out here?" For a man who moved with a limp and relied on a cane, he blazed a fast trail through the underbrush. They followed the slight path even after the grass and brambles swallowed it again.

Tyler stopped. He pivoted to face her. "Can I trust you?"

"I'd like to hope so." The uneasiness behind his hopeful expression sent tremors through her insides. "I mean, I'm aware I haven't been forthcoming about my life, but that will change over the course of the day."

He stared at her for long seconds before nodding. "I want to show you where the miracle tonic began."

"Are you sure?" She regulated her breathing as her heart pounded.

"Quite certain." He extended his free hand. "It's not far."

Julia slipped her hand into his. Her pulse accelerated as he closed his fingers around hers. About to see, with her own eyes, the proof of his lie, anxiety for his reputation besieged her. "You don't need to do this."

"I want to. It's time, and who better to reveal all to than you?" He squeezed her hand.

"Thank you for the confidence." Sweat accumulated on her brow, and she wiped it away with her sleeve. The stifling air in the wooded area made tramping through the underbrush somewhat trying. "Is this something you wish for me to remember for my article, or is it strictly off the record?" She lifted a handful of skirting in an effort to encourage a breeze beneath the heavy fabric.

"I suppose that depends on how the rest of the afternoon goes, so I leave it to your discretion." With one last tug on her hand, he pulled them both through a grouping of scrubby pine trees and into a small clearing. "This is where my side business found its roots."

The clearing itself was as large as a typical living area, but the focal point was the stream. Slim and unassuming, it cut through the woods as if fashioned by fairy hands. The meandering current of water gathered slightly on a rise before falling over an earthen and limestone shelf where it again pooled in another basin perhaps two feet deep. Gentle whirlpools and eddies churned with foam as the steam righted itself and continued its course through the trees. As shafts of afternoon sunlight glanced off the moving surface of the stream, it shimmered, sparkling as if diamonds lurked beneath the water.

"This is the mineral water stream?" She moved closer then kneeled on the bank in front of the waterfall. "It's a pretty area, almost magical."

"Yes. I bottle it here at the source, usually the morning of the sale. I want it to be as fresh as it can be." Tyler sat on a moss-covered boulder nearby. "So you see, I didn't lie when I told you it was mineral water."

"No, you didn't." She dipped a hand into the cool wetness and sighed. The relief from the humid afternoon was immediate. Cupping her hand, she brought the water to her lips and sipped. Cool, crisp with a hint of earthy sweetness, it tasted exactly like the tonic she'd sampled from his bottles. "You're absolutely certain it has no healing properties?"

"Again, that depends on the mindset of the person drinking it." Tyler's grin erased the lines of stress from his face. "You can call it a scam or a con, but I choose to believe in the hope this spring water brings. You can't put a price on that."

"For the moment, I believe you." Julia worked the buttons on her vest. She wriggled out of the garment, tossing it away some distance from the stream. "Also, for the moment, I will ignore you've chosen to sell ordinary water to the people of this city. No matter how I choose to portray it, that fact will be in the article."

"I understand. It doesn't bother you?" He followed her every movement with his gaze as she unfastened the buttons of her blouse. It slipped from her shoulders with a whisper.

"Not in the slightest, since it isn't my lie. In *this* moment, I don't care." The buttons at the waist of her skirt yielded to her manipulation next. The skirt slid down her petticoat and onto the ground. She kicked it toward the patch of grass where the vest and shirt had landed.

Tyler sat straighter, his hot gaze riveted on her. "Have you lost your faculties? This is hardly the place to disrobe, not that I mind."

She merely smiled as she bent and unlaced her boots. "There comes a time in everyone's life when they know beyond a doubt what they want and make steps to go after it." Both boots came off with little resistance, and then she made short work of her stockings. The grass tickled the soles of her bare feet.

"What it is you want?" Tyler had moved from the boulder, leaving his cane behind.

As Julia righted herself, she sucked in a breath, surprised at his close proximity. "I'm attempting to decide between a dip in your miracle stream or..." She stepped into the gentle current and sighed as the cool water lapped at her calves.

"Or?" Need roughened his voice. "What else do you want?" Desperation hung on the inquiry.

She glanced over her shoulder. "You." As if his reaction didn't matter, she turned her attention to the waterfall and put both hands beneath it, cupping the water then splashing it over her neck and chest. It dampened the thin lawn of her camisole and chased away some of the heat from the afternoon. "But if you're not in agreement..."

"Oh, I heartily agree to that plan." His low-timbered voice sounded in her ears followed by a faint splash seconds before he slid his arms around her waist. He pulled her backside flush against his front, holding her there. His insistent erection prodded the curve of her rear while he brushed the lower curve of her breasts with his thumbs. Her nipples tightened into hard peaks. "Very much."

"That's good to know since otherwise, it would have been a bit awkward to finish undressing in front of you." A shiver shook her as Julia recalled the last time she'd undressed in a man's company during those long ago days at Madame's school. With ruthless vengeance, she shoved them out of her mind in order to concentrate on the sensations dancing over her skin. That was the past. This coupling would mean something, be the beautiful expression she'd always longed for. She and Tyler would bond, and if all went well, they could begin a real courtship.

I cannot believe I'm so close to having a dream realized.

"Is that what you want?"

His question took her by surprise, as if he'd read her mind. She nodded in affirmation to both the spoken and thought-based subjects. "Yes, more than anything."

"Ah, then I can help you." He turned her in his arms until she faced him. The damp hem of her petticoat clung to her calves. "In recent days, it's all I've been able to think about. There's something about you, Julia, that makes me want to be in your company all the time."

"I hate to think of you suffering with no relief." She loved how the delicate skin at the corners of his eyes crinkled with his smile or how flecks of gold swam to the surface of those brown depths. She especially adored how he'd held back his urges until she was ready. "I hope you're proficient after all this bragging." Although verbal teasing primed her need, she craved his touch.

"I'll let you be the judge." He gripped her waist and lifted her onto the grassy bank. Seconds later, he untied the ribbons of her petticoat. "Are you certain this spot is ideal for your seduction? We can adjourn to the townhouse with haste."

"Hush, Tyler." She helped him push the embroidered fabric off her hips then stepped out of it. As they were nearly eye level, she held his gaze. "I don't intend to change my mind. This is a lovely place and obviously dear to you. Now it will be more so. It's perfect for new beginnings." Before she could say more, he neatly knocked her feet from beneath her, cushioning her descent to the grass with his body. On her back, Julia stared up at him, tremors roiling through her stomach. "You've done this before." The thought of him with other women made her burn with jealousy.

"I have, I won't lie, but you're the only one who matters." He nuzzled the spot where her neck joined her shoulder. "You're different, and I'm glad."

She glanced at the sun-dappled leaves above them, listened to the fairy-tinkle of the stream, and welcomed the heat of Tyler's body on hers. Her whole life she'd waited for someone to appreciate her for the person she was, desire her beyond using her body. How ironic she'd found that attention in the arms of a con man and a cheat. Deciding fate had a sense of humor, she closed her eyes and surrendered with a sigh.

She explored the breadth of his shoulders, traced the muscles of his back beneath his clothing. Would his body resemble how she imagined him? Anxious to find out, she plucked at his vest, the tweed rough at her fingertips, the metal buttons cool on her skin. "I need to see you."

"I'm happy to oblige." He lifted himself away, and stood with stiff movements.

Julia's breath shallowed as each piece of his clothing fell away. Never had she looked forward to seeing a naked man before. While at Madame's, she'd come to dread this very moment, would try not to gaze upon the men who'd visited her room. With Tyler, it would be a crime to compare him with those men. He'd not forced his attentions upon her, never once moving past kissing. This alone proclaimed him a truly good man. Her eyes pricked with tears. It was too good to be true.

Human nature had a tendency to deceive, yet he didn't know what she'd done. Maybe it didn't matter—

"Does your silence mean you've changed your mind?"

His question startled her out of her thoughts. "No. I was caught up in old ways of thinking." Julia blinked and refocused her gaze just as his drawers hit the ground, leaving him utterly and completely naked with the exception of black socks and the garters that held them up. She swallowed around unshed tears in her throat. That detail made him so endearing, so lovable she lost a piece of her heart to him in that instant. After long years of guarding against letting another person close, he'd gotten in with little effort—and she'd allowed it, welcomed it even. "Oh, Tyler."

An expression of satisfaction came over his face. "I trust that means you're pleased?"

"Most definitely." Heat rushed through her, centering between her thighs with pleasant moisture.

She levered onto her elbows as she swept her gaze over his body. Indeed, as impressive as she'd thought, he wasn't as pale or flabby as most men she'd seen. Broad shoulders, strong chest, and firm limbs spoke of regular physical work that had subtly defined his muscles above and beyond his apothecary duties. Black hair sprinkled his torso, weaving a gentle ribbon over a flat abdomen and ending in a soft nest of curls where his arousal jutted, curving back toward his body.

"I hope you don't intend to stand there all afternoon?" Julia gave him another once-over before meeting his gaze. "I'm rather lonely."

"Let me solve that problem." He winced as he lay beside her. "Turnabout is fair play, luscious Julia."

Ignoring his implication, she slid a palm over his shoulder and down his arm. "Does your knee pain you? Perhaps we should go back—"

Tyler laid a finger to her lips. "It's all right now that I'm down. Besides, my mind is occupied with much more interesting things than a war wound." He trailed his fingers past her chin, along the column of her neck and over the curve of one breast. "Let me work a miracle."

"That's what you told me about your tonic." She relaxed into the soft, fragrant grass as he caressed her breast through the camisole. "Surely everything you do doesn't end with such magic."

"You may tell me when we're finished." He pressed his body into hers, claiming her lips at the same time.

The kisses this time weren't tentative. Bold and full of masculine mastery, Tyler's embraces left her gasping for breath and longing for more intimate caresses. He traced her lips with bold strokes of his tongue. As soon as she let him in, he took possession of her mouth. Silky heaven descended as he explored the inside of her cheeks, her teeth, then used his tongue to fence with hers. During their kisses, Julia watched him. Would he grow weary of the preliminary introduction in lieu of ripping down her drawers and doing the deed?

Eventually, his eyes fluttered open and he ceased kissing. A frown marred his features. "Do you not enjoy this? I have many variations and can find a version to your liking."

This time, the warmth that infused her face had nothing to do with lust. Mortified, she buried her head against his shoulder. "Why do you bother when your ultimate goal is to find release?"

"This is a journey, Julia. During lovemaking, the power is balanced between both parties. One will not have pleasure without the other following. A couple works in tandem for the good of each other."

"Most men don't see things as you do." She squirmed beneath him. He wouldn't shift to let her escape.

"Perhaps, but then I'm not most men." His gaze burned into hers, sincerity blazing from his soul. "I won't hurt you. I promise."

Julia could do nothing except acknowledge the statement as truth as she fell further down the dark slope toward adoration. When she nodded, he grinned and resumed his conquest. She felt his touch everywhere at once. His hands on her breasts sent molten heat through her bloodstream. He teased her nipples beneath the camisole, and shivers of arousal climbed her spine. She arched further into his keeping.

So different from her other experiences, she sighed at the decadent glory of it. Her thighs fell open at Tyler's urging and he stroked her skin. With each pass of his hand, his fingers danced higher until they brushed against her fabric-covered mound. She gasped, stiffening. Sensations she'd not indulged in swirled through her womb.

Searching out his gaze, she bit her lip. "Will you do that again? It was nice." None of the other men had taken the time to caress her womanly parts, ensure that her pleasure wound so tight inside she thought she'd explode. They'd only been interested in working their dicks inside her, abusing her to find their own satisfaction.

"I will." He skimmed his hands up the outside of her hips then worked the ribbons at the waist of her pantalets. "First, I want to see you, tell you how gorgeous you are."

"You're a flim-flam man. Why should I believe you?" She lifted her hips as he worked the embroidered, lace-trimmed fabric down her legs.

"I may be a con when it comes to miracle tonic, but when I look at you, everything I say is God's honest truth." He tossed the garment away then parted her bent knees.

Her breath came in shallow pants. "Well?" Could he see her history just by looking?

"Beautiful." His appreciation showed in his expression. "You're wet for me." One hand went between her thighs and he strummed his fingers over her sensitive flesh. He found her swollen bud and rubbed it with his thumb. She bucked from the exquisite torture.

Tendrils of intense pleasure shot through her insides. Julia moaned. His touch felt like heaven and hell all at once, and it was worlds away from that horrible time.

"Tell me how you feel." Passion and a trace of insecurity roughened his voice as he settled between her legs.

Never had she known such a powerful sweep of emotion simply at the prospect of sharing intercourse. Tyler's reverence made her feel more feminine than she ever had in all her life, almost cherished. She touched a hand to his forearm. "I want you." Need coiled in her center, tightening, circling, the sensation throbbing into her core. "So much." Shock sank in to twine with her desire as she realized she spoke the truth.

He leaned over and dropped gentle kisses on her lips, her cheeks, her forehead. Holding his weight on his arms, he stared into her eyes. "You're special." The head of his member flirted with her opening, teasing, coated in her juices. "Never believe anything else."

The sunlight filtering through the trees gilded his head and shoulders, but the tears welling in her eyes blurred the image. Julia drew him closer, wriggled her hips in an effort to prompt him to further action. "Please."

He easily slid into her slick passage with one long stroke, filling her with a pleasant comfort. Just as smoothly, he withdrew, watching her. "Damn, you're warm and so tight."

Julia's world became a whirling vortex of bliss, friction and the earthy sound of Tyler's breathing and the slap of their flesh. Instinctively, she met his thrusts, tilted her hips to receive him time and again. As pressure built inside, memories poured into her mind of all the other times she'd had sexual congress before she'd realized fully what it meant. Faces haunted her from those years at Madame's school, the leering expressions taunting her. The stink of their sweaty bodies and foul breath so vivid she relived the terror and disgust of those days. Tyler's face disappeared in the deluge.

She squeezed her eyes shut and retreated into herself in order to shrink away from the man using her body for his own ends. Soon it would be over and he'd leave. She turned her face away, unable to bear a glimpse of her tormentor. Her body rocked as he drove into her passage. Julia clenched her fists. The feel of grass in her hands confused her as reality and the past collided into a jumble of thoughts and feelings. Her partner stiffened.

"Julia, darling."

Darkened memories reeled. None of her "clients" ever knew her real name.

His warm seed filled her channel, then the man collapsed on top of her, his breathing ragged in her ear. The scent of citrus engulfed her, hurling her into the here and now. Julia stirred. She forced her eyes open and stared at the mop of black curls. With a stroke of her hands, she acclimated herself to the feel of the masculine form.

Tyler.

She and Tyler had indulged in intimate relations, yet she'd missed the grandeur of it because she'd once again allowed her fears and memories of the past to take control. A wave of disappointment swept over her, so acute that she shoved at his shoulders as she fought its tide. Embarrassed and lost, when he lifted off, she scrambled to her feet, turning away.

"I'm sorry. You must hate me." At the moment, she despised herself. *Why can I not forget and move forward?*

"I don't hate you." Rustling clothing filled the silence.

Endless seconds passed, each etching new scratches on her soul as she waited for him to say something else. When he didn't, she swallowed the tears crowding her throat and pivoted. He faced the stream while he worked the buttons on his trousers. His bare shoulders were rigidly set. She could only imagine his expression as he planted his fisted hands on his hips and stared into the waterfall.

Julia's chest tightened. Her stomach pitched. She'd ruined everything. No matter how much she'd tried to forget, given herself permission to chase a new life, her sins had rushed in and strangled the budding dreams. At the moment, there was no escape.

"Tyler." Pain coated that one word. Her heart squeezed. She crossed the grassy expanse and laid a hand on his shoulder. When he flinched, hot tears sprang to her eyes. Quickly blinking them away, she sucked in a deep breath and let it ease out before speaking again. "There are no words to excuse my behavior. I wish things were different."

"So do I." Finally, he turned. His dark eyes flashed anger but also held underlying sympathy and understanding. He captured her hands in his, holding tight. "I want the full story, right now. I want the name of the man who stole your confidence and kicked the shit out of your spirit because I will personally track him down and end his pitiful existence."

The statement and the vehemence behind it, coupled with his willingness to continue acting as her champion despite her actions humbled her beyond everything else. She sagged against him, welcoming the quiet strength as he wrapped his arm around her, holding her next to his heart. The time for confessions had come. She'd already revealed her shame to Uncle George and Gretchen. Once she told Tyler her story, perhaps then her soul would be cleansed and usher in healing.

And, please God, let him still want me at the end.

Chapter Fourteen

"I mean it, Julia. Full story. Right now. We're not leaving this clearing until I hear it." He set her away from him. Tears wetted her cheeks; her hair had come loose from its pins and fell in thick waves about her shoulders. Grass blades and leaves clung to the tresses. "I thought you were enjoying what we'd shared," he gestured to the spot on the ground where they'd coupled.

Yes, it had bent his ego to discover he'd lost her interest. Beyond that, she'd acted as if he disgusted her as soon as penetration had occurred, yet it wasn't as if he could have stopped the act once it started. Tyler raked his gaze down her body. Her lower half was still bare. The thatch of dark blonde hair between her thighs heated his blood. Knowing what hid beneath those curls and how she'd begged him to touch her there was a direct contrast to how the afternoon's seduction ended. If he couldn't have her whole attention, there was no point in continuing.

He returned his attention to her face. The chemistry had jumped between them. It had simmered from their first meeting. Every teasing word, every action, every suggestive raised eyebrow had led them to this pass, except too many twisted memories still haunted her. It was time eradicate them permanently if they both hoped to move into something more meaningful. "Let me help you."

She took a deep, shuddering breath and let it out. "You're absolutely correct. You need to know the story. I had this same conversation with Uncle George not long ago. I should be used to the discomfort." When a fat tear fell to her cheek, she moved away from him and retrieved her drawers, slipping them on. By the time she'd fastened her petticoat around her waist, she'd composed herself somewhat. "I've always been headstrong. Call it a character flaw if you will, but I cannot change who I am now."

He made no move to go to her. Most likely she wouldn't have appreciated it—not yet. "I think courage and a backbone are needed in journalism. The meek don't chase down the news."

"No, they don't." With efficient movements, she donned her skirt and did the buttons. Finally, she shook out the blouse and vest then slipped them on, also closing the buttons as if presenting a proper appearance could shield her from the pain her story would cause. "As much as I'd like to say my troubles began at the finishing school, it would be a lie." She sat on the boulder he'd vacated earlier. "In my earliest memories, I can remember doing outrageous things to gain my parents' attention."

"I'm sure they love you." Tyler didn't know what to say that would alleviate the hurt in her voice.

"They don't. Over the years I've become convinced they never wanted a child, for it would take the focus off them. They're perfect, live a perfect lifestyle, and I have no place in that. So, the finishing school presented a grand opportunity to bring scandal to the family and put a dent in their perfect existence."

Cold chills dripped down his spine. "Oh, Julia. I'm sorry you had no guidance, no one to turn to." He couldn't imagine her formative years being as lonely as he feared, especially since his were completely an opposite experience.

"I had Uncle George, but I was too ashamed to let him know." Her shrug barely lifted her shoulders. "I cannot change what happened." She nudged his cane with her toe, coaxing it toward her. When it was close enough, she picked it up. "I came to The Ladies' School of Advanced Etiquette when I'd barely turned eighteen. It was no ordinary finishing school."

Tyler wanted to tell her to stop, but he knew an insane desire to hear the whole sordid affair, if only to put his wild assumptions to rest. "They were the ones who took the photographs. They were the people who initiated you into that life." Of course it was true. A young, virginal girl would have no reason not to trust adults in charge, and if that headstrong girl was stubborn to boot, it would have been a recipe for disaster.

"Yes." The muscles in her throat worked with the force of her swallow. "For days and days the photographers posed us and touched our bodies." A shudder wracked her shoulders. "The school staff rewarded us with money and all sorts of things to keep us happy — and quiet. That first year, my parents didn't stay home for Christmas holidays, so I remained at the school. I knew what I was doing was wrong, yet I'd hoped my parents would care enough…" She waved a hand. "That's when the next step of our education began — how to please men in bed."

A wave of revulsion rolled through his stomach, not at her, but at the people she should have been able to trust. Though he'd guessed the gist of her story, hearing it from her made it all too real. He hobbled toward her with silent steps. Julia didn't seem to notice, so lost in her memories.

"First, it was the male teachers. There was never any talking — we weren't allowed — no kind words, no kissing or foreplay from them either. They came in, mounted us, found their pleasure then left. For this new aspect of our education, we received payment." She gripped the brass head of his cane so tight her knuckles whitened. "I tucked it away, still have it hidden. I suppose I was too shocked, then too ashamed to leave the school. Though I was curious about the sex act, without being properly trained or taught, I didn't enjoy it, only knew that my body reacted to certain things but had no clue why or how. Eventually, I became numb to intercourse, pretended it happened to someone else. Some of it wasn't pleasant."

"I'm at a loss for words." He leaned against the boulder beside her, close enough for moral support but not touching her.

"Such was my uncle's reaction when I told him a few days ago." A hint of a smile graced her lips. "Gretchen says I should forgive myself, that it happened in the past and I'm not that woman any longer. My uncle said if I'd learned a lesson, I should take that knowledge and do something with it."

"What do you think?"

"He might be correct." Shadows filled her eyes. "It was stupid, but there's no sense lamenting the fact that it happened."

"I agree. You've kept it to yourself for so many years, and now you're telling your story to everyone you're close to. Doesn't that make you feel the tiniest bit relieved?" Gently, he touched a hand to her sleeve. She flinched but didn't move away.

"It does, slightly." Julia turned her head and met his gaze. "Do you remember that day in the church when you said I had to forgive myself in order to receive forgiveness?"

He nodded. "I do. It was the first time I saw you as a woman and not merely an annoying reporter."

"My perception of you changed then as well." Another smile tugged at the corners of her mouth. "I'm ready to start the process of forgiving myself. It's one thing to listen to everyone's opinions on the matter but a whole different thing to actually believe it for myself. Yes, part of it was my fault, and I take full blame for that. Some of it belongs to my parents and the administrators of the school. I can only be responsible for me at this point. I'm tired of living under that shadow."

"That, my dear, is a very mature attitude. I'd say you have grown up quite a bit in your self-imposed exile from the world."

"Thank you."

"Why did you never try to leave the school? Did they hold you hostage, threaten your family?" Why would someone as headstrong as her suffer through that?

A slight shrug moved her shoulders. "A few of the girls who did leave, who weren't pregnant, met with suspicious endings." She worried her bottom lip. "I didn't want that same fate, so I waited out my three years."

"What happened to the school then?"

"Once I'd signed an agreement to keep my silence, I came home. Mostly I did odd jobs before Uncle George took pity on me, but the school closed a semester later. Something to do with disgruntled parents of one of the girls. I'm afraid once I was out, I tried everything I could to not think of them again."

"I see." He pushed off from the boulder and claimed his cane. Some of the worry weighing on him lifted. He might spend his life selling herbs and tonics, but for this ailment, he knew an absolute cure. "Have you been back at the school since you left?"

"No. I've had contact with a few of the girls, but I never pass that way when I'm in the city, have never inquired as to the fate of it or the teachers. I locked them in a dark corner of my mind, hoping they'd smother under the weight of the years."

Tyler held out his free hand. A flash of pleasure coursed through his insides as she grasped it. "And the man who either wounded you deeply or abused you so horribly you retreat into memories? Do you have contact with him? I suspect you do, as witnessed at the evening of your parents' party."

She slid off the boulder with a twinkling of tears in her eyes. "I'd rather not say."

"Trust issues still, even after everything." Familiar bitterness welled in his throat. "Why can you not tell me?"

"No matter how much I want to, I'm bound by events not in my control." She laid his palm against her cheek. "There are more lives than mine at stake." Emotion akin to panic reflected in her blue eyes. "Please respect that."

"I will—for now. Can you not give me a name?" He wanted to settle the score, call the man into account on her behalf, fight all her monsters and bring her peace.

"I'd rather you not be involved."

"Soon, you'll have to accept I'll stand firm in your deepest moment of sorrow, pain or trouble. Even the strongest of women need a man behind them for support." He drew the pad of his thumb over her trembling bottom lip and fought the desire to cradle her in his arms, protect her from every ill in the world. "When you're ready, I'll be there. Now, if you'll indulge me, you and I are going to pay a visit to your old school." He glanced away, giving her a chance to compose herself.

His residual anger faded into a low flame. Not gone entirely, it wouldn't completely extinguish until he figured out the name of the man who'd obviously threatened her or was even now attempting to blackmail her. She had the right to her own counsel, but he had ways to ferret out information. He'd inform Victor of events. His friend could locate anyone.

An hour later, they alighted from a carriage. Tyler instructed the driver to wait as they wouldn't be at this address long. One of the neighborhoods west of Monument Circle had given up its life years ago. Derelict buildings crowded the streets. Weeds had grown between the cobblestones while some of the lots were given new life as dumping grounds for unwanted trash, broken pieces of furniture or carriage parts and heaven only knew what else.

He glanced up at the three-story brick building that once housed the fake school. Several window panes had been broken, giving the edifice a gap-toothed appearance. One of the double wooden doors hung ajar, squeaking as it moved in the slight breeze. He looked at Julia. "What happened to the people who once walked these halls?"

"Perhaps their deeds finally caught up with them." She took a few steps forward along the walkway. "I'm sad I cannot confront them and demand an apology for what they did, yet I feel relief they're not here to harm anyone else."

His heart hurt that such unscrupulous people still held sway over her. "Let's go inside. You can throw a rock through one of those windows as a symbolic gesture that you won't let this place hold you back any longer." He nudged her along the walkway. "For once in your life, relax your control and be a vandal — just don't let the word get out."

For the first time since he'd known her, Julia's smile seemed genuine and without guilt or shame attached. It was as if he'd seen the face of an angel. The vision planted itself in his soul. "You, Mr. Browning, are bad for a woman's motivation. No wonder you're such a smooth-talking salesman."

"It's truly a gift. Why should I not capitalize on it?" He held the door open then followed her over the threshold.

Silent minutes ticked by as Julia took him through portions of the school they could walk through. Internally, he raged when she showed him her old room and confirmed the furniture was all the same. No linens covered the stained mattress or decorated the dirt-streaked window glass. No trace of Julia remained in the hideous place. He imagined her quiet pleas for help or rescue, but bit back the sharp words he wanted to say. They'd do nothing at this late date and only make her feel badly. In another room of one of her friends, the story was much the same. In both there were dried white roses whose red centers resembled blood. One of the flowers in a hallway appeared semi-fresh. Odd to be sure, but again, the words stuck in his throat.

Julia ruthlessly ground the flower beneath her boot heel then continued onward. Tyler kept silent, knowing she did her best to banish the demons in her own way. Whomever the flower belonged to must have been decidedly abhorrent. When she needed him, she'd let him know, yet curiosity as to what the floral cast-offs meant niggled at his brain. He had to believe she'd tell him later in trust, and he also had to let her fly free. She'd never allow herself to be dominated or hurt again, that much was evident in her squared shoulders and proud carriage, but how he wished she'd ask for his help.

Can she not see I only want happiness for her?

He made a mental promise to treat her with the utmost care and respect. Julia was different than anyone he'd known. He wanted to win her heart without lying or cheating. Nothing else mattered.

At the end of their tour, she hurled a porcelain pitcher through a rear window. It crashed through the glass and broke into multiple pieces on the ground below. After heaving a sigh, she turned to him with delight lining her face. "That was by far the most satisfying thing I've done in a long while."

"I'm glad to be a small part of your victory." He leaned heavily upon his cane, the brass warm against his palm. "Shall we return home? I'm rather famished and a touch fatigued. It's been a trying day, as you well know." *Home.* Before, his townhouse seemed only a place to gain the basic creature comforts. Now, with a dash of Julia's personality, it had the beginnings of a true home, yet it was the early days in their relationship and tenuous at best. Would it last?

"I'd like that." She stepped closer to him and laid a palm on his chest. The heat from her fingers burned through the layers of clothing, branding him as hers. "I must apologize for this afternoon. I should have given you my full attention."

"Think nothing of it. You were under severe duress. Next time we come together, your mind will be clear to focus only on your pleasure." He snaked an arm around her waist.

"Next time?"

"Though that interlude didn't end as I would have liked, know I won't stop trying to see you into another compromising position. I want you to be happy."

"You're also a great tease, but somehow, I believe you mean it." Her smile brightened the dismal atmosphere. "I'd expect nothing less, and will in fact, encourage it."

Hope swelled his chest as his groin tightened. Perhaps fate had decided to bless him after all. He claimed Julia's lips, spending the next few minutes acquainting himself with her satiny soft mouth, tasting her sweetness, sampling her velvety skin, smelling her light floral scent. When he pulled away and peered into her eyes, there were no shadows in the cool depths, only a spark of anticipation. "Your carriage awaits, my lady."

It was more important than ever to square away his business with Joshua's widow if he wanted to make a bid for Julia's continued attention. He'd finish it at the first opportunity.

Dusk painted the sky with lavender and soft pink by the time the carriage bounced to a halt outside Tyler's townhouse. Julia uncurled herself from his side and exited the conveyance without his assistance. Drained from the events of the day, she barely kept her feet beneath her as she waited for him to pay the driver then escort her up the walkway. No sooner had Tyler opened his door than the other door sharing the same stoop swung inward and Victor stood in the doorway. The imposing blond man's gaze focused on her face, mussed hair and drifted over her wrinkled clothing and he swore as if he were a dock worker. He murmured an apology then shot past her and barreled into Tyler, pinning him against the wall between the two doors.

"How dare you violate a woman who's obviously had a less than ideal life?" Victor shook Tyler like a rag doll. "You promised you wouldn't harm her, wouldn't use her. I cautioned you against such an occurrence, now I find her in a disheveled state, following you into your bachelor lodgings no less." A violent shove accompanied the accusation.

"It's not what you think, Victor. I can explain." Tyler pushed at the other man's chest but remained trapped, his face reddening.

Julia teetered on the edge of decision: interrupt what was obviously a deep-set issue or let it run its course?

"I'm sure you can. You always fast-talk your way out of every situation." Victor pressed him more firmly into the bricks, his fingers digging into Tyler's jacket. "No more. I'm tired of saving your ass. People deserve to be treated better, and it's time for you to learn from your own mistakes."

Tyler shook his head. His frantic gaze landed on Julia. "Tell him I was helping you."

Warmth spread through her chest. She felt humbled knowing both these men would take such blatant steps to protect her. Perhaps human nature could be redeemed. "Mr. Archer, Tyler has done nothing unwanted or unwarranted." She tugged on his forearm. Raw power and the strength of his muscles flexed beneath her fingers. When he didn't budge, she wriggled between the men, pushing at Victor's chest with both palms, all the while extremely conscious of Tyler's body so near hers. "Indeed, without Tyler's interference, I'd be in a bad state." Squashed between the two angry gentlemen, she had no escape.

"You have debris in your hair, Miss Spencer. That doesn't happen unless one is horizontal on the ground." His gaze imparted significance, then shock crept into his expression.

Heat burned her cheeks. He knew, or at least suspected, what she and Tyler had done. "Thank you for noticing, but that's my business and none of your concern." She glared, refusing to back down until he released his hold on Tyler. "More of this sort of behavior will create a scene and have the authorities in your yard."

Victor nodded and released Tyler. He stepped away. "I apologize."

"Don't feel you need to, Mr. Archer. Between the three of us, there are too many secrets already. Tyler and I merely exorcised a few of them this afternoon." She glanced at Tyler, who rolled his shoulders. The color in his face slowly returned to normal. "Please, won't you come in? I'll see to a tea tray, and we can all have a polite conversation."

Victor curled his hands into fists. He looked past her to Tyler. "The woman is staying with you? Have you lost your mind?"

"The woman has a name." Tyler led the procession into the townhouse. "And yes, Victor. For tonight she's staying here, in my bedroom while I take possession of the sofa. It was necessary for her protection of which I will inform you about later, with Julia's permission of course."

"Can I trust that you two will remain civil while I make tea?" She encompassed both in her gaze as they sat at opposite ends of the sofa in the shabby living area. When they both nodded with similar surly expressions, she smiled. "I won't be long."

A quarter of an hour later, Julia returned with a tea tray and a plate of freshly-made molasses cookies she'd found in the kitchen, most likely courtesy of Tyler's housekeeper. The men still sat where she'd left them, except Victor had retreated behind yesterday's edition of the *Sentinel* and Tyler seemed engrossed in a copy of the *Saturday Evening Post*.

Not much better than suffering through tea with my parents.

Determined to restore an atmosphere of camaraderie, Julia handed out mugs of tea since Tyler had no proper china teacups. "How have you been, Mr. Archer? I'm afraid life has been busy since our picnic. I haven't had an update."

He lowered the paper a notch. "Why would you? It seems to me you and Tyler have been absorbed in other more *interesting* subjects."

The man made great efforts at being unpleasant. "What of your relationship with Gretchen? You two were very chummy during the outing." When she thought of that idyllic afternoon, heat slid through her insides. She and Tyler had kissed then as well.

That brought the paper down another few degrees. A flush covered Victor's neck and cheeks. "Your friend and I won't suit. Despite the initial attraction, after spending that afternoon with her I discovered she's a silly woman with a frivolous dog. I have no time for a female like that."

Julia gasped. Gretchen might be good-humored and enjoyed life to excess at times, but no one had ever described her as silly. "I'm sorry to hear it." Why had she not heard this news before now? She cast a quick glance to Tyler, who winked. Maybe she'd been a bit preoccupied.

"Indeed." Victor took an exaggerated sip of tea. "I must confess, finding you here with Tyler has me perplexed."

"How so?" Despite her best efforts at playing hostess, tension hung thick in the air.

"Enough, Victor." Tyler set his mug on a low table. "I told you why I invited her." His lips formed a thin line.

"While that very well may be true, I want to hear it in her own words." His attention once more slid to Julia, his ice blue eyes cold and hard. "Over the course of meeting you, I couldn't help but try piecing together details of your past, Miss Spencer. Are you taking advantage of Tyler? Is he paying you for services rendered as if he's a client?"

She choked on a mouthful of tea, resorting to mopping up the spill with a linen napkin. "I beg your pardon?"

"Just what I said. I have reason to believe your profession was much different before you became a journalist." Victor rose. He threw the paper on the table. "Tyler is my best friend, and if I'm forced to defend him from unsavory people like you, I will."

Julia's hand shook so badly, tea sloshed over the edge of her mug. She deposited it on the table and stood as well. "What is it you assume I've done?" Not willing to give quarter if he didn't know the truth, she narrowed her eyes. "I'm quite curious."

"This conversation has gotten out of hand." Tyler shot to his feet, glancing between them. "Let's all calm down. Maybe Victor should go home."

Victor crossed his arms across his chest. "I'd hoped not to come right out and mention it, but you left me with no choice." He cleared his throat. "You're a prostitute, and I don't appreciate you plying your trade in this neighborhood. Perhaps bars and gentleman's clubs are more to your liking since your picture graces one of them."

"You bastard." Tyler moved, outrage in his expression. He leaped over the table and crashed into Victor. They both went down in a heap at Julia's feet. Tyler grabbed Victor's collar with one hand, the other cocked back in a fist. "Apologize to her." Hardly two seconds went by before Tyler delivered a punch to Victor's nose. Blood spurted from the injury.

"Stop it!" Julia's pulse rushed in her ears. While it flattered her Tyler would defend her so vehemently, she hated that two friends were now brawling because of it. She yanked on Tyler's collar, pulling him off Victor who lay sprawled on the floor, a hand to his nose. She leaned down and looked in his face. "If that's what you think of me, I'm pleased to say you're completely wrong. The fact you mentioned it over tea makes you an ass."

She straightened then transferred her gaze to Tyler. "If you can eschew the childish behavior for a moment, I give you permission to relate my tale to your friend. Regardless, this stunt has tried the last of my patience. I'm going to bed. Goodnight."

Why did I ever want a man of my own? She lifted her skirts, stepped over Victor then exited the room with her head held high. Men were little more than grown up boys.

She had no desire to become a nursemaid.

Chapter Fifteen

Two evenings later, Tyler meandered through the City Market as he waited for Julia. He'd promised to treat her to dinner and also to tell her why he needed the money from the con. Working through her issues during that memorable afternoon at the spring, he hadn't been afforded the opportunity to come clean. He owed her that, especially after the poor showing he'd given her the night she'd stayed over. He'd begged her to remain beneath his roof, but she was strong willed and declined with assurances she could handle herself. He'd relented with promises of escorting her about town.

Once she'd retired that evening, he and Victor had come to an understanding. Though neither of them had apologized, friendship had cut deeper than current emotions and prompted the return of goodwill. Tyler had relayed everything Julia had told him then threw in his own suspicions. He'd asked Victor if he would discreetly inquire as to the men Julia might have had contact with all those years ago. When Victor had asked why the personal vendetta, Tyler admitted his fears regarding new threats he couldn't prove. There had to be truth buried within Julia's story, plus she'd do anything to protect her uncle. Victor had agreed and promised to report his findings in a few days.

Satisfied, Tyler had escorted Julia to the newspaper office the next morning, and once he'd ascertained her uncle was inside, made plans for the Market then threw his remaining energy into apothecary work.

Now, as he prowled the various stalls inside the building, anticipation tingled over his skin at the thought of seeing Julia again. Being parted from her for two days had left a gnawing hunger inside, not only for a possible furtherance of physical relations, but also to merely converse with her, cajole a smile from her and be in her company.

I've gotten myself into a fine kettle.

He grinned, probably looked very much like an idiot to the other folks perusing the vendor's stands, but he didn't care. If this was how the path to love began, then he refused to find a different route through life. With Julia, he felt as if he could do anything he set his mind to as long as she believed in him. For her, he'd be content working as a legitimate apothecary. He'd give up the miracle tonic business, he'd—

Tyler stopped. Cold chills raced down his spine. Two stalls ahead of his current position, Anna—Joshua's widow—stood bartering with the flower seller. Her child was nowhere around. He assumed Anna had convinced a neighbor to watch her. For the moment, she hadn't spied him. His heart pounded. His palms sweated. He wiped them on his trouser legs. What to do? He hadn't prepared a speech to Anna regarding the monthly payments. Yes, he'd made up his mind to finally lay the last piece of his past to rest, but without thinking it through, would it end in a scandal? He yanked off his wool slouch-type hat and raked a hand through his hair. Of course, he'd made that old promise in haste. It was only natural he'd end it in the same manner.

To win Julia's heart, it had to be done.

Replacing the hat, he squared his shoulders and approached her, edging around a hand cart filled with chrysanthemums, daisies, black-eyed Susans, sneezeweed, sunflowers and many others. They blazed in a riot of fiery autumnal color, but he found no joy in their beauty. The task before him occupied every thought.

Sandra Sookoo

"Good evening, Anna." He tapped the brown-haired woman on the shoulder, stepping back as she spun around. The flower vendor turned away to help another patron. "I had no idea you'd be here at this hour."

Surprise flitted across Anna's bland features. Her green eyes narrowed. "Tyler! How wonderful to see you." When she hugged him, his body stiffened, uncomfortable at having a female too near who wasn't Julia.

"Where's Rachel?"

Anna shifted her basket to the opposite hand. "My mother is looking after her. Thank you for inquiring." She tucked a tendril of hair into her bun. "Well, don't let me keep you."

Before she could vanish into the throng moving through the marketplace, Tyler said, "Anna, wait. We need to talk."

"About?" Mild curiosity clouded her eyes.

He wiped at the sweat forming on his upper lip. "I realize I told Joshua I'd look after you. I can no longer adhere to that promise."

A mask of anger twisted Anna's normally placid face. Twin spots of color jumped into her cheeks and brought out freckles on the bridge of her nose. "Are you sure this is a wise decision? After all, you weren't able to save my husband. I'd think you could manage to continue to support his wife and child."

A swath of guilt cut through Tyler's insides. "Be that as it may, I did apologize for Joshua's death. For years I thought it was my fault. Now I realize it was an unfortunate result of war. I did all I could." He would never have seen it that way had Julia not remarked upon it.

"Did you?" Anna moved closer. The hem of her skirt brushed his shoes. "To my way of thinking, if you'd done enough, Joshua would be with me today. I lost him to the grave, forced to raise a child by myself with little chance of a better life. If you take that support away, Rachel and I will be on the streets. That'll also be your fault."

As if attempting to move past Joshua's death wasn't enough. "Then it'll be a cross I'll bear alone."

"I never thought you'd treat me so badly. When Joshua wrote about you in his letters, I thought your character would be much more than what you've shown today."

He fought against the self-loathing. "As I said, circumstances in life have become such I cannot continue to indulge in the endeavors that bring in the money I've pledged to you."

Tears shimmered in Anna's eyes. When she blinked, one fell to her cheek. "We cannot survive without your help."

"You have your mother. From what Joshua told me, you have a large family in the city. Petition them, or you could consider joining the work force. There are plenty of positions available to women. If you'd like, I can assist you in securing a livelihood."

"And what then, abandon the search midway through like you did with Joshua's promise?"

How the hell did he answer that? Tyler rubbed the back of his neck where a flush warmed the skin. Had he not done enough? He fought off the memories of that earthen trench, ignored the echoes of gunfire in his head, Joshua's death gurgle. Wasn't it enough he'd tried, and had been there until the boy's end?

"I..." The rebuttal died in his throat. With one casual glance over Anna's shoulder, he spied Julia walking among the stalls. Every now and again she'd pause, chat with a vendor or purchase a food item or small trinket. A willow basket, similar to Anna's, swung from one elbow. A navy-dyed straw hat sat upon her upswept hair, matching the simple navy-and-black striped dress she wore. She seemed fresh and relaxed in the bustling market.

Julia turned her head and met his gaze. A smile tipped her lips. She waved, changing her course and heading in his direction.

His gut churned. He focused on Anna. His pulse tripped erratically through his veins. "Once again, I apologize. Is there any way we can continue this discussion at a later date?"

"Will you change your mind?"

"Unfortunately, I won't." Julia was nearly upon them. "If you will excuse me?"

A calculating light flashed in Anna's eyes before her appearance settled into its usual calm, no trace of tears evident. "I don't believe I will."

Before he had time to formulate a reply, Julia joined them. She raised an eyebrow in inquiry. "Hello, Tyler." The silence was deafening. She waited for an introduction, but what could he say? Her gaze jumped to Anna. "Who is this?"

Though hardly noticeable, he didn't miss the undertone of jealousy in her voice. He wanted to whoop at the small victory, yet a sick feeling inched up his throat. Having no way to avoid a confrontation, he uttered a small sigh. "Miss Julia Spencer this is Mrs. Anna Hobart. Her husband died years ago while in Cuba with me."

"Ah." Recognition flashed in Julia's expression. "I'm very sorry for your loss."

Tension filled the space around them. Tyler sweated beneath his suit. When both women stood there, staring at each other with reluctantly polite expressions, he blurted into the heavy silence, "In case you were wondering, Anna, Julia and I have recently begun our courtship." He glanced at Julia, hoping she wouldn't mind the little white lie.

Humor shone in her eyes. She bit her bottom lip but couldn't quite hide the smile spreading over her kissable lips. "Tyler is quite eager and excitable, and yes he's correct." This time the grin broke free.

His heart skipped a beat bringing with it a second chance at life. She didn't condemn his high-handed action, which must mean she agreed with his plans. That in itself could be construed as a miracle. "Well, what can I say? When I want something, I'll pursue it with enthusiasm." This evening hadn't gone badly after all. *I'm a lucky man indeed.*

A soft sound of derision from Anna brought his attention to her. "If I could wish you both well, I would. However, Miss Spencer has a right to full disclosure before you both go farther in your relationship."

He and Julia stared at her. Once again he broke the frosty silence. "What do you mean? There are no secrets between us." Except the small matter of not sharing why he ran the con. After this evening, it wouldn't matter.

"I'm truly sorry you think that." She laid a gloved hand on Julia's arm. "You need to know what kind of man he is. I'm with child, and he is the father."

Tyler reeled. His stomach bottomed out and he had the sensation of falling—straight into the pit of Hell.

Julia's world swayed for a few seconds before she straightened her spine and bit down on her tongue so hard tears sprang to her eyes. The pain focused her attention, allowing her to concentrate on the woman in front of her. "I beg your pardon?" Her voice sounded uncommon high. When the people immediately around them looked their way, she lowered her voice. "You're pregnant?" Uttering the word or even speaking in public about being "in the family way" could result in disaster within society's circles. It was taboo subject.

"Oh, yes." Anna transferred her basket to her other hand in order to rub her stomach with her right. "Almost three months, but I'm uncomfortable discussing such delicate matters here."

I imagine you are. Aloud, Julia said, "Fine. We'll move." She deposited her basket on the ground near the flower cart, then standing, grabbed an arm of both Anna and Tyler, propelling them through the crowd until she found a semi-secluded section of the market. "Have you consulted a doctor to confirm your story?" Forced into a reactionary stance, she shoved her feelings as a woman aside and embraced her instincts as a journalist. Doing so was safe, would protect her from hurt, and temporarily guard her heart until she could find the facts.

Anna shook her head. "Not yet. I wanted to be certain." She narrowed her eyes. "You aren't a mother, are you, Miss Spencer?"

"No." She crossed her arms over her chest and continued to stare the woman down.

"Oh, well, a nurturing woman just knows these things, especially after she's already had one child."

"I see." Although she didn't. Even examining Anna with a critical eye didn't reveal any sort of symptoms relating to pregnancy—no swell of the stomach, no tight-fitting clothing, no evidence of fatigue in the face. In fact, the woman appeared the picture of health. Julia transferred her gaze to Tyler. He looked green around the mouth, his complexion deathly pale. "Did you have any idea about this? Is there any credence to her tale?"

"I can honestly say I had no idea." He glanced between her and Anna then back again. "Believe me."

"I do believe you're ignorant of the knowledge." Julia glared at him. "What I want to hear now is if you've spent *significant* time in her company since Joshua's death." The remembered trek through the darkened streets a couple weeks ago confirmed he had, yet on that visit he hadn't stayed long enough for relations. Why did he see her?

Heavy silence stretched between the group. Tyler's jaw worked as if he wanted to talk, but no sound emerged.

Anna cleared her throat. "Obviously, there is much to discuss as it seems your romance has suffered a complication with my joyous news." Triumph flashed in her eyes. "I need to return home to my daughter. I have to watch my health you know." She touched Tyler's hand that rested on his cane. "I trust you'll call in the next few days. We haven't finished our discussion, and I'm certain you've experienced a change of heart."

He nodded. The silence fairly crackled with unspoken emotion Julia couldn't identify, didn't know if she wanted to try at the cost of her own heart.

She relaxed her arms as Anna departed. Being alone with Tyler now, after the announcement that had shattered her world, she couldn't ignore the emptiness in her middle that threatened to swallow her whole. She'd trusted him, allowed him close, and he still felt the need to lie to her. How many times would it happen? Why did she continue to be so ignorant of men's real motives? "Tyler, I want the truth. I have every reason not to believe her. I have many reasons to want to believe you. Please tell me you and she did nothing that could result in a baby."

Briefly, he closed his eyes, his lips moving as if in prayer. "Julia, sweetheart, I'm well aware of how this situation looks from your position. I wish circumstances were different." He visibly swallowed. "Yes, I have had contact with Anna over the years. I give her a monthly cash payment to fulfill the promise I made to Joshua as he died. I'd meant to tell you the other day, but there were much more important subjects to discuss at the time."

"I understand that, and probably would have supported it." She licked her lips. The reporter in her pushed for facts. "What of her pregnancy claim? Did you and she...?" She didn't have the heart to finish the inquiry.

The guilt that crept into his expression confirmed his involvement more than any words could. As he held her gaze, his eyes reflecting the same despair she felt, he finally nodded.

Acute pain tightened her chest as she fought off tears. Feeling more betrayed than she ever had at Madame's school, she stepped forward and slapped him hard on the cheek. In that moment, she didn't care who saw the action, didn't give a thought to what rumors it would start. He winced at the contact. "There are no words, Mr. Browning. I'm too angry to speak with any semblance of intelligence. Good evening."

"Julia, wait. Let me explain." He reached for her, but she jerked away. "Please."

"No. You had your chance. You disappointed me. I'm done with the lies." *Finished with having my heart broken.* Her hands shook so badly, she clenched her skirts in her fists to hide the level of her ire. "Don't trouble to call on me again. I imagine Anna will be more than available for your needs." Willing the tears away, Julia bolted from the open-air building, grateful for the crowd on the streets outside. Pushing onward, she made certain she became lost in the throng, not caring that she'd left her basket behind.

The sins of the past had once again ruined her chances for the future, only this time, they didn't belong to her. Why had she allowed herself to fall for his charm and easy charisma, his twinkling eyes and honey-sweet words? She should have known better. Being with a man always ended in heartbreak.

A scant half hour later, Julia alighted from a carriage, paid the driver with the last of her cash then stormed up the walkway to her house. She'd barely stepped inside the foyer when Bess materialized on silent feet. The housekeeper received Julia's hat, gloves and handbag.

"Miss Spencer, Miss Schmidt is waiting in the back parlor. As I had no idea you expected her, I don't have tea waiting."

Julia heaved a sigh. "If you can manage brewing a fresh pot of tea, I would appreciate it. In the meanwhile, I'll join Gretchen. Most likely she won't stay long. I wouldn't wish to trouble you with actually setting another place for dinner." Not bothering to see if Bess would respond, Julia swept past the older woman and made her way to the back parlor. As soon as she saw her friend, relief and exhaustion slammed into her. "I'm so glad you're here."

Gretchen stood. "By the time I got here, I remembered you'd be out, but your housekeeper offered tea..." Her voice trailed off. Her black hair fell over one shoulder in a shining waterfall. Concern filled her mossy eyes. "What happened? Where is Mr. Browning? You look as if you've seen a ghost."

"There was a bit of a problem at the Market this evening." She hugged her friend, grateful for a sympathetic ear. "Actually, it's more complicated than that."

"How so?" Gretchen pulled her down on the low sofa beside her. "In all the years I've known you, rarely do you let emotion consume you, but those tears you're holding back will break soon and once they do, you'll be too incoherent to talk. They've been brewing too long not to take over once you give them leave."

"Oh, Gretchen, what would I do without you?" Julia grasped the other woman's hands and held tight. "I fear I've made a mess of things, or rather Tyler did, and I reacted badly."

"Lord, did he draw you into a shadowy corner and have his wicked way with you?" When Julia didn't laugh or smile, a small frown marred Gretchen's expression. "Please tell me what happened."

Julia accepted the lace-trimmed handkerchief Gretchen handed her. "At the Market tonight, I met Tyler, except he was with another woman, the widow of a man he'd tried to save during his post in Cuba." She dabbed at her eyes. "He gives her a monthly monetary payment that stems from a promise he made the dying man."

"Where does the money come from? I doubt he makes enough as an apothecary to meet his own obligations plus hers."

"He never told me, and quite frankly I'm not sure I care now." Every time she thought about the damning announcement, her stomach pitched.

"That's not true. I think you care more than you want to admit. Somehow, Tyler did what other men never could. He made it through every barrier you put around your heart and you're annoyed about it, maybe a smidgeon upset because he didn't prove to be anything except a regular man after all." Gretchen patted Julia's hand. "It's a good sign. It means you're an ordinary woman, one whose scars haven't prevented her from living life."

"I'm not certain about that." Julia took a deep breath and let it ease out between her lips. "The widow announced she was with child and it belonged to Tyler."

Gretchen's mouth fell open. "Do you believe her?"

"I have no reason not to."

"True, but was there proof?"

"None I could see, but that doesn't mean she's lying." Julia wriggled off the sofa and paced the length of the room. "I cannot very well haul her before a doctor and demand an examination."

"Yet, without proof, you feel you cannot trust anything Tyler tells you from this point forward, correct?" Gretchen raised an eyebrow. "I assume he gave you damning information that placed him at her house, so indeed the alleged pregnancy could belong to him."

"I'm afraid so. That was the part I took issue with." Julia stared out the window. Two gray doves walked about the small patch of grass off the patio.

Rustling fabric indicated Gretchen had risen to her feet. "You desperately want to trust him, beyond this little issue. This bothers you because you're halfway in love with him."

Julia whirled around. A hot protest built in her throat but died an early death. Gretchen could see the truth anyway. Why deny it? Her shoulders drooped. "It's true. That man is good at thievery, and I suspect he's stolen my heart." Sharing the admission caused warmth to spread through her insides. It was wonderful to say out loud after so many years of thinking she'd never have the opportunity. "However, I still intend to write my article on him and expose his miracle tonic as a sham. I owe the city at least that. If, in the course of the continuing investigation, I find he was angling for two slices of cake by juggling us both, our relationship is truly over."

"I doubt it." Gretchen crossed her arms over her chest. "You like that Tyler walks the line between right and wrong. Deep down inside you know you won't be able to conform to society's rules either. He's your perfect match."

Julia nodded. "He is. I want to hope he's above blame in this fiasco."

"Before you do anything rash like write your article, or toss him out, give him a chance to explain. Can you really hold him responsible for something that might have happened in his past, before he met you? Ideally, the City Market wasn't the best place to have such a conversation, and if I know you, you left in a huff."

Heat jumped into Julia's cheek. "I did…after I slapped him. I told him not to call on me anymore."

Gretchen's laughter pealed through the room. "Oh, I doubt he'll follow that order. He's as lost as you are when it comes to matters of the heart. I've never seen two people more in love or quite so stupid."

"You could be correct." Shaking her head to clear the muddled thoughts, Julia returned to the sofa and sat. "I'll puzzle it out later." She glanced in Gretchen's direction. "While at Tyler's home, I had a conversation with Mr. Archer over tea. He indicated you and he would not suit. Is this true?" The best way to deflect her friend's delving into her love life was to poke around in Gretchen's.

"I'd forgotten I haven't told you about him." Gretchen collapsed next to Julia. "That man might be handsome and strong, but he's too regimented for me. I want to experience the baser side of life, and I certainly don't want it at the expense of making appointments for coupling or being told hugging and kissing in public are frowned upon."

"That bad?"

She nodded. "He needs a woman with a stronger constitution than me."

Julia sighed. "Unfortunately, I did glimpse a bit of that side of him. He's also very loyal." She clasped one of Gretchen's hands and squeezed. "Sorry, sweetie. You'll find a wonderful man soon, I'm sure of it."

"I'm not worried." Gretchen's eyes sparkled as bright as her smile. "Meanwhile, the chase is on, and besides, I need to keep my social calendar free."

"Oh, why is that?"

"To help plan your wedding, of course."

"Let's not rush things, all right?" The pit of her stomach roiled with uncertainty again. If only she knew whether or not Tyler had fathered Anna's child.

Life, it seemed, would always have its secrets.

Chapter Sixteen

The next afternoon, Julia ran her pencil lead through yet another line of text she'd spent the last ten minutes toiling over. At this rate the article would never be finished, and Tyler would get away with selling everyday water to the residents of Indianapolis. At the very least, he needed to be held accountable for fraud. When the third paper wad fell off the desktop, she threw her pencil after it.

It's pointless.

She couldn't concentrate. Yes, her mind dwelled solely on Tyler, but those thoughts were hardly the fodder for article content. Mostly they circled around the fact he'd spent time in Anna's company—enough time that the pregnancy could possibly belong to him. But what if it didn't? What if Anna had lied? Would he truly stay away simply because she'd ordered him to, or was he even now scheming up new ways to make her life miserable? Would he ever settle down enough to build a life, or was the craving for adventure and scamming too great?

The rapping of knuckles on the desk brought her back to the present with a start. Julia glanced up and met her uncle's concerned gaze. She scrambled to her feet. "Sorry, Uncle George. I'll clean the mess."

"Never you mind, darlin'." He perused the paperwork scattered on her desk. "Still workin' on the miracle tonic piece?"

She quickly gathered the handwritten pages into a neat stack. "Yes, and it isn't moving along as nicely as I'd thought." She rubbed her forehead. "I cannot seem to grasp the true essence of the story."

Uncle George came around his desk to her side. He wrapped an arm around her shoulders and drew her out of the office, then through the bullpen. "To get to the heart of the story, you need to delve into the heart of the man involved."

"I'm afraid that isn't possible at the moment."

"Ah, then I think perhaps you need to put your focus on somethin' else for a while. You're too close to the story." At the door to the reception area, he pushed it open, waited for her to pass, then followed her into the stuffy cubicle. "It happens to every journalist a time or two."

"How should I counter it?" Her uncle always seemed so sure of himself and his journalistic skills. She hoped one day to be as confident, as fearless, chasing a story.

A mischievous twinkle appeared in his eyes. "Your parents are attendin' a big to-do this evenin', some sort of musicale with local artist-types, featurin' that poet fellow, James Whitcomb Riley. You're always goin' on about his genius. Why don't you attend in a journalist capacity, then do a write-up? It'll get your mind off your young man."

"Another society piece?" Julia's stomach dropped to her toes. "I thought we agreed I'd do a real news story. You never take me—"

"Julia." His tone of voice brooked no argument.

"I apologize." Patience had never been a virtue she adhered to, but angering her uncle wasn't on her agenda for the day.

Uncle George nodded. "Askin' you to do this story doesn't mean I don't have faith in your ability, my girl. Just the opposite, and even a blind man can see the apothecary has you tangled up in knots—beyond worryin' over the article. Askin' you to write this story will offer you the chance to think about somethin' else for a while and maybe put other matters into perspective."

The urge to hide in her uncle's arms grew strong. Being an adult meant the loss of childhood comforts she'd taken for granted. "He and I are not talking at present. I'm afraid there are a few things we might not be able to mend."

"If the relationship is meant to be, all the ills will work themselves out. Love is stronger than everything else, though it feels much like work." She must have looked skeptical, for he continued, "You cannot expect a happily ever after to land in your lap. If you work hard for somethin', you appreciate it more."

Hasn't my life been difficult enough? Julia shook her head. "I don't want it to be easy, but now I that finally took a chance on a man, he hurt me, lied to me. How can I forgive that? I thought he was different."

"Haven't you done the same to him?"

She refused to look at her uncle as her cheeks burned.

"It's all a matter of perspective, my dear. Do you want to grow beyond the person you are now? Overcomin' obstacles in our lives makes us tougher to survive all sorts of other things, but you already know that. You'll either survive this relationship or you'll fix it."

She frowned, and finally met his gaze, not liking the good humor in his expression.

His broad shoulders lifted in a shrug. "Get yourself dressed in a pretty gown and cover the party. After that, you can tackle the miracle tonic story from a different angle. Regardless of the outcome, it's all experience."

"Maybe you're right." Her spirits perked and for the first time since the incident with Tyler and Anna, flutters of excitement tickled her stomach. "It'll be interesting to meet the famous poet."

"That's my girl. Always keep your eyes open."

Anxiety tightened her insides. "Mr. Hayes won't be there, will he?" The thought of needing to defend against his threats on top of everything else the evening would entail nearly made her ill.

Uncle George's eyes reflected uncertainty. "I haven't heard him talk of the event, but who can say. The man's a menace. Hints the sale of the paper is all but imminent. Stay vigilant no matter what." He chucked her under the chin. "I'll send a photographer along with orders for him to snap your picture for the paper. Unless you're afraid of drawing attention to yourself after that paintin'..."

She waved away his concern. "What's done is done and it's been hanging in that club for years."

"You're a smart girl." He tapped his temple. "Your young man might see it, realize he's been an ass and fall hopelessly in love with you."

"If only real life were as easy as a fairy tale, Uncle George." She exited the *Sentinel's* office. *But then, where's the satisfaction of fighting the evil enemy if I have to wait on a man to do it?*

As her carriage jolted to a halt outside a lush Italianate home on Lockerbie Street, Julia took several deep breaths to compose herself. Bess had fashioned Julia's hair into an elaborate creation of curls and twists, leaving a few tendrils loose to frame her face. Whatever else the woman was, she had a knack for hair dressing. The sheer amount of pins holding the art in place made her scalp ache. She poked at one and stared at the yards of fabric that made up her dress. A deep burgundy satin, tiny pearls and crystals had been sewn on the low, squared bodice and along the hems of her short, puffed sleeves as well as the skirt. They even decorated her matching evening slippers.

Julia sighed as the driver opened her door and helped her down. Since she'd been asked to cover the party on short notice, she'd had to borrow the gown from her mother's collection. Celeste had assured Julia the frock had never been worn since Mrs. Spencer hadn't liked the finished product. However, a few last minute alterations had made it perfect for Julia.

She nodded at the driver, who also ran the printing press at the paper. Uncle George was quite adamant he escort her. "Thank you. I should be finished here in two hours. Please come back for me then."

"Will do, ma'am, but if it's all the same to you, I'll cool my heels with the other drivers. Your uncle's orders, you see." He touched the brim of his bowler and winked. "Enjoy your evening."

With a smile, Julia walked up the path leading to the house. Dear Uncle George. She hoped she wouldn't need his concern tonight. Stuck in the crush of party-goers clogging the brick path and entryway, she concentrated on the facts she knew. That way, she'd have no time to think about Tyler.

The house belonged to Major and Mrs. Charles Holstein. According to the scuttlebutt around town, Mr. Riley rented rooms from them and in return, they hosted lavish parties with which to showcase the Indiana native's talent. Throw in a political hopeful or veterans from the War and they were instant people of import. What better backdrop to exchange fundraising promises or social invitations than a poetry reading and buffet dinner? Also attending the evening's events were William Merritt Chase, one of Mr. Riley's contemporaries and an artist in his own right, as well as attorney Charles Warren Fairbanks. A few years younger than the two other distinguished guests, rumor had it that Mr. Fairbanks had aspirations for Washington.

So lost in thought, Julia didn't realize the crowd had buoyed her along until she met the head of the receiving line, Mrs. Holstein. "Good evening, ma'am. You have quite a turn out tonight." She lightly pressed the matronly woman's hand, noting the peacock feather jammed into the woman's elegantly coiffed hair bobbed a perilous foot away from a candle flame.

"Of course, dear. Mr. Riley has promised to read his poem, *Little Orphant Annie*. That alone draws a crowd. It seems everyone was in a mad rush to make use of the invites."

A flicker of interest ignited within Julia's chest. "I cannot wait to hear it." To listen to him recite his actual work would be a special treat. Perhaps she should ask the poet for an interview and use that as the angle for her society piece.

Forced to traverse the remainder of the receiving line—Major Holstein, attorney Fairbanks and various other notables in society who she couldn't remember their names—she wandered through the rooms, taking in the ornate furnishings and beautiful painted ceilings that bordered on gaudy. Fall flowers and arrangements decorated tables and fireplace mantles while crystal chandeliers glittered in soft illumination.

From somewhere within the mansion, savory scents wafted to her nose. A rumble in her stomach reminded her she hadn't eaten since tea that morning. Off to one side, a sizable ballroom teemed with couples already engaged in a lively country dance. The colors from the women's dresses contrasted with the dark suits of the men.

She hesitated in the doorway and watched the dancers as they finished the set. In another lifetime, she'd enjoyed such a pastime. Now—

"Good evening, Miss Spencer. I'd be honored if you'd agree to a dance with me."

Julia gasped. She jerked her gaze to the speaker, but of course it would be *him*. The sound of his voice sent shivers of desire up her spine. "Tyler." Though the slow burn of anger still warmed her middle, her natural curiosity warred for dominance. She needed facts, yet at the same time, her feminine pride demanded retribution. "Why are you here?"

"To talk with you." He readjusted his grip on his cane. "I stopped by the newspaper office this morning on my way to the apothecary. When I asked your uncle about your schedule, he said you'd be at this party, and if I wanted my one shot in hell for redemption, I'd better ask you to dance."

"Damn you, Uncle George." He'd arranged the meeting. Vowing to take him to task later, she gave Tyler her full attention. Clad in the requisite dark evening suit, it gave him a dashing air, full of excitement and danger. He'd also gone to great lengths to tame his hair by parting it on the left and using pomade, but the curls slowly resisted the effort. It gave him a rakish appearance and sent a throb of need through her core. "I'm not here in a civilian capacity." *Concentrate on your job, Julia. Don't let him in again.*

"I'm aware of that. All I need is a few moments of your time. If, after our talk, you're still adamant about never wanting to see me, I'll not sour your life any longer." Though his gaze was as intense as ever, desperation lit the depths. He was uncertain of his reception, and that made him more endearing.

The thought sent shockwaves reeling through her. She heard her uncle's words in her head. *Sometimes folks have good reasons for what we think is questionable. Look past the surface stains and get to the heart of the matter.*

She nodded, unable to deny him. "I rather doubt you're capable of dancing with your injury."

A brief smile lifted the corners of his mouth. "It'll hurt like the devil later tonight, but one waltz with you is well worth the pain."

Why did he have to be such a charming ass? "I'm agreeing because I want you to tell me the truth about you and Anna."

"Fair enough." He rested his cane against the wall then held out a hand. "One dance will make you remember how you feel about me."

Julia fit her fingers into his palm. Flutters crashed in her belly. "And with every step I'll try to forget." She didn't know if the whispered words were for him or her. There was no time to figure it out as he drew her into the room and positioned them both on the dance floor.

"Why are you afraid of giving yourself permission to love?"

Did he want her love after knowing her past? The knowledge plowed through her remaining defenses and left her weak at the knees. Did she want him after his revelation? "I... too many people could be hurt." She glanced at the other couples. A waltz! How could he have known the next dance would be such an intimate one?

"They could, but how will you know if you never take a chance, take that blind leap of faith? Once in a while, people can surprise you." Tyler's dark eyes promised things she'd longed for, wished to have. "For this one dance, don't think like a journalist. Only feel as a woman."

The string quartet's opening notes sang into the sudden hush hovering in the air. With a strong leading move, Tyler guided her steps. They sailed along the outskirts of the floor as if they'd been dancing together all their lives. His fingers on her waist left heat in their wake. His hand holding hers tightened. They moved with fluid grace in ever smaller circles to the center of the room. He drew her so close their bodies touched enough to tease.

Julia's pulse raced. Her breath came in small pants due to the corset restrictions and his proximity. She moved her hand from his shoulder to lightly brush a gloved finger along the side of his neck, almost as if to remind her the evening wasn't a dream.

The music and conversation faded into the background. Her world became the feel of Tyler's body against hers, the clean, citrusy scent of him, the way his smoldering gaze turned her insides to liquid heat so intense her core throbbed. In his arms, she had the sensation of being safe, that everything would be all right and she could finally have the future she'd always wished for. She decided to give him the benefit of the doubt. They'd work through whatever it was he'd done or hadn't told her. Tyler's words from several days ago echoed back at her:

"When you find that one person or thing to believe in despite the odds, despite every doubt, your eyes will finally be opened and you'll give in. Life will indeed be as sweet as you dream."

It was time to start believing in him as well as herself. There was no reason she couldn't have everything she wanted. Her past was not an anchor, only a foundation. She wanted him despite the odds.

Near the end of the song, Tyler's grin turned decidedly wicked. He maneuvered his mouth close to her ear and whispered, "My dear, if you continue to look at me as though you'd like to devour me whole, we'll both have significant problems."

She grinned and nodded hello to an acquaintance in the crowd. "I've not forgotten your sins of omission, but this room is much too confining for private conversation." A new life would mean forgiving and practicing acceptance — taking him through the good times and the bad. It sounded like the best adventure. "Meet me in the carriage house in fifteen minutes."

"No, too much chance of discovery." Tyler made a misstep but quickly recovered enough to finish the dance. Once completed, he guided her to one side of the room, his hand hot at the small of her back. "I toured the grounds earlier. There's a collection of benches at the rear of the garden at the brick wall. I'll be waiting there."

"I understand." She edged toward the back of the crowded room.

Tyler followed so close his breath warmed her neck. "Once you arrive, I intend to kiss you as thoroughly as I want to do at this moment yet can't due to society's restrictions."

Spikes of need streaked through her body, tightening her nipples while moisture dampened her drawers. "I promise to be there." She parted with him. Tyler made his way toward the door with a more pronounced limp, presumably to retrieve his cane, and Julia shoved her way through the teeming throng on the outskirts of the dance area.

Thanking the heavens that someone had the foresight to open the patio doors, Julia rushed outside and let the evening air cool her overheated skin. She breathed in deep draughts as she strolled the stone patio area in the attempt to calm her nerves in preparation for the meeting. If she followed through on Tyler's hints and acted with her heart, a whole new world would open for her. Never had she looked forward to her future more. In one man's eyes, suddenly she was valuable, wanted, perhaps even cherished.

Once her heartbeat maintained a normal rhythm, she left the mingling people on the patio to follow a brick path toward the back of the property, not more than fifty yards from the house.

Organized flower beds lined the path. Tall hedges muffled the sounds from the party the farther she went. At a turn on the walkway, a man stepped from the shadows.

Julia stopped short, her pulse beating a wild dance. Jackson Hayes stood in front of her with a sneer on his lean face. A red-centered white rose lay against his black lapel. Trickles of fear seeped down her spine. "What are you doing here?"

He ignored her question. "Am I keeping you from meeting a lover, Julia?" Jackson's beady eyes glimmered in the faint moonlight. "Apparently, you've forgotten our earlier conversation, so I thought to stake my claim before you had the chance to join him. You belong to me and no one else. I hope you won't make me do something drastic as a demonstration in a very public place."

She took a step backward. "Get off this property." A glance over his shoulder didn't reveal any sign of Tyler. Had he arrived yet? Could he hear their conversation?

"I have a legitimate invitation." Jackson patted a breast pocket. "Besides, this is a party, not your drawing room or the newspaper office. You hold no sway here."

"Let me pass."

"I'm afraid I cannot do that." His sneer deepened to a smirk. "Since I have you to myself for the moment, I feel I must reprimand you."

"For what?" Julia changed tactics and stood her ground. He was nothing more than a bully. If she fought back, he'd leave her alone. *Please God, let that be true.*

"You're entirely too friendly with a certain apothecary. Have you told him about me?" Jackson darted, closed the distance between them and gripped her arms before Julia drew her next breath. "And your uncle is wary of me as well. Have you blabbed to him?"

"No, I swear to you. I didn't mention your name to either of them though I appraised them both of my past."

Her attempt to wriggle free only jammed her tighter into his clutches. She peered into his face. Confidence in herself surged. "Neither of them has judged me for it. Those memories hold no sway over me anymore."

"I don't believe you." He brought his mouth crashing down on hers in a brutal kiss that left her lips bruised and swollen. "You'll always be a whore, Julia, and any man who tells you differently is lying."

"No." Her shivering had nothing to do with the chill in the air.

"Do you honestly believe a man like Mr. Browning wants a woman who's welcomed a slew of men into her bed for money?"

"He certainly had no problems with the news a few days ago." The words slipped out before she could stifle them. When Jackson growled, she struggled in his hold, but he'd always been strong. He crushed her body against his.

"Poor, stupid Miss Spencer. Did you think he had feelings for you? Men can sense loose women. I'll bet he merely suggested it, and you did the rest because you don't know any better, because your body craves a man's touch, his domination."

"No." Is that what Tyler thought? Yes, she initiated relations that day by the stream, but he'd seemed as enthusiastic about as she had, and then his empathy for her once she'd told her tale had appeared genuine. Did it all stem from his belief he could have her whenever he wanted if he appeared understanding? Doubt crept in with all the insidiousness of a thief. No! She had to believe in him. Her nose almost touched the detestable flower on Jackson's lapel. She ripped it off the suit, regardless of the straight pin that secured it, and threw it down. As she wrenched away from his hold, she jammed her knee upward, connecting with the soft portion of his anatomy.

"Tyler would never think that. He might have lied about other things, but never regarding me."

Jackson cursed, called her vile names while he cupped his crotch with one hand. "Still too naïve for all your experience. Has he given you sweet words of a future with him? Has he offered marriage? Most upstanding men of society would at least do that before bedding a woman."

"We…" She trailed off. Did the fact Tyler hadn't done such a thing make a difference?

A gloating smile touched Jackson's lips, lifted the ends of his thin mustache. "Will he welcome you as the mother of his children? How will you explain your story to ladies' clubs and at socials if word gets out? Believe me, I'll do my level best to make certain this whole city knows of your reputation if you defy me."

She couldn't stem the tide of shivery fear that prickled her skin. What had started out as a night on the brink of wonderful now vanished under the pall of darkness. "Why would you do this?" How much hatred he must harbor to destroy lives.

He shrugged and took a step toward her, his expression dark. "I've always gotten whatever I wanted in life—money, control of the newspaper, the ear of a few politicians, and women. But what fascinates me is when someone refuses to bow to my demands. It becomes a challenge for me to bend their will, and now I want you simply on the grounds that you detest me."

"I would rather gouge out my eyes with a dull stick than do anything for you."

"Ah, such spirit. I love it when they fight." He stumbled toward her once more. " My offer still stands. Be my mistress, offer me your body on my whim, and I'll see your uncle retains a position on the paper once it's sold. If you don't, my new target will be the apothecary. I told you of my plans before. This time I won't hesitate to follow through, but instead of your uncle, I'll implicate Mr. Browning with the crimes."

The man was insane. "He's too smart for your petty threats." She hoped it were true. As her heartbeat pounded, she stood rooted to the brick walkway in fear. Jackson had enough contacts to cause widespread damage, yet she'd never lower herself and meet his demands.

"On the off chance you're correct, let me up the ante." Jackson sidled close enough to slip an arm around her waist. "I've had a man follow you these last weeks. How is your dear friend Gretchen?"

Julia stiffened even as her stomach pitched and bile rose in her throat. She stared at him in horror. "Leave her alone."

"If you don't submit to me, or if you breathe one word of my involvement and threats, I'll turn my attention to pretty little Gretchen. It would be a shame if an accident befell her to mar that beauty, wouldn't it?" He put his lips to Julia's ear and said, "She'd have no one to blame but you. In this case, I'm one journalist who will gleefully reveal his source."

She pulled away. The sour taste of fear sat at the back of her throat. "You wouldn't dare." Was this penance for her past or unfortunate bad luck?

"It's rather hard being a martyr with a past. I'll allow you a few days to make your decision." He sketched her a slight, mocking bow, then turned on his heel. "Remember, I'll dare to do just about anything."

"No." Tears slid down Julia's cheeks. As her hopes crashed into a million pieces, she made a silent vow. No matter what, she'd protect the people she loved — even if it meant destroying their trust in her. Above all, Uncle George, Gretchen and especially Tyler had to remain safe.

Chapter Seventeen

Tyler tightened his grip on his cane so much the etchings in the brass head left a mark on his palm. He couldn't believe the evidence before his eyes. As he'd meandered through the garden, he witnessed a kiss between Julia and a man he'd seen at the *Sentinel* a handful of times—the owner or some such thing, and a powerful man in his own right. A union between them made sense; he had the position to help her career. The two had instinct and drive in common whereas she and he—Tyler—had nothing in common except less than ideal pasts. He fisted his free hand. This wasn't how he'd hoped the evening would end. Tyler had ducked behind a grouping of evergreen hedges. What the hell had gotten into the woman? Not a quarter of an hour ago, she'd been ready to seduce *him*, now this?

Anger shoved into his chest. Did what they'd shared mean nothing? He swore he'd made his interest in a future with her clear. Perhaps he hadn't presented his case correctly. He pulled a few branches apart and watched the scene unfold. Julia and the man argued, but the words didn't drift to Tyler's position. Minutes passed. Julia's face paled then the man held her close, presumably to whisper private words in her ear. Tyler's ire grew. When the man traversed the pathway toward the house, Tyler ducked further into the foliage while the newspaper man gained the crowded patio.

Long seconds dragged by with only the faint strains of the string quartet and the chirp of crickets to mark the time. Finally, Tyler returned to the path, now empty. Julia had disappeared. He glanced back at the house but saw no trace of her rose-colored gown. Unease tugged at his conscience, prompting him to walk the path. Near the turn that led to the benches he'd mentioned earlier, he stepped on a white rose. He stared at it for the space of a few heartbeats. Where had he seen a similar bloom before? Not able to pluck the knowledge from the depths of his memory, he dismissed it for the time being, he continued around the hedge wall, only to stop short for the second time since leaving the party.

Julia sat huddled on one of the stone benches, her shoulders shaking. The soft sound of muffled sobs broke the silence. Her distress sent confusion crashing through his psyche. Why would a woman who'd just been involved in a passionate moonlit rendezvous let grief consume her not five minutes later? Unable to put his finger on why the situation annoyed him, he cleared his throat. "Julia?"

Her head jerked up and she twisted around. When she spotted him, her eyes widened with alarm. "Tyler." She stood, visibly shaken, her cheeks silver and wet with tears. "You need to leave. Immediately."

"Why, so your other lover can return?" He regretted the question the moment it left his lips as her eyes narrowed. "I apologize. I had no right to accuse you of anything."

"He's most definitely not my lover." A shiver wracked her shoulders. She stared at him, her expression a mixture of defeat and exhaustion. "You promised me the rest of your story, Mr. Browning." She wiped her palms on the waist of her gown. "I'd rather you did it sooner than later, as I wish to write up my notes before retiring."

"Damnation. I thought we'd moved beyond the formal?" It was almost as if she wished to put distance between them. "I thought our meeting wouldn't be about work. Have you changed your mind?"

"No." The word wavered though the hint of a chill in the air could have been conjured by the soft utterance. She waved a hand in dismissal. "This isn't the place to discuss private matters of a romantic nature." The tendons in her neck worked with the force of her swallow.

"Agreed. I'd rather our next time together be in a proper bed. I still have grass stains on my knees." When his joke didn't produce a laugh on her part, alarm bells triggered in his head. "Julia, what happened since we parted?"

"Don't ask. I cannot tell you, and even if I did, I doubt you could help." Tears shimmered in her eyes, silver in the moonlight. She caught one on her finger as it fell. "Please, our time is limited. We should conclude business for my article."

He glanced out the entrance to the partial hideaway. "Did that man threaten you, accost you in any way?" Had he misconstrued what he'd witnessed between the two?

"I beg you not to revisit the topic." She retreated toward the bench. "If you wish to remain here, you'll have to talk of why you need the money from your con and if you fathered Anna's child."

His past and future collided in the shadow-shrouded garden. Tyler nodded. "I do owe you at least that." He rubbed a hand along his jaw. "I promised Anna a monthly stipend to help raise her daughter and have the basic necessities. Since my income from the apothecary provides enough only for me to live on, I was forced to run the con. I knew I was good at fleecing good people out of their cash, but I had no idea selling the miracle tonic would be as lucrative as it was."

"How long have you been giving Anna money?" Julia's neutral tone revealed nothing of her feelings.

"Since I came home from Cuba. Of course, the military had already informed her of Joshua's death. I was released soon after due to my wounds. When I was able, I visited her. At the time, her child was two-years-old." He shrugged, staring evergreen hedges. "I felt bad she had no one and was glad I put forth my offer. Her gratitude confirmed her situation. Only afterward did I discover she has a fairly sizable family here in the city." An old familiar wave of bitterness hit him at the remembered omission.

"Do you want to stop the payments?" The question was so soft he barely heard it.

Tyler glanced at her. Julia's eyes, still luminous with tears, sparkled. She bit her bottom lip. "Yes. I want to be certain all ties to my con life are finished in order to start our relationship." He took in a shuddering breath. He'd stated, in a roundabout way, what he wanted. Not knowing what her meeting with the newspaper man had been about prevented him from sharing his true feelings. "That life is done. I'm ready to step into a new one." When he'd always been able to charm with words, they didn't appear that magical where Julia was concerned.

"I sympathize with you. When we make the decision to chase our dreams, ones we never thought we'd actually want, there's always a blockage in our path we never considered." Her voice wavered, thick with unidentified emotion. "Then other paths open from the first, and these we don't wish to ever travel, but we must, for the good of the people we love."

He moved close to her and dropped a hand on her shoulder, not trusting himself to do more. "Julia..." His chest hurt from the wealth of feeling jammed inside. In this moment, when the moonlight gently frosted the dark landscape and her lilies of the valley scent perfumed the air, he had to make her aware of his regard. "I need to say —"

"No." Julia slipped from his touch. "And the child she's pregnant with now? Did you have relations with

Anna?" She pinned him with a hard glare, the one he'd seen upon first meeting her. "The truth please."

"Do you want it to be true so you'll have an excuse to end what's between us due to your own fear of claiming happiness?"

"Tyler..." She looked so vulnerable the urge to fold her into his arms and protect her overtook him.

He fought it. The words had to be said regardless. She'd either want him despite them or she wouldn't. His pulse rushed so hard through his veins his fingertips throbbed. This was the last chain binding him to the past. As he gripped his cane, he nodded. "In a moment of weakness a few months ago, when I'd delivered a payment, Anna and I reminisced about Joshua. A glass of wine, a few tumblers of whiskey later, mutual grief tilted into a quick turn in the sheets." He hated the pain in her eyes, hated himself more for putting it there. "It meant nothing. We both realized that same evening it was a mistake and would never be repeated."

"Yet it resulted in a new life." She crossed her arms over her breasts. "You had to know this might have been a possibility, yet you reeled me into your sticky web with the bedroom as your goal." Her shoulders drooped.

"Honestly, it hadn't occurred to me. Once I met you, everything changed."

"I doubt you want a courtship. I've been told men don't woo women like me. Perhaps, after witnessing your behavior, it's true."

"That's a lie." He closed the distance, his knee and thigh flooded with agony from the sudden movement. "Look at me." When she didn't, he physically turned her around. Deep sadness and regret shadowed blue eyes that had been full of joy and life not twenty minutes ago. "Whatever that newspaper man told you, it's not true. How can he know what's between us, the level of connection we've shared, what we feel for each other? If you doubt, rely on what's in your heart. You cannot deny that."

"Perhaps this is for the best." She stepped away from him. "Don't feel obligated to me any longer. Marry Anna and make a life with her. That way, you'll no longer need to run cons to make money, and the baby will know its father."

Desperate, he took a step forward as ice coursed down his spine. "If you'll listen to what I'm actually saying—"

"Enough, Tyler. Enough." She wiped at the lingering moisture on her cheek. "I have all I need to finish my article, which is why I sought you out in the beginning. Everything else is irrelevant now. I intend to write the truth as I have come to understand it. If the words destroy what's left of your reputation, so be it. Maybe you'll think twice before you engage a woman's affections without being free of another."

Pain he never knew he could experience gripped his heart. He pressed his free hand to his chest and gasped at the thought of losing her. "Is this what you want?"

Julia nodded but remained silent, her eyes a stormy picture of denial.

"How did you feel when your reputation was similarly destroyed without regard to what was real? I beg you not to do the same to mine. If this is truly our last night together, I'd rather fond memories linger instead of the echoes of harsh words."

A sob escaped her, so intense her whole body shook. "Please, don't seek me out." She wrapped her arms around herself. "I cannot tell you why, but for your own safety and the solvency of your apothecary, you must let me go."

Everything that had built him into the man he was protested her wild plea. In a perfect world, he'd bundle her into his arms, ignore her orders and instead demand the last of her secrets then exact revenge on the person who brought her to this pass. As it was, his life was far from ideal; in fact, it was a tangled mess rapidly unraveling, and he couldn't in good conscience ask Julia to follow him through that thorn-strewn path. The knowledge left him broken and his soul bleeding.

Finally, he nodded though it went against every fiber of his being. "I thank you for the company you've bestowed on me. I wish you well in life, but know this." Tyler swallowed around the unshed tears in his throat. "No one will fault you if you ask for help. Don't give another person the right to belittle you, and don't give them power over you. I hope you realize that before it's too late."

When she didn't look at him, he left the sanctuary of the garden, steeling his heart against the near-hysterical sobs that followed him. She'd made her choice. In retrospect, so had he. There was nothing left to do except assemble the leftover pieces and hope to hell he'd survive the aftermath.

The battlefield contained fewer traumas than living through the knowledge he was hopelessly in love with the journalist without seeing that love fulfilled.

Julia had barely seated herself behind her father's desk in his study before memories of the evening assailed her. After crying out her grief in the garden, she'd composed herself as best she could and returned to the party, but it brought no enjoyment. She'd responded to acquaintances as if she were made of wood. Listening to James Whitcomb Riley recite his poem didn't capture her interest, and more importantly, she'd felt sick and on edge after spying Jackson lurking about the fringes of the gathering.

Not wishing to sit through dinner, she'd excused herself in order to ask Mr. Riley a few questions, but they weren't as in-depth as she would have liked. Her mind was too scattered. She hadn't seen Tyler since the garden incident and her parents were both in their element, being worshipped by local society as if they were the sun and everyone else little planets. Not able to stomach more of humanity's foibles, Julia had gratefully taken refuge in the carriage and returned home.

Exhausted and heartsick, she burrowed more comfortably in the supple leather chair that smelled of Uncle George—tobacco and peppermint. Where was her pillar of strength when she needed him the most? Doubts chipped away at her ability to do justice as a reporter. What if those obnoxious pups in the office were right and she didn't have the wherewithal to do the job? Certainly a man would never let the fragments of a love life deter him from his task. No, they wore relationship problems like war wounds. Did breaking a courtship promise even bother the male of the species?

It was no one's fault but her own.

She smoothed her hands over the papers scattered on the desktop. Her handwritten notes made no sense, her carefully thought out points seemed jumbled and petty, colored with too many emotions. Just seeing Tyler's name in stark black and white caused her throat to tighten. She'd driven him away, but it had been necessary to keep him safe. If he thought less of her for the words she'd spoken, she'd have to live with that. He'd be free with a thriving business and well out of Jackson's reach—unless she quelled that with the power of her pen.

Turning her attention back to the tonic article, Julia scribbled a few paragraphs, determined to finish the piece.

From day one, Tyler had lied to her. It was no secret he'd scammed the citizens of Indianapolis out of their hard-earned money, but then, after he'd told her everything earlier that evening, his cause had noble —if hugely misplaced—roots. Were the means worse than the end? When did charity become a cross to bear?

She tapped the end of her pencil against her chin. Were his actions really that abhorrent? He kept his promise the best way he knew how. Put in the same position, she had no idea how she'd respond. With the exception of courting her knowing he'd slept with Anna, wasn't he simply a common working man trying to meet his obligations and find a modicum of happiness? Perhaps he didn't deserve the public outcry and the backlash her article would bring. Maybe he already lived in his own personal hell as punishment for his misdeeds. After another glance at her writing, Julia tore it into small squares.

Why did she think she'd be qualified to judge another person's life when hers was shattered beyond repair?

Desperate to take her mind off her troubles, she cast her gaze about the desktop. She drew a long, wooden box toward her, lifted the lid and removed one of her uncle's cigars. Bringing it to her nose, she inhaled the delicate scents of vanilla and apples, as well as the more powerful overtones of tobacco and oak. The scent brought her a sense of peace and a longing for simpler times gone by, before she'd met Tyler and lost her heart, knew the heavy cost of loving him.

Uncle George appeared in the doorway. "I'd offer you a light, punkin, if I didn't think you'd react badly to your first bout of smokin'. Besides, if you want to go down the devil's own path, I'd suggest startin' with good liquor instead."

Julia summoned a smile she didn't feel. "I enjoy the smell of cigars. It reminds me of times before everything went wrong." She replaced the cigar and lid, then pushed the box away, even the small actions making her tired. "Do you want me to move?"

"No." He came into the room and closed the door behind him. "What's troublin' you, girl? These past days you've been a shadow of yourself, but now, you're a tad haunted as well. It's different than before." He leaned a shoulder against the door. "I assume meetin' your beau at the party this evenin' didn't bring the results I wanted?"

Her cheeks heated from his implication. "Just the opposite. I never thought you'd stoop to matchmaking, Uncle."

"Well, you're a stubborn woman at times. I had no choice but to involve myself."

"That I am." She rubbed her eyes then pinned him with a glare. "If you must know, Tyler and I have parted ways at my request. There are too many inconsistencies in his story for us to untangle quickly. At least this way he can mind his own problems, and I won't suffer the guilt of destroying his reputation."

"Sometimes, a heart can't heal in haste." A thoughtful expression creased his face. "I assume you've given up writin' about the miracle tonic?" Uncle George shoved off the door and approached the desk, dropping his considerable bulk into one of the chairs that faced it.

"I have." She gestured to the scraps of paper. "I'm unable to pen a story without coloring it with my own personal opinion, which is in direct contrast to the job of the press. There's no chance of neutrality in this matter." A wave of disappointment rose in her chest. Tears threatened, but she tamped them down. "I apologize for the failure."

"Darlin', I won't have that sort of talk." He stroked his mustache with a forefinger. "What you need is an article you have experience with and real heart-felt emotion behind." Uncle George tapped his temple. "If you want to be an unforgettable reporter, you need to get your hands dirty."

"Which means?" Julia pulled the pins from her hair and dropped them on the desktop. Once her hair fell over her shoulders, she sighed and massaged her scalp. "I don't understand."

"Write *your* story for the paper. I'll personally proof it and make sure it finds its way to the printer. I'll circumvent Jackson. He'll never know until it's too late."

"No!" Julia straightened her spine as she gazed at her uncle in shock. Her heart beat a wild tattoo. Jackson's threats jumped into her mind. "While I may have considered it weeks ago, circumstances have come to light that prevent me from ever sharing that tale again."

Uncle George gave her the look that had reduced her to quivering jelly as a child. It was no less effective now. "Of course there'll be fallout afterward. Your personal pain will be splashed across the city, but if you get a reader with emotion and it sticks in their heart, they'll never forget. What's more, they just might relate to the story. Hell, the same thing might have happened to them. Isn't that the reaction you're lookin' for?"

Julia squirmed under his stern regard. "It is, but..." How did she decline without revealing Jackson's name?

"My girl, listen to me." He leaned forward, resting his arms on his knees. "In your heart, I know you want to bring the man who abused you—the one who I suspect is even now causing you grief—to justice. What better chance do you have than now? The power of the press is at your disposal."

"Even if it means he'll go after you or others I care about the second he sees his name in print?" Above all, she had to keep Tyler and Gretchen safe, not to mention her uncle. None of them deserved a ruined life simply because she couldn't control hers.

"In everythin' there's risk. Ask yourself this: is the risk of scandal to you greater than it is to this man—Jackson?"

Her gasp echoed in the sudden silence. "How did you know?"

"I still have that instinct. I can add up an equation with the best of 'em. And I had enough hints from you and his words to string it together." His smile didn't light his eyes. "If enough of the public knows what happened to you and the other women from that so-called school, they'll have no choice except to be upset and will take up your plight for justice. Jackson will have to bow out gracefully or risk complete humiliation and possible incarceration. Besides, the *Sentinel* might as well go down fighting."

"He told me he has the ear of various politicians and police officials. Prison time won't be an option." She frowned and kept tight control on the frustrated tears crowding her throat. "It's a damnable mess I've landed in, Uncle."

"Oh, I won't deny that. You never did do things by half." His eyes twinkled. "However, you can make things right, and in the process clear your conscience and free your soul." He rocked to his feet and held out an arm. "Come here, girl. You look like you'll fall down in a gentle breeze."

Julia had no sooner stood than she crumpled, saved from hitting the floor by her uncle's protective embrace. "I have no idea what I should do." The coat of her uncle's evening suit muffled her words, the chain of his pocket watch cool against her blouse.

"I think you already know. I raised you right enough to say it. Also know this," he set her away in order to look into her face, "I couldn't be more proud of you. I sometimes think you have more integrity in your little finger than I do in my whole body. Whatever you decide, I'll support. Together we'll endeavor to beat that bastard at his own game. It's time for action and to do what we should have years ago. What I should have done years ago."

The deep rumble of his voice infused her with courage. Julia nodded. Briefly, she related the nature of Jackson's threat and how she scared Tyler off with the contrived argument, how she let him think his misdeeds were what tore them apart. "I refuse to let Jackson hurt you, Gretchen or Tyler. I'd rather give into his demands than see that come to pass."

"Over my dead body. If he touches you again, I'll personally beat him with the fireplace poker." He gripped her shoulders with his big hands as he scowled down at her. "Don't you worry about me. I'll take care of myself. If I have to, I'll strong-arm my brother, play on his sense of civic duty and familial pride to help. Jackson might know powerful people, but your daddy does too."

Emotionally drained, Julia giggled as she thought of it. The image of the two brothers bickering dispelled some of the tension in her body. "I wish you luck. You'll need an incentive that directly benefits Father."

"Never mind the how." Uncle George pulled her in for a tight hug before releasing her. "One more request. For the love of heaven, forgive Tyler. Give that poor boy a chance. He's had a hard enough time without you addin' your female angst to the mix."

She wiped at the tears on her cheeks. "Why are you so anxious for this match?"

"I want you to be happy. If this man makes you feel special and cherished, don't discount him so quickly. He may surprise you after all."

"I'll bear that in mind." She crossed the room, pausing at the doorway. "I'll also consider your article request." A hard swallow banished the last of the tears. "I love you, Uncle George. You've stuck by me through everything. I cannot express how much that means."

A red flush sprang over his face. "Aw, get on with you now, or you'll make an old man cry. Just promise me a dance at your weddin'."

"Don't rush to put that in print without facts." She left the room with a smile tugging at her lips. By the time she'd climbed the stairs and took refuge behind her closed bedroom door, exhaustion had taken hold, prompting her to fall onto her bed, fully dressed.

All her decisions would keep until tomorrow.

Chapter Eighteen

Tyler lifted the half-empty bottle of Kentucky's finest bourbon to his lips and took a deep swallow. Long past the witching hour, he'd returned home an hour ago, after wandering the streets and visiting various pubs and saloons since leaving the party—and Julia. Now, with dawn not far off, he felt anything but sleepy. Fortified with liquor, occasionally chased with cold cuts and baked goods his housekeeper had left, he'd planted his rear in a wingback chair and stared at the Oriental privacy screen that partially hid the bathtub in the parlor.

"You know, Victor, I do believe Julia left me because of that damn tub." He gestured at it with his bottle. The deep amber liquid sloshed inside. "She may have seemed interested in it before, but I can sense the truth."

"You're an ass and well on your way to being drunk." Victor leaned across the side table and yanked the bottle from Tyler's hand. "She left because you couldn't keep your dick in your pants, and then you tried to justify the crime with a mountain of guilt. What the hell else was she supposed to do?" He set the bottle on the floor beside his chair, out of reach.

Tyler narrowed his eyes. His vision briefly blurred. "I'm not drunk. Won't be until I finish that entire bottle." He ran a shaking hand along his stubble-covered jaw. "Learned how to hold my liquor from you in the service, remember?"

"I taught you more valuable skills, too. All of which you seem to have conveniently forgotten in this latest wallow of self-pity."

Tyler shook his head. If he kept a constant supply of liquor in his system, it would keep his heart numb. "Can you blame me?" Jack didn't give him the bottle. He watched his pal through half-narrowed eyes. Victor had kept him company since he'd come home earlier in the evening, fumbling with his key and telling the door he wasn't good enough for the likes of Julia Spencer. He hadn't lectured during the following hours where Tyler had begun to hate himself, his bad luck and his life. Mostly, his friend relieved him of bottles or anything he deemed dangerous and listened. "All my life I've worked my ass off just to survive. Look where it's gotten me."

"Exactly where you deserve, in the dregs stinking of liquor and reaping what you've sowed. You're a thief and a liar, Tyler. What do you want me to say?"

"Empathy would be a nice start."

"So would throwing your ass on the first train out of town." Victor stood, clasped his hands behind his back as he paced the length of the small room. "But I won't. Do I think you've been justified in running countless cons? It's a fine line. Should I feel sorry for you because you might have gotten Anna pregnant then went and broke Julia's heart? I think not." He stopped short and pinned Tyler with a dark glance. "You lay with the down-trodden widow. This is your own mess."

"Obviously." When his friend didn't look away, Tyler stood. "It happened a few months ago. I wasn't thinking. It hasn't happened since, and I rather doubt it would have happened at all had I not been slightly drunk."

Annoyance flickered over Victor's features. "There is a chance the child could very well be yours."

"Yes." A sharp shaft of guilt lanced through Tyler's chest. "Unfortunately."

"You never did have a care for your future. Now you may not have the chance."

"Thanks for the sympathy. It must have cost you dearly to say those words." Bitterness coated his throat like two-day old coffee. He moved across the floor and stood by a window. The glow from a gas light softened the empty streets and cut through the darkness. "Regardless, I suppose I should do right by Anna and marry her."

"What of Julia? I suspect you've also bedded her in your mad rush to antagonize every woman in this city." Victor crossed his arms over his chest. "What of your responsibility to *her*?"

Julia. Her name caused his heart to seize. "I have no other option except to do as she asked and let her go." Despite his best intentions to ignore it, the dull ache throbbed through his chest.

"Is that what you want?"

Was it? He thought over their time together, the flirtations, the intimate moments, the vulnerable sides they'd both shared. Never had he formed such a connection with a woman. The prospect of attaching himself to a different one who had no feelings for him at all, with whom he felt nothing but guilt, turned his blood cold. "Does it matter?" he finally asked. "I've made a mockery of my own life and am trapped by it. I'm surprised she didn't set me loose before now."

"That's how this whole drama will end? You're giving up? After all the sacrifices, never mind the cost to your friends, you've decided that's it?" Victor strode across the room and shoved Tyler into the wall. "You listen to me, soldier."

"Ease off." Tyler pushed back. Victor was stronger. "We're not in the military anymore and you're not my commanding officer."

"That may be so, but nothing's changed except the uniform." He shook Tyler's shoulders. "As much as I felt bad for Anna when Joshua died, I'm of a different opinion now. She's seen how she can manipulate you from that guilt, has used it as a weapon all these years. You've given her the ammunition by offering her the cash payments."

"What else was I supposed to do?"

"Let her muddle through. People die in wartime. You can't claim a personal responsibility to every one of them. It wasn't your fault. Besides, I'm certain she's receiving some sort of benefits from the government or other agencies for being a war widow. She's not exactly as destitute as she's claimed."

Tyler stared at his best friend, taken aback by the livid anger and pity reflected in his eyes. *How could I have been so stupid?* "Oh, God." Thinking back over that horrible scene, he realized the truth in Victor's words. More men than Joshua had perished that day, and he'd felt nothing except a brief, momentary sadness. It hadn't occurred to him that Anna also had another avenue of funding. "I never saw it until now."

"None so blind, eh Tyler?" A tiny amount of wry humor clung to Victor's question. "Did you tell her the payments would stop?"

"As a matter of fact, yes, just before I met Julia at the City Market." He pried Victor's hands from his lapels. "Anna said she'd be on the streets and mentioned the pregnancy to Julia at that time. That was after I told her Julia and I were courting."

"It's a wonder you survived the Cuban conflict." Victor shoved his hands through his hair. "Of course, your mind wasn't consumed by a woman at the time."

"Is that an apology?" Tyler cocked an eyebrow. Victor lived life the way he saw fit. When he'd commanded their unit in Cuba, every man had to follow his orders to the letter.

"Hell, no. You, my friend, are a mess. The only way to fix this is to beg Julia's forgiveness. Under her management, you'll stay out of trouble and I won't have to worry about keeping an eye on you. Believe it or not, I do have aspirations above and beyond playing nanny."

"No one asked you to." He glowered. "Although, if it weren't for you, I'd probably be in prison."

"You're right. Now, about winning back Julia's regard?"

"Easier said than done. The woman is adamant." Tyler turned to the window. He stared at his reflection in the darkened glass—haggard, unkempt, hair wild. His evening suit was wrinkled and hung at awkward angles on his frame. "In retrospect, I could have made better choices had I known winning Julia was at stake. I suppose the punishment of losing her is fitting."

"That's pathetic, even for you."

"I didn't think you'd understand." Tyler spun around and waited for the room to stop wobbling before he continued. "You've always been above reproach. You never make mistakes. Your clothes are always pressed, your days strictly regimented. Hell, I'll bet the chances of you finding yourself in a female's bed are slimmer than the odds of women getting the vote this year."

"My romantic life isn't up for discussion. I'm perfectly content on my own." Victor's expression remained closed. "You're addicted to your past, Tyler. You enjoy clinging to your mistakes, all the ills that have befallen you. They're cozy, familiar and grow into excuses as to why you're unable to have a future, live your dreams. It's time to stop. Be a man and take responsibility for once. Life goes to shit sometimes. Walk through it and leave it behind."

"I'm doing that by asking Anna to marry me."

"Damnation, you're a bigger idiot than I'd thought." Victor took up pacing once more. "Anna is using you. She's running a con on you in the form of your guilt. In fact, I'll wager one hundred dollars she's not with child."

Tyler reeled as if he'd been struck. He made a jagged path across the floor then collapsed into the chair he'd vacated earlier. "Can a woman do such a thing?"

"I'm afraid so." A warning flashed in Victor's eyes. "It's been my experience women will do anything in order to manipulate a man."

"That's a risky scam. Time, of course, will prove her wrong if she's lying."

"Any manner of excuses can be manufactured in the meantime, and you'll be caught in a marriage you'll hate more with each growing day."

"What should I do?" Despite the weighty subject matter, a swath of excitement slipped through Tyler's gut. "Openly accuse her?"

"No. Simply advise her of your interest in the coming birth. In your fondness for impending fatherhood, you'd like to be certain she's in the best health possible. Offer to pay for her visit to a good doctor in town. If she is pregnant, she'll be grateful for the attention. If she isn't, she'll invent a reason to avoid it. She's already experienced in pregnancy. It won't be hard to lie."

"And then?"

Victor's grin reminded him of the moments when they'd run a military operation. "Go in for the kill and confront her about it. Directly asked, a con who has no confidence in the game or herself will break. Anna won't bother you again."

For the first time since that moment in the Market, Tyler relaxed. "Excellent idea. Once I have confirmation, I intend to go to Julia's home and demand she speak with me. Petition her uncle if I have to. Hell, I'll let her destroy my business in the paper as well as cut my reputation to shreds if it means she'll have me."

"One step at a time. The first thing you need is to sleep off the alcohol. No woman in her right mind would want you in this shape."

Tyler rocked to his feet, swaying slightly. "One question first." He eyed the bourbon bottle then focused his gaze on Victor. "I thought you didn't trust Julia? The last time you were in her company, it ended badly."

"I've changed my mind." No embarrassment or discomfort showed in his expression.

"How so?"

"I figure if she's not running a scam on you, and after everything she's been through in her own life she still wants to be with you, she can't be that bad."

"Except she tossed me aside last night." Tyler worked the buttons on his waistcoat with one hand. "Granted, there were tears involved, but the result was the same. She's a great actress that one."

Victor rubbed a hand along his jaw. "You have the brains of a cooked noodle, boy. Think! Your woman orchestrated the argument as a catalyst to remove you from a situation she assumes she has no control over. She wants to protect you, God knows why. I suspect she's being threatened."

Tyler snapped his fingers as another moment of clarity clicked into place. "That newspaper fellow! His name escapes me, but there's something odd about him."

"Exactly. Go sleep off the liquor. I'll see what I can dig up about our beady-eyed friend."

"You're a good man, Victor." Tyler stumbled over to his friend and clasped his shoulder. "I won't forget this."

"Good. Promise me you won't run anymore cons and we'll call it even."

"Done." As Tyler climbed the stairs, he grinned. In a matter of days, he'd walk into a new life with Julia—if he could convince her to have him. *Shouldn't be a problem. I've sold water to folks who can have it for free.* Selling Julia on a future with him would be child's play, but he'd need a plan.

Two days later, Julia walked into the *Sentinel* office, took a seat at behind Uncle George's desk and wrote her article longhand. A bottle of miracle tonic sat on the desktop as inspiration. She ignored the noise and activity from the bullpen as she crafted the new piece that had brewed in her mind ever since the talk with Uncle George. During the midday lull, her uncle brought her a cup of tea and a sandwich, but generally left her alone. He worked from Frank's desk. She nibbled at the offering, then returned to work while moving to the typewriter. She barely glanced up as Gerald and Frank returned to the office, fresh off their trip from Texas with stories of adventure and drama.

Her masterpiece held her full attention. She'd catch up with the guys later. Eventually, the journalists trickled out of the office and left quiet in their wake. Julia pecked at the keys, steadily filling page upon page with lines of words.

"Julia, darlin', it's nearly dinner time." Uncle George cleared his throat and rapped a knuckle on the desk. "I know you're workin' real hard, but I'd prefer it if you'd leave with me. Plenty of time to finish tomorrow."

She looked up. "Uncle, I appreciate your concern, but I'll be fine. I promise."

"You're certain?" His expression reflected deep doubt.

"Yes. I don't intend to stay long. A half hour at the most. I'll be home in time for dinner, or just slightly later. I promise not to linger." She nodded for added emphasis.

"I'd rather not leave you alone—"

"Uncle." She interrupted him with an exasperated breath. "I have two more pages to type, then I'll come home and proofread. After that, I'll let you read it. In the event there are changes, I want the opportunity to work on them first thing tomorrow. Besides, I think Mr. Hayes is out. I haven't seen or heard him for as long as I've been in the office."

"I'm trustin' you, girl." His eyes softened and shimmered with familial affection. "I assume you took my advice to heart?" He gestured at the typewriter with his chin.

"Absolutely." Julia grinned and tapped a key with a fingernail. "I realized this piece isn't fully about the miracle tonic, though the water played a part. It's more of a cautionary tale for all women. It's my hope the story will do good and heal others above and beyond me."

"Glad to hear it." Uncle George's gaze drifted to Jackson's office before focusing on her. "Will you, ah, call Jackson to task in the article?"

"Of course. It'll be the public's responsibility once this goes to print. I hope justice will follow." She leaned back on the wooden chair. "In a way, writing this article has been the best catharsis."

"I can imagine." Uncle George came around the desk and squeezed her shoulder. "It'll be good to see you smile again."

"Thanks. It feels as if all that drama happened a lifetime ago. Maybe it did. I'm no longer that woman." Unbidden, her mind jumped to Tyler. Tendrils of sadness twined around her heart. A part of her expected to see him burst with jaunty confidence into the newspaper office, while another part of her hoped he never came around again. She had no doubts Jackson would carry out his threats. "I'm anxious to find out what else I'm capable of."

"Whatever it is, you'll raise eyebrows and captivate the city. But just in case, I'll close the office door."

"Thank you." Once he left, closing the door as promised, Julia turned back to her typewriter. "Work your magic," she said to the keys.

Another thirty minutes slid by before she finished and pulled the last slip of onionskin from the machine. Evening's shadows fell heavy through the room. She'd forgotten to light a lamp in her fervor to finish. No matter. As she gathered the ten pages into a neat pile, she read over the opening paragraphs to herself.

"To all my sisters of Indianapolis, this tale is for you; to their male counterparts or family members, I implore you to read this as well if only to draw them close and protect them, so you'll understand the world can be a horrible, ugly place if you lose your perspective. I've chosen to share this story with you in the hopes you will never find yourselves in the same place.

"My intent was to write about a certain apothecary on Washington Street and its owner Mr. Browning, and to bring attention to what I believed was a crime, but I've since changed my mind. Yes, there's danger in becoming involved with a con artist, but only because I might have been a victim of the master criminal—myself. Compared to Mr. Browning's deeds, what I hid from the world is larger and more damning in scale. I took the advice from the Good Book and decided to remove the plank in my own eye before pointing out the splinter in someone else's."

Julia chuckled over the witty insertion.

"However, over the course of my life's journey, I've come to realize redemption starts from within, and it's oftentimes sent on hidden angel's wings as my revelation was. For that, I wish to personally, and quite humbly, thank the man responsible, Mr. Browning himself. If he hadn't shared his heart and allowed me to open mine, I shudder to guess where I'd be today. My story follows. I urge you to answer this tale and the blatant threats you see in print with honesty and the search for justice."

She hadn't realized she'd finished by reading the last paragraph aloud, but upon hearing the words echo shallowly in the room, she smiled. If luck was with her, Uncle George would sign off on the piece without too many revisions. He'd personally hand it to the printer at the last second, by-passing Jackson altogether and maintaining the element of surprise.

When Uncle George's office door flew open and slammed against the wall, Julia gasped. Jackson stood in the frame. She'd thought he was out… She quickly folded her pages and jammed them beneath the typewriter. "Your time of reckoning has come, woman."

Fear trickled down her spine as her gaze locked with his across the small space. Livid rage purpled his face. His eyes flashed hatred. His heels rapped smartly on the hardwood as he advanced toward her. "My answer hasn't changed." She stood, trying to portray an image of calm and not call attention to the pages she'd hidden. God, had he seen her try to stow them away?

"That's unfortunate, Miss Spencer. Almost as sad as your uncle asking vague questions of me."

"If he knows you're involved, it's probably because you've gotten sloppy, Mr. Hayes. Not to mention you've made vulgar insinuations to him about me. My uncle is a smart man. He'll puzzle it together without my involvement."

"How adept you've become at falsehoods. There has also been an unknown gentleman tailing me for the past few days. I have it on good authority he's an acquaintance of your beau. It's only natural to assume you mentioned me to the apothecary even after I explicitly told you not to at the party the other night."

"I didn't." She revisited her conversation with Tyler, assured she'd not breathed a word to him. "I broke our relationship. He knows nothing. Leave him alone."

"Not unless you agree to my terms."

Julia swept her gaze to the door. He stood between her and the only escape route. "Go to hell." Maybe if she had the element of surprise?

Jackson stopped in front of the desk with one hand curled into a fist. "You're aware of the ramifications of this choice?"

"I am." Her heartbeat slammed through her veins. She swore she heard it echo in the gloom. "My body is my own. Never again will I allow it to be abused." Belatedly, she realized she should have gone home with her uncle. Would she forever put herself into trouble in the quest to write?

"You've grown a backbone." He shrugged. "No matter. The more spirit you have, the harder I'll break you. It'll be much more fun than years ago."

"Do you want to know what I think, Mr. Hayes?" Julia edged around the desk though he was still between her and the door. "I think you're too much of a coward to cause a scandal. Your career, as well as your reputation, depends on you playing nice while in society's eyes."

"Correct, but what I have planned for you will never reach society's ears."

She stifled a shiver of revulsion. Never again would his hands know her body. "In that you are very wrong. Your deeds are close to bursting onto the public eye."

"Ah, now you threaten *me*? Few have done so and lived to tell the story. How do you think I gained this position?" He moved slowly, as if he stalked her like a jungle cat, rounding the first corner of the desk as she

Sandra Sookoo

scuttled around the other. "Try again. Your argument only whets my appetite."

Julia's stomach tightened. She went the opposite direction, matching his pace. "You may think I'll capitulate, but that'll be your misstep. I've written an article for the paper implicating you in every crime you've committed against me and the young women from Madame's school. Unfortunately, those are the only transgressions I have proof of. I'm sure a man of your ilk has many more."

"You can depend on it. As for this so-called article, let me remind you I'm editor-in-chief. If I don't want it printed, it won't be. End of discussion. Plus, once this rag is sold, you'll never work in the industry again. I'll guarantee it." He rounded another corner as Julia retreated. "Last chance, Miss Spencer. My bed or three lives destroyed. That's a hefty weight to carry within your soul."

"I've considered it, and while at one time I would have gladly exchanged my body to keep my friends and family safe from your vile tongue, I'm not that woman anymore." Julia paused, determined to stand her ground and face him. "Today, I have much better methods of keeping you at bay."

"I'm very sorry to hear that."

That brought her up short. "How so? I doubt you've experienced a change of heart."

"Of course not." Jackson moved so quickly she wasn't prepared for defense. He grabbed for her. Julia sprang away with a few ripped buttons on her blouse. "Since you refuse to come willingly, I'm forced to provide incentive."

No sooner had she fought off Jackson's next strike than he delivered a hard slap to her right cheek that had her seeing stars. She sagged against the desk, her skin hot. As she attempted to move away, he lunged. When he fisted a hand in her hair, her head whipped back. Searing pain screamed along her scalp. She struggled, but that only worked his fingers deeper into the tresses. "Let me go." An attempt to kick him between his legs failed. He was wise to her tricks.

"I think not. You owe me and know too much besides." His face loomed close to hers, his breath stank of onions. She sank to her knees. "Women like you don't deserve rewards." Flecks of spittle clung to his lips. "If you think you'll ever see your name as a featured columnist, you're sadly mistaken. You're a whore, Miss Spencer." The growl in his voice was the stuff of nightmares. "Never will you be anything else."

"Only in your eyes, but never to the people who matter most." Tyler's face flashed across her mind, seconds before Jackson slammed her head into the edge of the desk. Black spots floated in her vision and agony exploded at her left temple. "Bastard." She scrabbled for purchase, to remain upright, but her limbs wouldn't obey her command.

"Why change now when the title fits?" He wrapped an arm around her waist and hauled her against him, supporting her weight, his fingers digging into her side. "My carriage is waiting. Now that you're in a more docile frame of mind, it's time to adjourn to a more private location to conclude our business."

Hot saliva filled Julia's mouth as he dragged her out of Uncle George's office, through the bullpen and into the reception area. Pain pounded her head in overwhelming waves that hinted at nausea. "No." She pushed at Jackson's chest, attempted to pry his arm from her person, but her actions were feeble, slow at best. Simple movement of any sort caused her vision to swim and darken.

"I see you need a different sort of motivation." He pushed open the outer door and yanked her onto the street. Pedestrian traffic flowed around them. Jackson reached into his jacket. "If you think I won't use this in full view of these people, you don't know me that well."

He shoved something cold and metallic beneath her left breast. She felt its bite through her clothing. Fear kept her paralyzed. "A pistol?"

"Indeed." He edged them to a closed, black carriage that waited at the curb. "All these people will know is you're a desperate woman, down and out, not able to make a living due to your unfortunate past. You turned to pick-pocketing. The story I'll spin will have the pistol belonging to you, which you turned on me after I refused to hand over my money. I wrestled it from you and it went off by accident, sadly killing you. But perhaps it was for the best as it put you out of your misery."

The last of Julia's strength gave out. Her knees wobbled and she slid toward the ground. Why did she ever think she could handle Jackson by herself?

"I thought you'd come around to my viewpoint." He hauled her up, keeping the nose of the pistol in her ribs. When he nodded, the carriage driver opened the door. "After you, my dear."

Chapter Nineteen

A battery of blows at the front door roused Tyler from his doze on the parlor sofa. "Who the hell wants me at—" He glanced at a brass clock on the fireplace mantle. "Nine o'clock?" He rubbed the gritty sleep from his eyes and stumbled into the entry where the knocks had turned urgent and obnoxious. "Enough." He jerked open the door. Victor stood on the stoop, his blond hair wild, his face haggard and creased with alarm. "What?" Instantly alert, Tyler stood aside and let his friend pass. "You have that look."

"What look?" Victor paced the short length of the entryway as if he were a caged animal.

"The one you used to get right before our unit went into battle." Tyler gently closed the door. "Tell me."

"Miss Spencer may be in dire trouble." Victor stopped his restless energy to pin Tyler with a pained expression. "I had a late meeting with another member of the banking community this evening. As I walked toward the cab stand, I passed the *Sentinel's* office."

"And?" The hair on his nape prickled.

"She got into a carriage, or was helped into one, by a gentleman."

"Maybe it was her uncle or one of the other reporters, or a new beau she had a dinner appointment with?" He shrugged in the hopes he'd portrayed a nonchalant attitude.

Victor's eyes narrowed. "Don't be an idiot. Neither was dressed in evening clothes. If you can't see she's in love—well, never mind. The whole event seemed rushed. Julia moved too stiffly to be in a beau's company."

"And it took you hours to come over here to tell me? Obviously, you're not that concerned or else you—"

"Damn it, Tyler, do you care for her or not?" Victor grabbed him by the collar and hauled him into the parlor. "Listen to me. Of course I didn't sit around before telling you. I have more brains than that."

The news must be bad if Victor was this upset. Tyler ran a hand through his hair. "Tell me."

"After that incident, I took note of their general direction, but lost the carriage in the crowd. I stewed on the problem." He crossed his arms over his chest. "Something about it didn't ring true, so I did what any good solider would. I visited her home."

"Why didn't you ask me to accompany you?" A slow burn of anger built in his chest. If Julia was in peril, he should have been notified.

"God, lose the high-horse mentality and think logically. It would have taken an hour to get across town. I wanted to follow my hunch. As it was, I wasted precious minutes due to a carriage accident that blocked one of the main thoroughfares. By the time traffic was allowed by, it was well after seven."

"What did you find out?" He grabbed his vest from the back of the chair where he'd slung it prior to dozing.

"Both her uncle and the sour-faced housekeeper confirmed Miss Spencer never returned home for dinner. The uncle was visibly upset, said he should have stayed with her, but assumed she would walk through the door any moment. The housekeeper seemed almost pleased and told me some habits must be too hard to break."

"That woman needs her employment terminated." Tyler shoved his arms into the garment and buttoned it. "What happened next?"

"The uncle had an enlightened moment. He cursed everyone up one side and down the other, then stormed into a back section of the house. The housekeeper asked me to leave, so I did."

"Damnation, Victor. She could be anywhere by now, but I can tell you this, Julia did not leave of her own accord." Tyler donned his suit jacket and strode past his friend. "We have no time to spare. We'll find her friend, that annoying woman with the dog, what was her name? Surely she'll know where—"

"Gretchen, and don't you think Miss Spencer's uncle has already gone through the conventional routes?" Victor joined him in the entryway just as Tyler wrenched open the door. "You and I will return to the newspaper office, look for clues to her whereabouts."

"I'll kill whoever has her." Tyler started when Victor dropped a hand on his shoulder. "In recent days, there's been no excuse for my behavior. You're always there to sweep up the pieces of my broken life."

"Not for long." Victor nodded. "In a matter of days, I plan to hand off that responsibility to Miss Spencer. After that, I'm taking a holiday." His expression softened. "We'll find her alive and unharmed. Trust me."

Tyler shot out of the house into the night. Though he hoped with every fiber of his being Victor's reassurances would be proved correct, he'd seen more than his fair share of humanity than to believe it himself.

"What the hell do you boys hope to find here?" The raw voice of Julia's uncle scraped across Tyler's ears as he and Victor burst into the *Sentinel's* office.

"Sir, if you don't mind, the more help you have in finding Julia, the better off we'll all be." Tyler met the older man's gaze. His chest tightened at the pain there.

"We'll find her. Can you tell me where she works while she's here?"

"Certainly." He heaved his bulk off a chair and strode over the floor, weaving between a few desks then entered a private office. "She uses my desk and my typewriter. I'd thought she'd be safe. She sounded so confident she could take care of herself."

Tyler nodded. What else should he say to a man who was obviously frantic to locate his niece? "I'm Tyler Browning, by the way. We've met a few times yet never had a chance to formally chat." He sat in the chair while Victor wandered about the room.

Julia's personality poked through some of the items that no doubt belonged to George. Scattered with crumpled bits of paper, pencils and copies of various newspapers from around town, it gave off an air of determination and independence. A few ink stains and smudges decorated the edges, but nothing provided a clue to her whereabouts. Not even the bottle of his miracle tonic that rested near the typewriter. Why had she'd kept it?

"I'm well aware of who you are. Julia has been in quite the tither since meetin' you." A Southern drawl clung to the baritone voice, most likely brought to the forefront from stress.

"Is that a good or bad thing?" Tyler pulled open a shallow drawer beneath the desktop. A few papers rested within, along with a handful of hairpins, more pencils, pencil shavings and a pearl button. He closed the drawer with a snap then opened a square-shaped drawer at one side. The navy-blue straw hat he'd first seen Julia wear laid in the deep compartment.

"For Julia? I hope it's good." He extended a large hand. "George Spencer. If you find my girl, I'd be glad to welcome you into our family."

Tyler shook the proffered appendage. "I appreciate the trust, sir." For Mr. Spencer's sake, he vowed to locate her. No one should have to suffer the loss of a loved one.

"You haven't won it yet." He stepped away, clearing his throat, his eyes suspiciously moist. "I've already checked with Julia's friends and any contacts she's had in the last month. None have seen her recently, though I have a feelin' I know who she's with."

"What about men from the paper?" Victor perched on one corner of the desk. "Was she working closely with any of the journalists?"

"Ah, no. She and the boys have creative differences most of the time." George glanced out of the office. "When I left before dinner, Julia assured me she was the only one here."

"What's this?" Victor hopped off the desk, leaned closed then pulled a wad of papers from beneath the typewriter. Seconds later, he scanned the top sheet. "You should read this." He handed over the sheaf of onionskin. "Maybe she hid it in haste"

Tyler smoothed out the papers. "It appears to be a rough copy of an article." Some words were underlined with pencil, some struck through by typewriter keys. On other pages, handwritten notes occupied the margins.

"She was workin' on that when I left." George came over and peered at the pages. "She was all-fire excited about it, said she hoped it would set a few things right."

As Tyler read through the words, his sense of urgency grew. On occasion, his name jumped out of the other words. In those passages, she'd either praised him or called him to task for the miracle tonic con, but by the end, tucked into her heartbreaking tale, Julia had forgiven him. She'd even mentioned the need to keep him and others safe from the threats of one man—Jackson Hayes.

All roads came back to that man. "Where is Mr. Hayes right now?"

George shrugged. "I have no idea. His door was closed when I left. I assumed he was either out or buried with work. He'd have no need to come out as there is a small water closet attached." Again, the older man's gaze jogged to the office, where the door hung unequivocally open. "I'm an ass and failed Julia. Again. I should have stayed with her or demanded she leave with me, but you know how stubborn she can be. You think that bastard took her?"

He did know, which is why they needed to find her quickly. He heard Victor curse softly under his breath. "What?" Tyler swiveled to face his friend.

"There's a drop of blood on the floor here." Victor stooped at the front of the desk. "And another not far off. Whatever happened, I'm convinced Miss Spencer didn't go willingly."

Tyler shot to his feet. "Do you think she'll return to us alive?" He hated to ask, but they needed to know every eventuality.

"Who can say?" Victor stood. "Knowing Miss Spencer, she probably fought like a cornered tiger, which would have made her attacker angry, and since both she and this Mr. Hayes are no longer here, logic tells us they're together." He moved closer to George. "Mr. Spencer, perhaps now would be a good time to divulge any other information you might have regarding your absent editor-in-chief. I followed him extensively yet there is much information missing."

While the other men conversed in low voices, Tyler fought down a wave of anger so intense he wanted to punch a wall. He hated feeling helpless. Knowing that man had threatened her, but she hadn't asked for assistance or protection, sent his stomach into knots. He should have rejected Julia's decision in that garden, should have come around every day, followed her and badgered her until she let him back into her life. He listened with half-hearted attention. What was happening with Julia every moment they delayed here? Where the hell was she?

Not having an answer, he shuffled through Julia's pages. A passage swam before his eyes, the implications of the words cutting through him with the force of a knife. He read it aloud.

"It wasn't until I saw Mr. Hayes at an event we both attended that my suspicions regarding him were confirmed. Had I harbored any doubts, the white rose with the blood-red center made my mind clear. He was the one who'd violated me so harshly years ago. He's the one I fear most now."

As Tyler looked at the other two men, he remembered the times he'd seen such a flower—once on the path at the party when Julia broke their relationship, and once at the dilapidated school in the hallway. *Damnation. Jackson Hayes has some balls.* He folded the papers. "I know where they are."

Both George and Victor turned to regard him.

Tyler nodded. "The school where all Julia's troubles started is still standing, though it's in disrepair. That's where Mr. Hayes has taken her. We need to hurry. If the blood is any indication, a fight was certain. If she was rendered unconscious after entering the carriage, I doubt she'd remain in that state for long."

Victor frowned. "How can you be sure?"

"Just trust me. Too strong willed to give over that much control." He shoved the papers into George's hands. "When's the next time the paper goes to print?"

"Mornin' after next." The man battled with shock and fear. "Why?"

"Is there any way you can put out a special edition tomorrow morning? Make sure you put this memoir in it. If that jackass Hayes gets out of this situation without me killing him, I want the assurance the public will get the job finished."

"Done. I'll use the copy from the next edition and get right to work on it. We'll simply skip a day." Victory lit George's eyes. "Go rescue my girl, Mr. Brownin'. I'm countin' on you."

Tyler returned to the desk and retrieved the bottle of miracle tonic. "Come on, Victor. I think I've got one more con in me." He hoped to be convincing enough to save the most important life—hers.

Julia's head raged with pain. She tried to turn over in the hopes a more pleasant position would alleviate the agony, but her body wouldn't obey and her arms felt odd as if they were suspended above her head. She cracked open first one eye then the other and moaned at the situation that greeted her. An oil lantern burned low on a grit-covered floor, in a room she knew only too well—her old lodgings at the abandoned school. The door, with its covering of peeling paint, gaped half-closed, a maw of darkness beyond.

Her heart sank. As she attempted to move off the dusty, stained mattress, pressure on her wrists prevented that movement, tied as they were to the rusting iron bedframe. By the flickering light and in the shifting shadows, she ascertained she was alone for the moment and unable to tell how long she'd been imprisoned. Her skin crawled as a wave of fear crept over her. What did he plan? What had he already done?

She raised her head and ignored the lingering pain. For the moment her clothing seemed to be in place. Relief filled her chest and she sagged into the nasty mattress once more. Jackson must have wanted her alert when he began his violation. Julia fought a wave of nausea. She recalled entering the carriage with him earlier, remembered the desperate bid for freedom as the conveyance had slowed to take a street corner. After that, there was only darkness and the scent of stale cigar smoke and onions. The back of her skull throbbed. He must have hit her with his pistol. No wonder she'd blacked out. Worry for her health overtook the fear. Was she even now bleeding, in need of medical care? Worse yet, did he plan to kill her once he'd finished?

Not while I have breath left in my body.

Julia twisted her wrists. The stiff fibers from a frayed rope bit into her skin. She cast her gaze around the room, but nothing came to mind that she could use to free herself. Acting on the sense of urgency flooding her body, she ran her fingertips along the iron frame. Rust and chipped paint flakes poked her, yet the rod securing the rope loop had a weakness. A connection point with another portion of the frame held a jagged crack. She craned her neck in the attempt to look at it better. Yes, if she had enough time and luck, repetitive sawing should cut through the rope.

The door swung inward. Jackson stood on the threshold, a thunderous frown on his face, his dark eyes glittering in the poor light. He entered the room and laid a scuffed, dusty doctor's bag on the top of a bureau. "So glad you woke. I want you cognizant for the night's activities." With deliberate movements, he spread a handkerchief beside the bag. After opening the satchel, he removed various items. Lamp light winked off the wickedly sharp metal implements.

266

"What are those for?" How had he come into possession of medical equipment? Probably she didn't want to know. He was an unscrupulous bastard. Cold sweat broke out on her forehead as her imagination ran away.

"Patience." He shrugged out of his jacket then tossed the garment over the back of the lone wooden chair. Eddies of dust swirled into the air. "I'll admit it took a considerable amount of willpower on my part not to take you in your unconscious state."

"Be careful or else one might think you have morals." Julia moved her wrists until the rope binding them to the framework landed at the jagged crack. "If finding pleasure was your goal, you could have done it and been well away from here without anyone the wiser." She had to keep him engaged in conversation.

"Oh, that's only one part of it." He undid the buttons of his waistcoat then flung it away. The butt of his pistol gleamed from his waistband. "If all goes well, I'll make a lasting impression on you, one that'll prevent you from enjoying relations with any other man. I must warn you. There will be considerable pain on your part when I mark your body after I have my enjoyment."

Disgust clamored through her stomach with the fear, yet she relaxed slightly, still covertly working the rope. "Ah, then you mean to keep me alive."

A cruel grin slid over his face, the shadows twisting his features into a grotesque mask. "That largely depends on how you perform for me. Too much of a struggle and a bullet will find its way into your heart. Too little and I'll be certain the wound will ensure a slow, lingering death. Of course, all of this will occur after you experience the bite of the scalpel." He met her gaze. "Don't look so alarmed, my dear. How often does a person have the opportunity to choose the outcome or length of their life?"

Tears crowded her throat, enhancing the hysterical thump of her heart. "What is wrong with you?" She'd thought he was terrible for his threats, kidnapping and attempted rape, but the rest of his plan left her gasping in outrage. "You're mentally disturbed. Is mutilating living, breathing people a new hobby, or have you done it all along?"

Jackson took his pistol in hand, laid it on the bed. His trousers hit the floor. He stepped out of them and spent time folding the pants and draping them over the chair back. "I've left my mark on a few women who've impressed me over the years." Clad in his shirt sleeves and drawers, he grabbed the gun and approached the bed then perched on the edge. The mattress sagged beneath his weight. "You've irritated me from the first."

"How?" As discreetly as she could, she worked the rope over the sharp edge of the metal. Her previous efforts had frayed the fibers but there was much work still to go.

"You're too outspoken and full of confidence. Women like you are trouble and will corrode the structure of our society, asking for privileges like the vote, better pay, cleaner working conditions."

"As it should be. The world is changing. Women won't be repressed for long."

"Perhaps." His shoes dropped to the floor with dual thuds. He kept the pistol beside him. "You're nothing better than a prostitute. Imagine my surprise when I saw you working in a highly-visible career with an interested beau."

"Why does any of this bother you? People change, mature, and learn about life along the journey." Julia continued to saw the rope. "None of it concerns you. Why not mediate the paper's sale and go away?"

"It does when you pretend nothing in your past happened." He fisted a hand in her skirt and yanked her lower body toward him. "No one forgets me. Now, I intend to make certain you never will."

"You can try, but you'll fail. My body is no longer yours to command." Julia kicked at him, pointing her feet to utilize the hard toe of her boots. She knew victory for a few seconds as she connected with his ribcage, but the feeling vanished as he fought back, ultimately stronger. When he shoved the nose of the pistol into her stomach, she went pliant.

"Smart girl." Jackson threw his body across her legs, immobilizing them, then he sat upon them, fumbling at her skirts with his hands. "I guess it'll be a quick death after all."

One of the cords in the rope snapped. Excitement streaked through her. Julia risked a quick glance at her binding. Two more remaining. Jackson's hands beneath her skirts focused her attention. Unable to use her arms or legs, she squirmed, desperate to keep him at bay for as long as possible. With a growl, he shoved the fabric. The bunched skirting blocked her view. His fingers were on her drawers, pulling, plucking at the thin cotton. Seconds later, the sound of ripping cloth met her ears then his vile hands were on her skin and the cold bite of his pistol pressed against her private parts. Terrified of what he'd do, she clamped her thighs together as she continued to saw at her bonds.

"Let her go." The command rang from the direction of the door.

Julia sucked in a surprised breath as first Tyler came into view, closely followed by Victor. "Help!"

Before the newcomers could advance halfway into the room, Jackson twisted, his pistol cocked and pointed at them. "That's far enough, boys. You move again and I'll shoot one of you. Doesn't matter who."

Victor put his hands in the air. "Settle down. We just want Miss Spencer."

"That's the problem. I'm not finished with her. Now, if you fellows know what's good for you—and her—you'll turn around and walk out of here."

"Not until you hand over that gun." Tyler took a few steps forward.

"Sorry." Jackson swung the pistol, this time pointing it at Julia's head. "I guess since you two don't listen well to instruction, I'll give you a different incentive."

Julia yanked at her bound wrists. Another cord gave way. "Tyler, Jackson is insane. He's a monster."

"Oh, I have a fair idea of what he's about." Tyler advanced another step. He put a hand into his jacket pocket. Seconds later he pulled out a slim bottle of tonic water. "Look here, Mr. Hayes. You're troubled, but I have something that can help."

"Spare me the rhetoric." Jackson dropped his arm but remained sitting on Julia's legs. "You're nothing more than a snake-oil salesman, and we both know it."

"Are you one hundred percent certain about that?" Tyler moved another step closer, holding the tonic aloft. In the dim light, it looked mysterious and thick as clear honey. "One sip of my miracle tonic and you'll feel the effects instantly. Ingest half a bottle and anything that's wrong will start to heal."

"Stop it! There's nothing wrong with me."

"There could be. Mental instability is never caught in time, and the medical profession doesn't understand it thoroughly. Why else are asylums crowded?" Tyler wiggled the bottle. "Just one sip. How will know you otherwise?"

"Annoying pup." Jackson scrambled off Julia's legs to stand on the floor. An erection tented his drawers. "You're too late. I have the advantage. Even if you or your friend takes me down, there will be enough time for me to get off one shot." He aimed the gun at her side. "Miss Spencer will meet her reward tonight."

Tyler paused. He exchanged an inscrutable glance with Victor, who stood a few paces to his left. "What's the plan?"

Victor shrugged. "Hard to know. The man is plain crazy."

"Should we both rush him like that one time in Cuba?"

"Worth a try I guess."

"Gentlemen, please. He'll shoot." Julia's breath came in shallow pants. Her head pounded in time to her rapid heartbeat. She silently implored Tyler to leave, but when he turned his head and met her gaze, nothing except grim determination lined his face. "Tyler, maybe it would be best if you go."

He shook his head. "I've long thought you needed a protector. This predicament drives home the legitimacy of that thought." When he took a step forward, Victorson swung the pistol around and trained it on Tyler, his back now fully toward her.

"Easy now, Mr. Hayes." Tyler tossed the bottle of tonic on the bed. It landed heavily between Julia's legs. "I'm letting you have that at no charge. I know once you taste it, you'll want more."

"Out, now!" Jackson gestured with the weapon.

"I'm on Washington Street, you know. Plenty more where that came from."

"Damn it, boy. I'm not messing around." The room echoed with the pistol's report. Jackson's arm jerked from the kick back.

Julia screamed, yanking down hard on her bonds. The rope gave but didn't break. A thin veil of smoke floated through the air. When it settled, Victor sat slumped on the floor, one hand pressed tight against the opposite shoulder. Thick, dark blood seeped between his fingers as the color slowly leeched from his face. A streak of blood decorated the wall behind him. He seemed as shocked as she felt.

"Take Victor to a doctor. He doesn't look good." *God, let him be all right.* Her wrists burned. Her arms ached from being tied above her head for so long. Because of her, Victor was injured, might possibly die. The cocking of Jackson's pistol rang in the silence. "For all that's holy, Tyler, please. He'll shoot again."

For the first time since he arrived on the scene, Tyler's expression reflected fear. "I won't leave you, Julia. I promised I'd look after you. I aim to follow through on that."

Jackson snickered. "Too little, too late. I suppose it'd be fitting for you to watch the last humiliation of your lover. No difference leaving one body compared to three."

Panic shot into Julia's bloodstream. She gave the rope a hard tug and it gave way. Euphoria flooded her. Finally, she had the ability to use both hands again. She pulled herself into a ball, keeping her movements slow so as not to give away her new freedom.

Tyler's eyes lit as he caught the change in her situation. "Mr. Hayes, men like you are too chicken-hearted to do much besides bully your way through the population." He edged forward a step, which forced Jackson back, nearly level with Julia's shoulders. "One of these days, someone will come along who won't take that sort of intimidation any longer. It'll almost be as if you'll be hit upside the head with that knowledge."

She glanced at Victor. He lifted one eyebrow and gave a subtle nod.

Jackson scoffed. "No one has bested me yet." He drew the pistol upward, training it at Tyler's heart. "Any last words of undying affection?"

Julia kneeled while grabbing the bottle of tonic water. The bed springs creaked. As Jackson pivoted to face her, she rose on her knees and brought the bottle down on his head with all the force she could summon.

Confusion and pain clouded his eyes. A stream of blood trickled through his pomaded hair and along his temple. He raised his pistol in a shaking hand. "Why are you so damn difficult?" Terrified that he'd fire, she stood on the mattress, and taking the bottle's neck in both hands, brought it down again on Jackson's head. This time the glass shattered. Water splattered to the floor seconds before the editor-in-chief dropped to his knees, then finally slumped into a prone position amidst the glass fragments.

She gaped at the unmoving man. "I guess that really is a miracle tonic. It stopped Jackson when nothing else would." As if she moved through cold molasses, Julia climbed off the bed. The torn remains of her drawers slipped down her legs and tangled around her ankles. She didn't care. Tyler was there and he put his arms went around her, supporting her as she sagged into his familiar body. "I'm so glad to see you." With a sigh, she surrendered to the pounding in her head and the fuzzy darkness in her vision.

Chapter Twenty

September 30th, 1900

Julia leaned back against the sloped side of the bathtub. A sigh of appreciation escaped her lips as the warm, rose-scented water enveloped her, the bubbles on the surface bobbing on the gently lapping water. She dragged her hands through the heavenly liquid. Her aches and pains faded away beneath the surface, all but forgotten as she relaxed. She'd adored the bathtub with the lion's feet the moment she'd seen it in Tyler's home all those days ago and had known then she'd somehow find a way into it.

And so she had, with help from Victor. He'd let her into Tyler's home where she then implored the housekeeper to heat countless pots of water to fill the tub. Once that had been accomplished, she'd informed the woman of her plan to pull a declaration from her charge and make him an honest man. The housekeeper had wished her good luck and with a big smile, left immediately following. Now all she needed was for Tyler to come home. She grinned as she rested her head on the lip of the tub. Victor had been nothing but lovely to her after the terrible events three days before. Maybe being shot had given him a different perspective and made him into a softer version of himself. She chuckled and bent her knees. Not likely. He was still in a fair amount of pain from the shoulder wound. The bullet had gone cleanly in and out, and Victor was under the influence of doctor-monitored morphine. Yet, his eagerness to help her win a meeting with Tyler had been genuine.

Perhaps he had his own reasons. Perhaps he humored her. Either way, she couldn't fault him. She only hoped he'd find someone or something that would chase away his demons.

Down the hall, keys rattled followed by the sound of the door opening then closing. A masculine groan wafted to her location. Papers shuffled. He sneezed.

Julia giggled. "Tyler, is that you? Won't you come into the parlor please?" Utter silence followed her request. She imagined his puzzled expression as he attempted to make sense of her presence in his home.

"There'd better be a damn good explanation..." His voice trailed off the moment he gained the parlor. "My God, you're naked. And in my parlor." He glanced about. "What did you do with the privacy screen?"

That's what he'd fixated on? "Very observant." She devoured him with her gaze. Brown tweed trousers, topped with a matching waistcoat over an ivory shirt, he was the epitome of his profession. Not having seen him for days reminded her of how much she'd come to anticipate their time together. "I temporarily moved it because I wanted you to see me thusly."

"Julia." He took a few steps toward her, his gaze sweeping over the bathtub the fire in the fireplace, the golden wash of the few candles illuminating the evening shadows before returning to her. "*Why* are you naked in my parlor? Who let you in?"

"You can thank Victor for that. He came by yesterday to check on me. I told him how I'd missed you and wanted to talk. Together we devised this plan."

"My *friend*, my *neighbor* Victor suggested you should bathe in my parlor?" Confusion ran rampant in Tyler's expression. He shoved a hand through his hair, leaving the curls in disarray. "When I called the day after your rescue, you said you wanted to be left in peace." He gripped the head of his cane hard.

"I did, but you took it out of context." She lifted a leg partially out of the water. Steam rose from the appendage. Thick suds clung to her skin before she put the limb back under the liquid warmth. Tyler stood, apparently transfixed in place, attempting to look anywhere but the tub or her. She smiled. Feminine power bolstered her confidence. "I was exhausted and in pain. I needed to understand my mental state and my feelings for you before we sat down to a conversation."

"Ah, and you are in my house now because?"

"I thought since our courtship has been rather unconventional, this most important meeting should be no less, and I want your full attention. I have one request."

He met her gaze, his twinkling with unidentified emotion. "That would be?" This time he couldn't keep his attention from wandering down the length of her body.

She shivered under his intimate scrutiny. "Don't look too long upon my face. The bruises and lacerations don't lend themselves well to aesthetic beauty." Her stomach pitched when she thought about the mess her face and head were in after Jackson's violent abuse. Even now she'd left her hair down since wearing pins hurt her scalp.

A strangled sound issued from Tyler's throat. He leaned his cane against the edge of the bathtub then lowered to his knees. "To be honest, I didn't notice your injuries until you mentioned them." He stroked a hand along one side of her face. "Your natural beauty makes a man forget any imperfections you think you have."

"Thank you for the compliment." She grasped his hand, regardless of her wet state.

"As if you weren't hinting for it." He waggled an eyebrow. "Let it be known, when I'm in your company, I'm more attracted to your inner radiance, the indefinable confidence and determination that defines you." He brought her hand to his lips and placed a gentle kiss on her fingers. "There were moments when I wasn't certain we would find you alive."

"Tyler…" Her heart lurched at the raw emotion in his voice.

"No." His Adam's apple bobbed with the force of his swallow. "The aftermath could have been so much worse."

"But it wasn't. You did a masterful job distracting Jackson from his murderous intent."

"If I hadn't seen what you were doing with the rope, I'd never have made the move. Most likely, Jackson would have gone on to shoot me, then done God-knows-what to you."

"Hush." Julia sat up, took his face between her hands and lightly kissed him. "Perhaps instead we should thank God none of those things occurred and we're both here, preparing to indulge in much more pleasant pursuits."

"Why, Miss Spencer, are you propositioning me?" He leaned over the tub as she relaxed against the back once more.

"Do you want me to?" Flutters tickled her belly. This was what she'd missed being separated from him. The teasing, rife with sexual tension, the companionship. More than that, she'd longed for him alone, seeing his smile, hearing his voice, matching wits with him.

Uncertainty shadowed his eyes as he held her gaze. "Do you want me, without reservation or shadows from your past?"

Would this always be an issue between them? "It's a fair question." She grabbed his hand and placed it on her breast. Her nipples pebbled at the brief touch and need lodged between her legs. "I cannot help my past, yet neither do I begrudge it. I've learned many lessons since that time, but the more important one is never doubt that I'm deserving of respect."

"Ah. I'm glad to hear it." He slid his fingers over her erect nipple before he dipped his hand lower to follow the contours of her body.

Her sound of exasperation ended in a low moan. "You'll torture me until I say it, won't you?"

"It would be nice to hear, especially after all we've been through." He moved his hand over her thigh and brushed the curls covering her sex.

"I want you, Tyler. Desire you." She opened her legs with the hope he'd alleviate the unrelenting throbbing. "I knew the moment I tore up my article about the miracle tonic I'd fallen in love with you. I couldn't, in good conscience, paint you in a derogatory light, even if your tonic is bunk."

"While I appreciate that, I had the chance to read the piece that actually went into the paper." He stroked his hand along first one thigh then the other, never once touching the spot where she wanted him most to be.

"What was your opinion?" She'd written her heart into that article. In the event Jackson's threats had come to fruition, she wanted Tyler to know how she'd felt, wanted the city to know he was a decent and honest man deep down.

The grin that tugged at his mouth spoke of wicked things. He glided his fingers over her folds, stroking the sensitive flesh. "I enjoyed it so much I bought a few copies."

"To read again in the future?" When he circled her swollen nub with his thumb, Julia's concentration fell into a cloud of bliss.

"Not exactly." Tyler remained quiet as he spent a few seconds teasing her nubbin as he peered into her eyes. "I'd thought to put them away in order to show our children one day, tell them what an extraordinary woman their mother was during a crazy time in her youth, the day she became the first female reporter on staff at the *Sentinel,* or rather the *Indianapolis Star* now."

"Oh, Tyler." Her heart skipped a beat. Tears crowded her throat and welled in her eyes. Hearing those words made her prouder than when her uncle had praised her article the morning it came out. "You truly want me to be the mother of your children?"

"Yes. I can't think of anyone else who would put up with a con man like me and want me in spite of it." His fingers worked more magic. "Is there a problem?"

"No." Julia's eyes drifted closed as pleasure became her world. Desire coiled low in her belly, pushing outward with each pass of his fingers, each insistent touch of his thumb. When the heated sensations broke, her feminine walls contracted and her toes curled beneath the water. Sensation raced along her skin, alternately chilling and warming her. The desire she'd felt upon seeing him this evening was far from satisfied. "That was unexpected." She sagged against the tub, as limp as a dishrag. "But wonderful."

"It proves sexual acts can be very different when you're with the right person." He pulled his hand from the water and dried his arm with the towel folded on the floor. "If you'll indulge me, I plan to show you lovemaking can be better than you've dreamed." He clambered to his feet, then winced and rubbed his left thigh. "Damn shrapnel."

In a daze, Julia gripped the sides of the tub and stood, accepting the towel he handed her. "You want to be with me even knowing of my past?"

"Beyond any doubt. You're my biggest distraction and also my greatest inspiration. My life is better from knowing you and will be better still from winning you." He lifted her out of the tub but kept his arms around her as he set her down and bundled the towel across her breasts. "Does my reporter have any more questions?"

It was uncanny how well he understood her. "It doesn't bother you that everyone in the city knows what happened to me?" How would it affect her children's chances in society? "That I have a secret shame?"

"Not in the least. Besides, you don't seem haunted by it any longer. You laid your past to rest when you attacked Jackson with that tonic bottle." His grin flashed slightly crooked white teeth. "Everyone has skeletons in their closets. If a person won't overlook that or won't forgive you for it, you don't need to have them in your life." Tyler pressed her closer to his body. The rigid length of his arousal prodded her stomach. "Are you done?"

"Almost." She twined her hands around his neck. Without their anchor, the towel fell, slipping away, caught between their bodies. His citrus scent teased her nose; the strength of his arms comforted her and kept her upright while she asked the difficult question. "What of Anna? You have a responsibility to her." In all the drama, she'd forgotten about Tyler's obligation.

"That's what I wanted to discuss with you a few days ago had you let me say my piece." He bent and placed one arm under her knees then effortlessly picked her up off the floor with a small grunt.

"Put me down. Your leg doesn't need the added strain."

"Hush, woman." He captured her lips in a feather-weighted kiss. "Anna lied, plain and simple."

Relief shuddered through her. "You're free?" When he nodded, she stifled the urge to clap her hands. After all, it would be in poor taste.

"Apparently, she suffers from acute jealousy. When she learned of our courtship, she panicked and thought her monthly support payments would stop—which they will. I'm adamant regarding that."

"Meaning?" She held his shoulders as he carried her through the parlor and up the stairs to his bedroom.

"I'm not giving her any more money." Tyler gently laid her on the bed. He trailed his lips down the column of her throat then traced her collarbone with his tongue. "I've come to realize that while it's perfectly acceptable to feel guilt for Joshua's death, hiding behind that guilt and being a prisoner to it is not a good thing."

Julia shoved his shoulders until he lifted off. "I have the solution." *It's perfect!* She couldn't hold back her smile. "Finally, I can tie this thread."

"Oh?" He shed his waistcoat and shirt. They fell unheeded to the floor. "Please enlighten me."

"I tucked away the money I earned at Madame's school. I could never spend it, didn't want to buy things that would bring me pleasure with tainted cash." She levered onto her elbows. The expected heaviness of shame never came. "I'd be happy to give it all to you for Anna. It's a few hundred dollars but will give her security for a while."

"Are you certain? That's a fair amount of money." He edged off the bed and planted his hands on his hips. "I'd hate for you to give it up on her account."

"I want to. If we don't let her have use of it, that cash will simply sit in a jar at the bottom of my closet for the rest of my life. At least this way, she can use it and I won't have the reminder every time I see that can."

Tyler stared at her as if he'd never seen her before. "You're a marvel. Is it any wonder why I'm so lost in love with you I never want to find my way back to reality?"

He loved her. What a wondrous thing to hear. "Anyone would have done the same."

"No, they wouldn't." Shadows filled his eyes, gone as quickly as they came. "Although, you should only give part of that money to Anna."

"Oh?"

"Yes. The other part should be used to buy that damned painting in the gentleman's club. If it takes all my life, I will track those other pictures down and attempt to purchase them too." The passion in his voice moved her.

Warmth flowed through her. Tears prickled her eyes. "It's such a small thing, but I feel as if I've been cleansed of a terrible disease or awakened from a nightmare. All because of you."

"Aw, Julia, don't cry." He shed the remainder of his clothing. "I merely told you how I felt."

He seemed so uncomfortable at her abundance of emotion she took pity on him. "This is true and what's more, you're showing me. Come to bed." She held out her arms, and when he followed instructions, she pulled him close. "Since those dark days at Madame's, I never thought a man would feel such a thing for me, let alone choose to love me despite my past. Or that I could look past those years and let such a man into my heart."

Tyler nuzzled the tender spot where her shoulder joined her neck. "How could I not? A fiercely independent woman who's beautiful to boot? What's more, she's caring, generous and has turned a blind eye to my cons."

"Let's say a severely disapproving eye. Without them you and I would never have met." Julia ran her hands down the length of his back and caressed the small dip at the base of his spine. Tyler's hard cock pressed against her thigh. She kissed him and put every ounce of longing into that simple joining of mouths. When she pulled away, she said, "Like you, I'm no longer a prisoner of my past. Knowing you, loving you, has given me new life and set me free."

"I guess we've both been redeemed."

"I won't dispute that claim." She couldn't deny the love that blazed in his dark eyes. She felt its answering echo deep in her soul. "Thank you, for taking a chance."

"Thank you for believing the con."

Conversation ceased in lieu of the heated exchange of mouths. Julia met each thrust of his tongue with enthusiasm, matching him stroke for stroke. He slid his hands over her body. He rubbed her nipples into twin peaks of arousal with magical fingers. She arched beneath him and sighed as he closed his lips over a tight bud.

Desire tightened in her belly. Passion throbbed in a frantic rhythm between her thighs. Coupling this time would be different. There was real emotion behind it, a joining of souls, a promise made. "I need you inside me." She wriggled in anticipation while his tip kissed her wet opening. "Hurry. I cannot wait any longer."

Tyler entered her in one long, forceful push then paused. He kept his weight on his forearms and stared into her face. "Don't close your eyes. Keep focused on me. It won't be like all the other times. I promise. I won't let you be lost."

She pulled him close, tilting her hips to take him deeper. "I know." Julia smoothed her palms up and down his arms but never broke eye contact. "I'm ready, and I want you."

As he claimed her lips, he withdrew from her passage only to re-enter with greater intensity. After a few thrusts, she matched his rhythm. She bent her knees, drawing them toward her to allow deeper penetration. Pressure bore down from within and mingled with spirals of pleasure that increased with each thrust. Their labored breathing filled the silence. Sweat broke out on her body and she felt a light sheen on Tyler's back as she held him.

He moved his hips faster and more franticly. She mimicked each movement. The friction of their bodies rubbed against her sensitized nub. "Tyler, I need..." She had no idea what she needed since all her attempts at carnal relations had ended when the man was spent.

"This." He angled a hand between them, while slowing his thrusts. One finger found her swollen nubbin. He tormented that bit of flesh then withdrew his hand as she whimpered.

Julia gripped his shoulders. The dam holding the growing pressure broke and sent her hurtling into a warm, dark void of bliss. She dug her nails into his skin as he continued his movements. Her core contracted, each sending her crashing through pleasure that stole her breath. Seconds later, he followed her into that unexplainable place and his warm seed shot into her channel. When he collapsed on top of her, she wrapped her arms around his waist and held tight.

Her eyes drifted closed. She listened to the rapid beat of her heart, felt the answering thunder of his pulse beneath her fingers, and sighed. Finally, she'd found the missing piece of happiness her life lacked. In Tyler, she'd gained acceptance and redemption. With him, she would build a future and find a home.

With a sigh of contentment, she shifted her weight beneath him and stroked the side of his face. "I believe, Mr. Browning, you have ruined me for other men."

He lifted his head. A smug grin brightened his features. "That's good to know." As he rolled, he took her with him, tucking her against his side. His breath warmed her ear. "You have my promise I won't run any more cons. I have everything I've ever wanted."

"Fantastic news. I'd hate to lose you to the authorities so soon in our relationship." She relaxed into his embrace. "I'll still work at the newspaper." A twinge flared in her stomach. Would he expect her to stay at home and practice domesticity?

"I wouldn't want less and feel quite confident you'll set this town to buzzing. Since your Uncle George is the new junior editor, I won't worry about your safety."

This was true. Shortly after her unconventional article had run, Jackson had been hounded by police, angry citizens and various reporters from other papers. The next day he'd fled the city for parts unknown with the police in pursuit. Uncle George had gratefully stepped into the gap Jackson had left and had eased the *Sentinel's* staff into the buyout. He'd been adamant they all kept their positions.

"Unless I look for trouble?" The warmth of new love crept over her skin.

"Sweetheart, it has no trouble finding you."

"What about your miracle tonic business? Surely more people will ask about it."

"For me, it's already done its job, not to mention I know where the source of the water is." His deep chuckle sent tingles of renewed arousal through her body. "I intend to say I had limited quantities. They should have bought into it earlier."

She wrapped her arms over his and settled more comfortably against him. "Life with you will be interesting."

"I expect so. An ex con man-turned apothecary partnered with a former prostitute-come-journalist." He pressed a kiss into her hair. "What will people say?"

"That we're lucky indeed." Julia didn't care what else they'd say. After all, it wouldn't matter. For the first time in years, she was happy with him and with who she was as a person. There was no greater feeling in the world.

The End

About the Author

Sandra Sookoo is a bestselling author who firmly believes every person deserves acceptance and a happy ending. Most days you can find her creating scandal and mischief in the Regency-era, serendipity and happenstance in Victorian America or snarky humor in the contemporary world. Reading romance is a lot like eating fine chocolates — you can't just have one. Good thing books don't have calories!

When she's not wearing out computer keyboards, Sandra spends time with her real life Prince Charming in central Indiana where she's been known to goof off and make moments count because the key to life is laughter. A Disney fan since the age of ten, when her soul gets bogged down and her imagination flags, a trip to Walt Disney World is in order. Nothing fuels her dreams more than the land of eternal happy endings, hope and love stories.

More Victorian-era stories from Sandra Sookoo

Cairo Nights

Losing something you want the most makes you stronger — or an easy target.

Joy Debinham, daughter of an English missionary, hides a secret heartache while working with Egypt's poverty stricken. As she attempts to save the children from easily curable diseases, she has another interest — keeping Egypt's treasures in the country. But the arrival of Quinn ignites her banked passion and becomes the obsession that might put her life in danger.

Quinn Handry, an enterprising American from humble roots, has come to Egypt for one reason — the money. He's done many things for a buck, but brokering stolen antiquities is the most lucrative. In order to reclaim what he lost years ago, he's always on the hunt for treasures until the day he meets Joy and everything dims compared to the desire she invokes in him.

During perfumed Egyptian nights, the heat between them flares while acquaintances conspire to destroy them. Danger doesn't stay confined to tombs and pushes them to finally realize what matters most — if they can live long enough to claim it.

You can find this book at any book retailer in both digital and paperback formats.

Winner Takes All

Lily Henderson's greatest passion is knowledge. Christopher Farnsworth thrives on order and decorum. But her penchant for Suffragette rallies and logical reasoning soon clash with his quiet, controlled ex-military lifestyle over a bowl of potato soup.

The two agree to a wager and love is the intended outcome. The premise? A suitable match by Easter. If he loses, he'll attend Easter church services dressed in one of his aunt's outrageously colored and beaded gowns. If she loses, she'll ride, Lady Godiva-style, around the heart of Indianapolis.

The problem is neither Christopher nor Lily can find matches as good as themselves. Romantic sabotage is the order of the day. The original wager is forgotten when the only thing the pair gamble with is their hearts.

You can find this book at any book retailer in both digital and paperback formats.

A Wolfish Scandal

He has nothing to live for. She has nothing to lose. Together, they have everything to gain.

Lyndal Carson's life is at a premium. Afflicted with a heart ailment wherein she can drop dead at any time, she makes a pact with herself to create one scandal and to really live before she dies. Tired of being a handmaiden to her family, she writes the letter that will change her destiny.

Grey Rutledge, a werewolf who is hounded by a reporter and haunted by memories, endeavors to provide a diversion large enough that the paper will forget its interest. He invites twelve women to his estate on the premise of choosing one of them for his mate. After the loss of his family, the only thing he wants is heirs and a woman by his side.

As the days go on, both Lyndal and Grey find that elusive piece missing from their lives. When their respective secrets are revealed, they both run the risk of losing everything. Danger catches them unaware during an innocent afternoon but it's what is decided as life hangs in the balance that will change their lives forever

You can find this book at any book retailer in both digital and paperback formats.

Unraveled Souls

Noelle Radliffe can communicate with ghosts. They haunt her nights and show her dreams of things that haven't yet occurred. When she has a vision of a dead lion and sees the name of a man, she searches the city to find him and warn him only to become sidetracked by an addiction she can't fight.

Enter Nicholas Pemberton. Although charming and charismatic, he hides a secret, one that is deadly as well as mysterious. He's a shape shifter and the urge to change into a lion is a battle he constantly wages with himself, second to the obsession he feels for his recent acquaintance, Noelle.

As the two fight their mutual attraction to each other, Nicholas attempts to elude the local authorities who are intent on linking recent murders to his name. Noelle continues to seek peace from her visions and to understand her purpose. But the connection between them is too strong to ignore. As passion ignites, so does the danger. Lives are threatened and destinies collide, but will love be enough to save their souls?

You can find this book at any book retailer in both digital and paperback formats.

www.ingramcontent.com/pod-product-compliance
Lightning Source LLC
Chambersburg PA
CBHW051243260626
47162CB00002B/587